# Jack's Passion

# Jack's Passion

Bill Kinsella

RESOURCE *Publications* · Eugene, Oregon

JACK'S PASSION

Resource Publications
An Imprint of Wipf and Stock Publishers
199 W. 8th Ave., Suite 3
Eugene, OR 97401

www.wipfandstock.com

Library of Congress Control Number: 2019911534

PAPERBACK ISBN: 978-1-5326-8299-5
HARDCOVER ISBN: 978-1-5326-8300-8
EBOOK ISBN: 978-1-5326-8301-5

Manufactured in the U.S.A.                                     08/08/19

For "GiGi," Georgette Underwood Kinsella

## Acknowledgments

The author wishes to acknowledge Maureen Brady for her insight and encouragement throughout the writing of this book.

The race is not to the swift,
Nor the battle to the strong,
Nor bread to the wise,
Nor riches to men of understanding,
Nor favor to men of skill;
But time and chance happen to them all.
For man also does not know his time:
Like fish taken in a cruel net,
Like birds caught in a snare,
So the sons of men are snared in an evil time,
When it falls suddenly upon them.

—Matthew 10:38


And he who does not take his cross and follow
after Me is not worthy of Me.

—Ecclesiastes 10:11–12

# 1

Early June, 2001

As a young man he had his whole life ahead of him but just after graduating Duke, he still hadn't heard from the Wall Street firm most likely to bring him to New York. Jack Conroy always thought he'd end up on Wall Street. He felt that was his inheritance. It had to do with his father who worked there and with his mother who liked that his father did. And because of his competitive nature and need to continually prove himself, Jack thought he wanted to work on Wall Street. But so far the firms who'd responded to his interest encouraged him to go on and get his MBA and then reapply.

Consequently, Jack found himself forming a contingency plan; an interim solution to the problem of what to do should Wall Street pass on him this time around. The odd thing was he wasn't that upset about it. You could even say he felt a sense of relief, as if he'd been spared or released.

He thought he might be able to work the summer at the Durham Nursery. The owner of the nursery liked him. He had worked there throughout college part time and felt confident he could again. This morning he got up with the sun and drove out to talk to Carlo Bellini.

The nursery sat in a valley some ten miles out of town. This morning the valley appeared as peaceful as heaven, bathed as it was by the soft light of the new day. The sun ascending seemed to grow larger before Jack, like a giant golden eye that watched and followed him. A spotless sky assured their communion. For him, being in the country early in the morning with the sun coming up always felt like a blessing. His eyes brightened taking in the countryside: mist clinging to poplars along the river outside of town; dew softening the hard edges of clumped grasses in an expansive field he passed by; and then, too, the luxuriance of late spring flowers that seemed to spread everywhere around him.

He knew what to expect at the nursery at this time of day. Bustling activity: flatbed trucks crawling out of huge garages, dump trucks loaded with soil, grinding their gears pulling onto the roadway, fork lifts scurrying about like giant yellow bugs, moving stacks of fertilizer. At the center of it all, directing everyone and everything, stood Carlo Bellini, a bulky, tall man, waving his arms like a traffic cop and grumbling out directives to his small army of workers. Jack exited his Jeep eager to be recognized. Always aware, the man with fingers the size of sausage waved hello. "Jacky," Bellini said in clipped speech, his voice as resonant as a kettle drum. Jack smiled and waved and stood to the side waiting for Bellini to approach him. The big man read his expression.

"Give me a minute," he said, one arm waving rapidly in a circular motion to get a sleepy truck moving. That finished, the stirring lot became suddenly calm and Mr. Bellini walked toward Jack. Watching him walk, Jack imagined he could feel the ground absorbing the shock of each step. When his old boss stood before him, looking like an Italian Paul Bunyan, Jack wondered if the man had ever been small.

Bellini relocated to North Carolina from Brooklyn thirty years before to open a nursery that, he was proud of saying; he'd started from seed and grown into a good business. Jack began working for him his freshmen year. They got along well immediately. Jack regarded Bellini as an unpretentious, hard-working man, who admired those qualities in his workers.

"I thought for sure you'd left for New York," Bellini said.

"Not yet."

"Nothing from the Street?" Bellini asked.

"I'm still waiting to hear from one firm."

While he said he was still waiting to hear, Jack's mien suggested he was also fairly certain what the reply would be.

The two walked together toward a large warehouse that resembled an airplane hangar. Jack was nearly as tall as Mr. Bellini but more slender although more athletically built. His broad shoulders outlined against the white linen shirt he wore suggested power at rest. He had on faded jeans and sandals with thick leather straps and his golden hair shone brilliantly in contrast to his companion's thick crop which was as black as a crow's wing. Bellini's power was the power of raw nature, as if he were the marble mountain from which the beauty of Jack had been carved.

The inside of the warehouse was as long as a football field and had a cool dampness the way large warehouses can. They walked under fluorescent lights past rows of stacked planting materials: fertilizer, manure, peat. Strangely, Jack felt his muscles relax to the familiar alkaline smells of fertilizer and lime that gave way to the pungent odor of peat as he made his way down a wide, brightly lit, corridor between the floor-to-ceiling shelves that loomed like mythic giants on both sides.

Just past the shelves of manure, Bellini said something he always said at this point, "Smells like shit in here but I love it." Jack laughed on cue knowing it would please Mr. Bellini. Today, Jack laughed more loudly perhaps, feeling comforted by the predictability of the remark which he found especially reassuring.

They reached the end of the corridor and turned right and walked to a tight corner where the owner entered a small office. Jack followed him in. Behind a desk that looked too small for him, his boss sat down in the same squeaky swivel chair he always had. Then with a huge hand he grabbed a coffee thermos and with the other motioned for Jack to sit down.

"What's on your mind?" the big man asked as he poured a cup of steaming coffee into a mug as big as a bowl. Jack expected Mr. Bellini to know right away why he was there and to offer him a job without him having to ask. It'd always been that way.

"I came to see if I could work the summer here," Jack said.

Bellini became more serious and sounded apologetically answering, "Sorry, Jack, I got all the summer help I need."

Jack felt hope sink, and what's more, something like a suspicion begin to emerge.

"I thought for sure you were gone," Bellini explained.

"I understand," Jack said.

"But here you are."

Bellini got up and walked toward a steel file cabinet in a corner of the cramped room. "I want to show you something," he said.

Jack had no idea what he might be shown. All he could guess is that Mr. Bellini might have gotten a ton of applications for summertime help. He watched politely as his old boss attempted to retrieve whatever it was he felt he had to show him. The big man couldn't get all the way to the cabinet because bags of a new grass seed blocked the way. He bent down and began moving the bags. Jack assisted, clearing the bottom bags but stopped abruptly after moving a few. A small bird, a gold finch, lay dead on the floor.

The sight of the diminutive creature, lifeless, startled Jack.

His eyes filled with a kind of sad confusion.

"You should have been outside in the open fields," Bellini said to the creature as he disposed of it, "shouldn't have been in here." Then turning

3

to Jack, "It happens every so often. A bird will come in to feed and get smothered."

The power of Bellini's voice snapped Jack out of it. He observed the big man gently dispose of the bird by wrapping it in a small burlap cloth which he then slid into a receptacle.

Then Bellini went to the now accessible file cabinet and looked in a couple drawers until he found what he wanted. He sat down again and handed Jack some papers. "You recognize these?" They were landscape design sketches Jack had drawn over the years working at the nursery.

"You still have these?" Jack said.

"Yeah, and I've used them," Bellini said, running a finger over his thick black mustache.

"You've got talent for this, Jack," said Bellini, holding up the sketches, "I've said it often. And if you want to, you can work for me full time. It won't be New York but you won't have to wait to prove yourself either."

Jack didn't know what to say. There was no question the offer pleased him, for he instantly felt a weight had been lifted from him. But working full time at the nursery? He never seriously considered that because of Wall Street. Yet the idea was a revelation. What if he could bypass Wall Street and have another life. He listened to Mr. Bellini explain.

"I'd have asked before," Bellini offered, "but thought for sure you were headed to New York."

"New York," Jack repeated automatically.

"You'd do well here," Bellini said.

Jack wanted to say yes but remembered his upcoming trip.

"I'm taking some time to visit family, Mr. Bellini. Would it be okay if I let you know after that?"

"That's fine," Bellini said.

Then the two walked side by side outdoors. Mr. Bellini got into his pickup truck and beeped as he drove away. Jack watched the truck disappear and wondered.

# 2

From the nursery Jack headed for Duke. The Year End Relay was today. He got there quickly and drove toward the aquatic center. With school just out the campus was dead and he felt like the only one there?

Underwood Aquatic Center sat at the far end of Duke's East Campus away from the academic departments, separated from them by a stand of Magnolias. Situated on a rise, Underwood appeared to hang above the Magnolias like a castle in the air and the tops of the trees seemed to reach up toward it. At least that's how it struck Jack this morning as he pulled into the parking lot. He had graduated two days before on June 3rd and might have felt differently approaching the center if it weren't for two things. First, the job offer from Mr. Bellini gave him the opportunity to stay around. If he decided to, he'd be back in Durham by July still near Veronica, who'd just finished her junior year, and working for Bellini again. If he did that he'd visit the pool all the time. Secondly, even though he was officially finished with school he still had this last meet to compete in before completely ending his Duke swimming career.

Since the regular season had been delayed due to pool problems, all conference meets had been compressed into a shortened season with no time left for the traditional Year End Relay. The Year End Relay was a long-standing event at Duke where the best seniors competed against the best juniors in a medley relay. The juniors would still be at school anyway preparing for the summer Nationals. So all that was needed for the meet to occur was for the seniors to hang around a few days after graduation; they agreed instantly.

The junior class had one of the most all around talented group of swimmers to come to Duke in years with strong swimmers in every stroke. It was primarily because of them the Duke's Men Team had won the conference title in the regular season. The seniors were good, too, but not exceptional except for one: Jack. Jack had been All Conference this past season, winning the one hundred yard breast stroke competition in the championship meet by a tenth of a second over another Duke swimmer, Phil Dayton. Dayton was a junior who hoped to replace Jack as team captain next year. The two shared a healthy, if uneven, rivalry. When you added the other strong junior swimmers to Dayton, though, the junior medley became practically unbeatable. Certainly, everyone thought the Year End Relay would be a cinch for the juniors. Everyone, that is, but Jack.

Jack had been raised precisely for the kind of contest he was about to take part in. Whenever there was a situation that somehow figured against him, he approached it with a daunting single-mindedness. It was as if all things in life other than that specific one disappeared, and all that remained on Earth was him and his goal. Perhaps, it was the need to reaffirm his parents' assessment of him that drove him to such myopic perfection. Or perhaps it was the basic nature of him as a person that compelled him to bear down, zero in, and forge ahead. Whatever it was, Jack was at his dazzling best whenever he or the team he was on was assigned the role of underdog.

As he came into the facility this morning he thought to himself briefly, this would be the last competition he'd ever participate in at Duke. That thought brought a momentary shudder. He paused, and then proceeded through the large glass entrance doors to the natatorium. Once inside Underwood, nothing bothered him. His focus became the meet. He went straight to the locker room. As usual, he was the first one there. He suited up and strode to the pool deck by way of a connecting door. He walked to the far side of the fifty meter racing pool and began his pre-meet ritual. He gazed down the pool, following the almost undetectable sway of the blue-white water. Duke Water he called it since above the pool Duke blue and white flags spread over the water in streamers adding their tint to the clear water. Jack bent down, took his hand, cupped it, and pushed the cupped hand out away from him. The water felt colder than usual today. He watched the ripple he'd made until it reached the dividing wall at the far end where the racing pool adjoined the diving tank. He was flat on his stomach, level with the pool, and so close to the water he got a good whiff of chlorine. It acted like smelling salts, bringing him up out of his deep concentration.

Standing up, his vision ranged past the racing pool to the diving tank beyond. His eyes climbed the highest platform and he imagined looking down on the race from up there. Visualizing his race before it happened, he saw himself start, saw where he would hold back, how he should handle the turns and stay under as long as possible, and where he must accelerate to eat up water. They'll dictate the pace so I must be stronger longer he said to himself. He tapped himself twice over the heart with V-ed fingers.

His swimming senses were so tuned into the physical conditions of the pool and his own body, that he noticed how the hair he'd let grow out, just slightly, absorbed the pool's moisture more than it ever had before. He was totally zoned-in and ready to get in and warm up.

Entering the water, he heard the chatter of his teammates who had now arrived and were milling around the coaches office. Then, he heard something unusual: Bursting from the P.A. system exploded the full throttled energy of the Beatles singing Help.

Jack looked up.

Phil Dayton had just come out of the media room adjacent to the coach's office. His junior teammates were gathered around him chuckling. Dayton walked down pool side to be near where Jack was warming up and addressed him.

"I know how much you love your father's music," he said to Jack, "and I think this song is apropos for you guys today."

Jack stood up in the water listening to the music, overlooking Dayton, and then shook his head as if to say you don't know what you've done. "Dayton," he said, looking at his smug teammate, "you've pumped me up big time." After that, he dove under. His back submerged with such power Dayton's smirk disappeared, replaced by an expression of irritated concern.

After warm ups, Coach Ross assembled the swimmers near his office. "I've decided to alter the medley somewhat by putting the breast stroke last."

Jack understood exactly what the alteration meant. He and Dayton would go head-to-head one last time.

Then Coach Ross walked, clipboard in hand, down the side of the pool to the far end where the starting blocks stood. Jack watched. The relay was ready to begin. The coach surveyed the fifty meter pool that lie before him, its water still calm. His assistant coaches would officiate. He had directed one to the middle of the pool and one to the dividing wall at the far end. Then he told the swimmers to take their places.

Above the pool, lamps spread the entire length, radiating heat and light. Jack glanced at the line of swimmers before him as they passed directly under the lamps heading to the starting blocks. They looked illuminated. Flashes of their Duke blue and white swim trunks stood out as they moved. The entire natatorium seemed aglow and a palpable energy suffused the air.

Jack stopped as if to take it all in; perhaps conscious of the fact he was looking at his 2001 team for the last time. He looked briefly up at a banner behind him. It read Duke Men's Team-2001 Big East Champions. Then he turned back toward the pool. He heard the coach announce, "Swimmers, let's go."

The relay teams lined up, Jack included. Juniors took lane three, seniors lane four.

The back stroke would go first. The swimmers involved entered the water. Coach Ross checked his officials and then raised the starting gun. Bang, the race was on.

Indiscriminate cheering came from the sides of the pool from underclassmen who looked on with admiring zeal as they watched the junior back-stroker immediately pull ahead. After the first hundred, the juniors were ahead by half a body length. The second leg commenced with butter fliers bolting out from the blocks into churned up water, their arms flying out, up, and over in syncopated unison down the fifty meters where the swimmers dipped into their turns at the wall before blasting back up, all the while kicking, arms turning, and the junior lead growing to a full body length.

Then the third leg, free stylists set free into the water, their streamlined elegance returning some measure of calm to the hitherto agitated pool. Bulleting down and back, they raced faster with this more graceful stroke. But now the junior was not able to sustain the half body length per every hundred lead set in the first two legs. So that coming into the last leg of the relay, the juniors would have to settle for Dayton having just over a body length lead on Jack. Dayton waited to watch his teammate touch the wall and then launched out. Then the senior touched and Jack was in.

He had stood atop the block like an artist's sculpture of the perfect swimmer: V-shaped, finely wrought, powerfully contained. But when the touch came he uncoiled, exploding off the block, instantly enlivening the race. His long muscular body glided over the water before perfectly piercing a calm pane of it, like light going through glass. Underneath the water for what looked like a third of the pool, his arms pressed against his sides and extended down to his straightened knees, he torpedoed toward the far wall before breaking the water's surface without resistance. Then he pulled his body in the shape of a cross, the ideal consequence of a beautifully performed stroke.

Dayton fought to hold his lead but where he fought, Jack flowed, the water yielding to his masterly stroke. In a steady, powerful rhythm, Jack surged onward, gaining on Dayton. His kick was so powerful he covered greater distance with every surging stroke. He was a demonstration of the ultimate breast stroke rhythm: pull, breathe, kick, glide . . . pull, breathe, kick, glide . . . gliding powerfully up toward Dayton. So that while Dayton still held the lead going into the wall at the turn, time turned with Jack favoring him going into the last fifty. Dayton fought the water and the clock as Jack, almost breathlessly, came on. One body length from the lead was gone. And then by mid pool in the last fifty, half again of the junior lead disappeared. And there Dayton might as well have stopped for looking back. He turned to see where Jack was and that was all.

The juniors on the side of the pool numbly witnessed the dissolution of a sure thing. Jack took one deep breath and returned Dayton's glance with a kick and glide that brought him side by side with his rival. And then it was as if Jack had found another gear, as if some invisible motor ignited inside him to propel him. He broke ahead in a surge that didn't fade. Power gliding to the wall Jack touched first, a half body length ahead of Dayton, setting a school record for his split.

"Christ," Dayton yelled, coming out of the pool. But Jack didn't get out. He swam back and grabbed one of the Duke flag lines flying over the pool. Then with flag line in hand, he did an exhilarated lap around the perimeter of the pool, the blue and white flags trailing behind triumphantly, seniors cheering in delight, juniors awestruck, underclassmen swearing to God to be like Jack. Chant-like, the underclassmen passed the name among them as if they were passing a word made flesh: Jack.

Out of the water at last, Jack was raised up by the jubilant seniors and admired by the entire team. Even the juniors were amazed. Coach Ross cut short the adulation, but he too reveled in the result.

"Seniors, line up," Coach Ross said, "Team, meet them."

Everyone knew the drill. The senior swimmers formed a line facing another line made by the rest of the team. Then one by one each underclassmen swimmer went down the senior line touching elbows with the seniors like fish touching fins, all the while cheering Duke . . . Duke . . . Duke . . . until after the last underclassmen touched the last senior all hands rose in a wave, like a swimming stroke, up into the air and then down again, and in unison Duke Blue punctuated the finish.

After pitched emotions subsided to a more down-to-earth level and the aura of spectacle gave way to post meet banter, several senior and junior swimmers exchanged competitive jabs going back to the locker room, Jack not among them.

"You guys won for one reason," Bob Evans, a junior, said to some seniors, "Jack."

Dayton, who was next to Evans, cringed at his remark saying sarcastically, "Praise be to Jack."

His voice smacked of envy and Evans responded, "Dayton, you sound sour. None of us could have held Jack back today. He was just too good."

Dayton peered at Evans. "Yeah, well I guess I forgot that while I swim in water, he walks on it."

Jack had joined the others now and heard Dayton's remark. He raised his head, his jaw firm, and its muscles stiffening into an expression of reluctant consideration for someone whose ego had been bruised.

"Dayton," he said, trying to console the perturbed junior, "I'm sure next year, you'll get my record."

"Oh my God," Dayton said, "not only do you crush me but you have to be nice about it. You're both a strong and kind God. Is that right, Jack?"

"Dayton," Evans said in disgust, "you're a terrible loser."

"Stay out of it, Evans. I don't like being patronized by Jack is all. We all know the truth. There's no way I'll get his record next year. Just like there's no way Jack will get to Wall Street without an MBA. I won't ever be the swimmer you are, Jack. But I'll be damned if I don't get to Wall Street before you. I'm taking a full year of MBA courses next year, did you know that?"

Jack looked at Dayton with a kind of hopeless dismissal, as if to say you just can't be nice to some people.

"Have you heard from the Street?" Dayton pressed, his lower lip stretched in cynical anticipation of Jack's response. But Jack continued to ignore him infuriating Dayton into eruption. "When it comes to Wall Street, Conroy, I'll leave you in the dust."

Jack turned to Dayton, his eyes full of contempt. His stare froze the tormented junior. Coach Ross interceded, "That's enough, Phil. Don't ruin our tradition by thinking only about yourself."

"Who should I think about, Coach? Jack?" Dayton couldn't let it go.

"You might," Coach Ross said. "Jack's always put the team first and whatever he chooses to do, I know he'll lead others doing it."

# 3

Jack returned to his apartment late that afternoon. He got permission from the landlord to extend his lease for a couple of months. Before going upstairs the landlord gave him his mail, mentioning he'd signed for one of the items. Jack didn't look at the mail right away but immediately began packing for his upcoming trip to his aunt and uncle's. He quickly filled a canvass duffel bag then returned to the bureau where he'd set his mail down.

There were a couple of bills, one from the phone company, another from a utility. There was a letter addressed to Recent Graduate from a credit card company offering a new Master Card account. Under the credit card letter was a business sized envelope with a certified mail sticker attached. This was the letter the landlord had signed for. It was upside down in his hands. He felt the envelope as he removed the green sticker, then turned it over to read the return address. The envelope was of fine quality paper, with a texture that made it feel as if it had been minutely stitched together the way a fine piece of cloth might be. It was off-white, with embossed, thick, black typing. The print was elegant and bold and the return address read Sanders Brown. It was the last letter he'd been waiting for from Wall Street.

Jack sat down on the bed to read the letter but shadows in the room made it difficult to read and he chose not to turn on the lamp. So he got up and went to the window in the living room and broke the seal of the envelope by tearing the left corner of it open. He took out what he thought was the only page of the letter, not realizing that when he'd torn the envelope, he'd separated the first from the second page of the letter. He discarded the envelope with the second page still inside.

The first page looked like a complete letter. Jack read carefully:

Dear Mr. Conroy:

Sanders Brown Company has carefully reviewed your letter of interest, college transcripts, and personal references. We are pleased to be able to extend to you an invitation to interview with our firm. We will be conducting interviews during the second two weeks of

June. Please contact the undersigned by June 15 to arrange for an interview.

Very Truly Yours, Cliff Sutton
Manager Human Resources

He had ten days to respond. But he was leaving for his uncle's the next day and wouldn't be in Claremont Hills until the fifteenth. If he wanted to set up the interview, he should do it first thing in the morning. But he felt reluctant to do so. He'd dragged his feet about sending letters to Wall Street in the first place. Veronica thought she knew why, although Jack had never come right out and said it. That was because, intermittently, he still did want to go to Wall Street. But, lately and increasingly, his feelings about working there, when he admitted them to himself, were negative. He didn't explore the reasons but that is how he felt. He didn't want to go. His father had urged him to send letters. His mother and father had expressed disappointment about him not getting his letters out sooner. They wanted him near them.

They would be proud and delighted if he went to Wall Street. It was his dad, also, who'd suggested Jack provide both his school and home address for response, fearing Jack's delay in contacting firms might result in their responses coming to Duke after he'd already left school. Jack had forgotten about that and since he didn't see the second page of the letter, didn't realize a copy had been sent to his home. He never read the following:

CC: Mr. John Conroy, Claremont Hills Estates, Claremont Hills, NJ

All Jack could think now was that he wished the letter had not come. He'd waited most of the semester, thinking secretly: I hope I don't get an interview. Now that he'd gotten an offer to set up one, he felt sick to his stomach about it.

What he craved was the feeling he'd had that morning after Mr. Bellini had offered him a job. He'd been happy. It was true, at Underwood after the relay he'd wished he was going to Wall Street. But that was to beat Dayton. Dayton had made him feel less enthusiastic about staying in Durham, making him think that by working for Bellini he'd be shirking responsibility. Then, too, Coach Ross's comment, while it was meant to make him feel confident, further dampened Jack's excitement about taking the job at the nursery. In his mind, Jack could hear Coach Ross saying: "Whatever he chooses to do, I know he'll lead others doing it."

So this letter might have made him feel that he was back on track. Dayton would have to eat crow if Jack beat him to Wall Street by getting a job with Sanders Brown. And Wall Street's future would be in better hands. These thoughts passed through his mind and momentarily pleased him. So did the ideas his parents would be proud and Coach Ross would be proud. But all of that incidental pleasure dissolved into a sinking feeling when Jack thought about not working at the nursery, about being in New York instead of Durham, about being away from Veronica.

Then the letter took on a different quality. It became like a draft notice sent to him during wartime bringing with it an array of implications, of certain limitations, and affecting him so somberly that his plan to work for Bellini and be near Veronica seemed hopelessly naive-a pipe dream. It occurred to Jack that what he'd arranged was a young man's oasis from the real world. Real possibility presented itself with the letter that came late but not late enough.

Time, too, took on a different quality with the letter. Confusion spoiled time and expectation turned it into a kind of battle ground. Time, so long his patient escort, now seemed an urgent usher directing him to the nearest exit of his present life out into a chaos of nows. Now, he must decide what to do, where to go, whether he had to leave or whether he must stay. Now, now, now is all he felt, and he wasn't at all sure what to do now. Jack needed perspective but felt incapable of obtaining it in the swirl of the moment. He stood in his apartment taking inventory of its contents, all the paraphernalia of four years at Duke, not sure whether he was coming or going in the larger sense. He went back into his bedroom, stood still and stared at two maps and a photo between them that he'd used as wallpaper for the past year.

One was a map of Durham and Duke, the other a map of the world. Between them, a photograph of a lake he'd liked going to in the country outside of Durham fit neatly into the scheme of the maps and acted for Jack like their key. Seeing the lake photograph always soothed Jack. He'd thought of it as God's eye that he could look into and find his own soul and be calmed. Seeing the lake, he could somehow manage with whatever went on in school and the world, remaining hopeful.

He'd blown the photo up into a poster the same size as the maps and it had seemed the perfect link between where he'd been and where he felt he'd be going. Today, though, the lake photo did not provide its usual solace. Something about the sudden acceleration of purpose Jack felt upon receiving the letter thwarted the photo's calming effect.

He had expected graduation to be liberating. But as he stood there in the room, now gazing at his diploma which lay flat on the surface of a dark table, he felt like he had just gotten a summons to appear on trial where what was at stake was his very being. He felt duty bound to be all that he could be, but apprehensive about needing to be that in New York.

He paced the rooms of his apartment, grappling with his feelings, stopping in front of the same window where he'd read the letter and watched the sunset. The sun setting cast that section of Durham where he lived into soft, gray shadows. Everything outside appeared indistinct, only vaguely what he knew it to be. And at that moment, the quality of the outside world's appearance struck a sympathetic chord in Jack, as if it reflected his hazy notions of future. The light in his apartment had also diminished with the sun going down and seemed on the verge of disappearing altogether. So as Jack stood at the window, it was as if he was positioned between two worlds of growing darkness, of dubious certainty, of nebulous meaning. In the thralls of this fade out, peering back into his darkened room, Jack felt a sudden, terrible loneliness.

Veronica, his girlfriend, would be coming to the apartment soon and that reassured him. But now, alone, he felt lost. He couldn't wait for her to leave the school library where she worked. He thought of calling her and asking her to come home now but that seemed too extreme.

He thought of calling home and telling his parents about the Sanders Brown letter but couldn't bring himself to do that. If he conveyed any hesitation about New York, he knew his parents would dismiss it. They'd say what he felt was just temporary and normal, call it post graduate jitters naturally setting in as he prepared to begin again. They'd definitely say any fear of his, if that's what this hesitation was, was baseless. What, after all, did he have to be afraid of? Hadn't he just graduated from Duke? Wasn't that more proof of his exceptional nature, more proof that he'd be up to any challenge, handle any adjustment, his post college life might deliver?

Jack knew that's how his parents would react. They couldn't possibly understand the depths of his present loneliness. For it seemed, even to Jack, baseless. After all, Veronica, his girlfriend would remain his girlfriend even if he went to New York. So what was it? What was it but some overwhelming sense of finality, inexplicable in terms of his present situation?

He stood a long while in the fading light, clutching the letter in his hand. He looked at his packed duffel bag and felt a sudden urgency about getting away. He wanted to take Veronica that instant to Taylor Island.

Moreover, he wanted to return to Durham after the 4th of July as he'd told Mr. Bellini he would. He felt paralyzed. Then he heard footsteps on the walkway leading up to the house his apartment was in.

He looked at his watch. He looked down to see Veronica about to come inside. His jaw stiffened, his hand tightened. In an impulse, he took the Sanders Brown letter with both hands and tore it up, and then threw it the trash. When Veronica came into the apartment and stood before him, he felt better. "Hello, V," he said, looking at her like he hadn't seen her for years. "I want us to leave tonight instead of tomorrow."

Veronica gave a puzzled look. "What's up?" she asked.

In the dim light of the room Veronica appeared like a dark outline of herself and Jack wanted to be able to look into her eyes. He turned on the lamps in the room. Now he could see into her eyes and it was like looking into the lake. He put his arms around her waist and pulled her close to him. "I missed you so much today," he said softly.

Veronica returned his affection with a peck on his cheek. "You're not telling me something," she said. "Did something happen today? You seem preoccupied."

Jack let go of her waist and took both her hands in his. He turned and gazed out the window at the now quiet street. "A couple of things happened," he said.

"Well?" Veronica queried.

"I beat Dayton in the relay," said Jack, smiling.

"That's good," Veronica grinned, "next?"

"Mr. Bellini offered me a job." Jack pulled back from Veronica into attention, waiting for her reaction.

"Jack, that's wonderful!" Veronica lit up in delighted surprise. "That means you'll be staying in Durham, right?"

She hadn't thought that would happen. Tears came into her eyes. "Jack," she whispered.

Then as an afterthought, "But why should we leave tonight, everything seems to have turned out wonderfully. There's nothing else, is there?"

Jack gazed at Veronica. He traced the outline of her face with his hand then placed his hand softly on her dark hair behind her neck and stroked it.

"Everything's good, V, I just want to go away with you, and be with you, and show you things and can't wait."

"Okay." Veronica sighed, relief and happiness both in her voice. "Okay, Jack."

# 4

As a sophomore, Jack had been asked to escort entering freshmen around campus on their orientation day. He knew instinctively how to put the incoming freshmen at ease and liked being chosen for that. He could place himself in their shoes and anticipate what might interest or intimidate them. As a guide that day, in a friendly and effective way, he began their adjustment and made some friends doing it. It was always about making friends with Jack. One of the friends he made was Veronica.

Jack led his group of twenty-five freshmen to a hillside garden that displayed magnificent clusters of yellow roses. The roses spread around the garden in various beds of different sizes and shapes that interestingly complimented one another while accentuating the whole. Walking through the garden, it was impossible not to be pleased. The sheer number of roses presented such a powerful display of beauty that the freshmen were awed. It was a tangible treat-they smelled the sweetness of the roses and were dazzled by the odd and brilliant arrangements of them.

As a way of setting a tone for taking in all that was new to them, the garden walk worked marvelously. The new students forgot themselves amid the beauty Jack brought them to.

"These roses are unique and wonderful," he'd pointed out. "They bloom the entire year. I come here when I'm fed up or overwhelmed. It's far enough away from the rest of the campus so that I feel like I'm outside of myself and can get perspective and solace just knowing that, despite all that seems so monumental and insurmountable, these flowers still bloom."

In the back of the group that day, anxiously listening, Veronica Cashmiris stood out. She was tall, slender, dark and lovely and Jack couldn't help but notice her. She'd stood back, shyly, but clearly listening to Jack's every word. He knew she was listening and had adjusted his talk to see if he could get her to smile. Eventually she did and he smiled back at her only to watch her look away in a nervous retreat from further eye contact, a slender finger on her demure hand twisting a strand of hair around and around. He continued talking calmly about school, his message resonating reassurance, his clear blue eyes fixed all the while on Veronica and at last her deep brown eyes warmly returned his gaze.

Veronica didn't see Jack after that for several weeks. School took over. She was the first of her family to attend college and felt compelled to start out right. Caught up in the hectic pace of her first month, she'd been carried along by freshmen's continuing obligations. Everything was unfamiliar and both exciting and intimidating. Things happened constantly that felt foreign and compelling. Veronica hoped for calm so that the fuzzy picture of her new world might come more clearly into view. For her, it was that groping time . . . that dumb beginning that takes you and, like an anesthetic, allows things to happen around you that you are only vaguely aware of. Then all of a sudden a month and a half had passed and midterms arrived, knocking loudly on her freshmen door with frightening prospect.

She stirred like a blender, she rushed toward midterms like a person running blindfolded down a city street. Churned up, hell-bent, fearful and determined, she felt a world away from being at ease. These were her first tests at Duke and she needed desperately to do well. It was not that she hadn't studied or didn't understand her courses. It was that she felt a burden as the first of her family to go to college. Also, she was worried that the grant she had been given by Duke might be reduced or eliminated if she didn't prove herself worthy. Frazzled, she longed for a time out.

She remembered Jack. What was he doing? How did he handle it? And she recalled his talk at the garden.

He had mentioned swimming on the college team. She got up, dressed and headed to the Underwood Aquatic Center hoping to see him. It was as if Jack, because of his talk of solace, had become the solace he'd described. He wasn't at the pool. She considered where he might be, those gardens.

She walked back past a row of sturdy Magnolias that with their waxy green leaves and bursting saffron flowers seemed a line of boutonnièred Generals, too sweet smelling to stand with such decorum in so grave a place. She walked beyond them and beyond all the august halls they seemed to guard. She walked down a small flight of stairs to a parking lot, crossed the lot and proceeded across a wide sun-filled meadow. The fall sun warmed her face. Then a slight breeze blew toward her and refreshed her. She felt the wind gently push back her hair that shone chestnut-colored in the sunlight. She walked on steadily and halfway across the field saw on the terraced ground above the field dots of color that were the flowers of the garden Jack had shown her group on orientation day. She gazed behind her. All the gray-stone lecture halls and buildings of the academic departments were bathed in a soft, golden light. From where she stood, they seemed less and less intimidating as they sat quietly back, like unused books on a library shelf.

She came to a rise in the field at the far end where it swept upward to meet the garden. Now the tiny dots of color she had seen at a distance enlarged before her into yellow roses, extending toward her like welcoming bouquets. She gazed around the garden into the maze of beds. What at first seemed a confusion of colors had settled into an articulate pattern of beauty—balanced, accented, and amazing. Here, the gardener's design had met God's so that grace and beauty bloomed together in a brilliant spectacle. It seemed a symphony of color that she could all but hear. She turned and paused.

At the intersection of two lines of roses, recumbent on a patch of earth just large enough to hold him Jack rested, his arms stretched at right angles from his sides. He looked as if he might be sleeping until he sat up. He wore headphones and in one hand held a book. Veronica thought to move away, afraid she might be intruding. But he saw her.

"Hello," he yelled, forgetting the headphones.

Veronica laughed. Jack understood why and removed the headphones. Then in normal volume he said hello again. A long silence followed within which Veronica's mood turned like a weather vane blowing in the wind. At one moment she felt comforted by Jack's presence and in the very next disturbed by it. What'd been really only a momentary silence seemed an eternity until Jack focused on her and spoke.

"Midterms," he said.

His one word summed up everything. Veronica realized he knew exactly how she felt. She'd been understood.

"Do you get used to all the work?" she asked, rushing her words.

"I come here quite a bit," he said.

There was an easy going attitude about Jack and it worked like a charm. In his presence she felt less frazzled, more optimistic. It was pleasing and peaceful to be with him in the same way it was pleasing and peaceful to be in the garden. Jack made a gesture toward a bench in the garden and they went and sat down together.

They sat without speaking and with little need to. But rather than causing additional apprehension the way silence between two people new to each other sometimes can, the quiet moment contributed to their affinity.

Next to each other the two made a remarkable looking couple. Veronica, half Lebanese and half Italian, was as dark in complexion as Jack was fair. She had long dark brown hair that shined chestnut colored in the sunlight. Untied, it fell down over her shoulders in a luxurious wave. Her eyes were almond shaped and deep brown, lending an exotic and alluring look. If those two people had been flowers, they would be a yellow rose and light brown orchid. But they were a young man and woman, beautiful as they were. Glowing in their beginning, radiant in their freshness and magical in their natural state-no more was needed for them to be all there was and ever could be.

"You know what amazes me," Jack said after a while, scanning the garden. "We can get these flowers to grow all year, but we never take the time to smell them."

"Sometimes it does seem to me that everything is a mad rush," Veronica said, gazing around the garden too.

"We have to slow it down. Each person has to regulate their own clock to keep a more even pace," Jack added.

"How's that even possible today the way we live? I mean everything we do is done at warp speed. To do otherwise is to be left behind," Veronica countered, still talking quickly as if to reinforce her point.

"I think it's as Gandhi said," Jack went on. "We have to be the change we want to see in the world. There's no other way. And as I see the world today, no other choice."

"You're an idealist," Veronica said, turning to Jack with a skeptical smile.

"God," said Jack. "I hope so; I don't want to be anything less."

"Okay, but what do you do now? How do you slow it down and reduce the constant tension? I mean we all take midterms, even dreamers, right?" There was a certain street wise quality to Veronica's analysis.

"I'll show you how I do it. Come on," Jack said, getting up.

Veronica followed Jack across the field to the student parking lot. Jack's maroon jeep was far down in the lot in the sophomore section. They got in and he sped out of the lot and off campus onto the open road. Veronica, bemused, sat beside him with childlike curiosity about where they were going, happy to be getting away from the intensity of campus, instantly trusting Jack.

"Where are we going?" she asked after a moment, her dark hair pushed back by the wind blowing at her with the Jeep's top down, her intensity abating, giving way to the animated interest of a fun-loving kid.

"Does it matter?" Jack questioned.

"No, not really," Veronica chuckled, her dark eyes drinking in the open road.

They took a drive out into the country. They did not go very far, just far enough so that you could feel the pace change. All the activity of campus passed away behind them. It was as if they had been listening too long to music played too loud and now, with the drive out into the country, that annoying music stopped. The country was slow-paced, unobtrusive, and open. No uproar-no rush, toned down, nothing but open space. It was the perfect antidote to the tumult of campus before midterms.

The sun shone brightly on the road before them; the air was clear and pleasant. Long stretches of road rolled under the jeep's wheels in an easy, rhythmic flow. And Jack drove on, apparently without any specific destination-relaxed, just going with the road.

"Sometimes I think the dynamos out of control," he said.

"We do seem a tormented lot," Veronica agreed.

"Not out here, we're not," Jack said. "We have to get back here to the country and, somehow, we have to take it with us wherever else we go."

As he said that he slowed down to make a turn. They had come to a ridge where a dirt road crossed their road. A vista of burgundy grass extended away from the intersection toward hills in the distance on both sides. The grass swayed in a mild breeze so the field looked like a crimson wave moving toward, then away from them from north to south, the wave broken only where the road cut into it. He turned right, off the road, onto the dirt road and headed south toward some hills. He drove three or four miles over dusty roads, like a boat sailing through a choppy red sea until he came to a second ridge. He climbed the ridge and then started slowly down the other side. As the ridge dropped down they could see, well before the hills but framed by them, a crystalline lake. The lake sat like a blue jewel in a sea of blood red grass. It was a narrow but long lake fed by a small river that entered and exited in the middle on both sides. Jack looked at the lake in awe.

"It's something, isn't it?" he said.

"It looks like a Cross," Veronica commented.

"I know," Jack said.

"Are you religious?" she asked.

"The Cross means something to me," he said.

"What?" she asked, looking at the lake.

"Sacrifice, renewal," he said, "and goodness." Jack continued gazing at the lake.

"God, I love the outdoors. That's why I like it here so much. I guess you could say this place is my church and my religion."

"Meaning?" Veronica asked.

"Meaning this lake with its shape and with its own special beauty is my symbol. We all need working symbols," Jack said.

"Is it just symbolic for you, then?" Veronica inquired.

"No. It's real, as real as you are," Jack said, "and it kind of blows me away, like you do." Jack shifted his gaze from the lake to the sky and back. "It's starting," he said.

"What is?"

"The show, look."

With light playing over the field and lake, first illuminating, then muting both, a magnificent display occurred. All in an instant the wide field flamed a burning red and then the flame diminished to a ruddy glow. The blue lake sparkled and shined, then darkened, subdued to navy in the shade. Jack had been here before and knew the light and how it changed and how the colors did. He pulled the jeep to the side of the road and stopped. For several minutes the entire scene played out repeatedly, as the light came and went, shined and died. It was like watching a magical stage from perfect seats where not a nuance could be missed and the stage genius operating the lights, with utmost dexterity and keenly aware of his guests attention, did not fail to put on his best show. There was such ineffable magic going on in such a golden silence. And through it all, Veronica, with Jack beside her, felt a child's sense of wonder. Never had she felt so immediately attracted to someone and not nervous about it, but joyous.

"This is amazing," she said.

"If you get too close it's not the same. You have to know how to look at it," Jack said, "and it's the same with school. It's probably the same with everything. You just have to know how to look at it."

Veronica thought about everything they'd seen: the ride out, the rolling country road and the quiet, beautiful, hills. She thought about campus, subdued by distance and mood now. She thought about seeing things with Jack. She looked at Jack and couldn't stop looking.

In the afternoon's falling light he glowed intermittently-like a flickering candle. His tousled hair was burnished gold, his bright blue eyes warm and clear with kindness and attention. His eyes were the eyes of someone who had just given a special gift and couldn't help being a little delighted. Delightful is how she saw him. There is magic in the world. That is what she knew. He proved it. There was never any rush. It all came naturally after that. Two hands, warm together.

Once they had met, their life together felt as if it were lived outside of time with the only urgency their love. Their seasons were seasons of affection and they followed an orbit that had them revolving around each other.

But now, at the hour of their departure to Taylor Island, an alien quality emerged, a tension hitherto unknown. It was as if Time had caught up to them and they heard at last the inevitable tick tock of its breath.

Veronica had readied herself according to Jack's desire and met him outside her apartment. Jack's reassuring smile put her more at ease and he loaded her bags into the jeep. Then he got behind the wheel and Veronica took the passenger seat.

"I feel like we're escaping from something," she said with a look of still unsatisfied curiosity. Jack squeezed her hand in his.

"Not escaping, embarking," he answered, aglow with anticipation. "Other worlds than this await us."

"Do they?" Veronica worried.

# 5

Jack and Veronica stayed the night in Boston, and took a bus to Cape Cod at an ungodly hour to make the earliest ferry to Taylor Island.

The prow of the boat cut a V-shaped wake through the smooth water heading toward Taylor Island. It would get into Chimera harbor at 7:15 where Uncle Browne would meet them. Taylor Island had two main towns, one at either end. Chimera on the Northwest side and Cythere, fifteen miles away, on the Southeast end of the Island. Jack's aunt and uncle lived in Cythere.

It was a pleasant morning, not as chilly as usual coming across the sound, so Jack took off his parka and placed it on a white steel bench next to Veronica. They were up top in the open air. Veronica sat, busily trying to push her camera back into her over-stuffed backpack. Jack stood at the rail, watching as the boat glided over the water, searching ahead for the outline of Taylor Island. He wore a long sleeved white linen shirt, tan khaki pants and penny loafers. As the sun rose, it made his hair shine reddish gold. His clear blue eyes eagerly looked out toward the island.

With the commotion Veronica made, Jack turned to watch as she wrestled with the back pack, determined by sheer force of will to get every-thing into it. Amused, Jack commented, "V, no sense stuffing the camera back in, you'll just be taking it out again in a minute."

Veronica hesitated, not sure whether to put the camera in the bag or use it at that moment to snap a photo. She scanned the view before her.

"You said it's lovely here, and it is," she commented, the camera now raised and ready to shoot.

"I said lovely? That sounds like your word. I said it's cool here," Jack responded, eyeing Veronica. She wore a light silk rainbow scarf to keep her neck warm, and her chestnut hair cascaded around her shoulders and over the top of her iris-blue blouse. She had on thick, black, sunglasses Jack had bought for her. She could have been an Arabian princess, and Jack loved looking at her. "Veronica," he said, "you look great this morning. Maybe we can get someone to take our photo."

A young ship's assistant passed by and Jack asked him to take their picture. Standing against the railing of the boat, with the sun rising and the island coming into view behind them, and with the calm, aquamarine water in the background, they looked splendid.

In a few moments the ferry horn sounded and the ferry slowed as it came into the channel to dock. The captain swung the boat around to back it into its slip and that gave Jack and Veronica time to get their things together. Veronica scudded about, picking up her things, looking around for anything she might have left behind, making a small uproar by her anxious movements. She started putting the camera away again but stopped when she noticed Jack watching her. He was just about to laugh.

"What?" she asked. "What's so funny?"

"You, you seem altogether discombobulated."

"Thanks a lot," Veronica grinned, "guess I'm nervous about meeting your aunt and uncle. Do you think they'll like me?" she asked beseechingly, at the same time abandoning attempts to control everything around her and trying to relax for a moment.

"I know they'll like you," Jack said confidently.

"How do you know that?" Veronica asked.

"Because they're nice," Jack insisted.

"But why will they like me?" Veronica pleaded, raising the sunglasses off her eyes so they rested on her forehead and Jack could see her anxiety.

"Because you're nice," he said, walking up to her and warmly gazing into her eyes to reassure her, "and you have nothing to worry about and we'll enjoy ourselves, right?" Jack had placed his hands on Veronica's shoulders so as to steady her and he felt her body relax under his touch.

"I'm being absurd, I know," Veronica said.

At the dock it had suddenly begun sprinkling even while the sun still shone.

"Island weather," Jack said, "you never know."

Uncle Browne wasn't there yet. Jack had called the night before and given the arrival time. He explained to Veronica, "He's never on time. I think he goes by a different clock." But Veronica's insecurity had resurfaced.

"I hope it has nothing to do with my coming. You're certain they know I'm coming, right?"

At school she was usually confident, doing Dean's list work every semester. But she was insecure about Jack's family and their affluent background. And recently she'd started to imagine Jack's aunt and uncle as aloof snobs, probably because they lived on this well-to-do island, out of circulation with the average world, where many of the islanders were, in fact, rich. "Stop it, Veronica," Jack laughed, "you remind me of a kid about to perform in front of an audience. Trust me; you'll like my aunt and uncle." Just as he said that a car horn beeped. It was a high pitched, squeaky sounding beep, as if the horn had just inhaled helium or came from a child's bath toy.

"That's my uncle's car," Jack said excitedly, "no mistaking it." They turned together. At the curb a tall, thin, man exited a cobalt blue Mercedes coup.

"Jacket!" he called out.

The Mercedes had its top down and the driver waived a hello with one hand and held an open, pink, umbrella in the other. He had silver hair with bushy, protruding, eyebrows that looked like white caterpillars resting horizontally above his eyes. He wore a pale blue blazer and navy polo shirt and had a red bandana tied around his neck in a makeshift ascot. When he spoke his eyes moved all around with great animated interest—up and down, then wide open, and then almost closed. And the eyebrows, with all of this expressiveness, resembled white moths jumping around a wild-eyed flame. Uncle Browne walked over to Jack.

"Damn switch to the convertible top is broken and I never know when the top will go up or down. I was lucky your aunt left this umbrella in there," he said, waving the umbrella like a sword at the sky and letting go a burst of laughter in his frenzied jubilation.

"Uncle Browne," Jack said affectionately, shaking his uncle's hand.

"Jacket, boy-you're the spitting image of your young dad, and even more handsome if that's possible. Sorry I didn't make it to your graduation but we had one of our own, you know. I'm so happy you came up," he said, embracing Jack. Jack stepped back to stand beside Veronica.

"Uncle Browne, this is Veronica," Jack offered proudly.

Uncle Browne took a step backward. He was a tall man at six foot four, slender and genteel looking. His silver hair was long and brushed back and he had an aquiline nose. When he stood tall and held his chin up to contemplate something, he looked distinguished and formidable, like some early American aristocrat poised around a table as some important document is signed.

"Veronica," Uncle Browne said dramatically, "how nice to see you. My nephew talks about you with hyperbole, you know. But I must say it turns out to be understatement."

"My uncle's an English professor at the community college here," Jack explained. "He's the only person I know who talks about usual things in unusual terms. He once told me I was the personification of youthful splendor. Isn't that what you said, Uncle Browne?"

"I did and still do," Uncle Browne proffered.

"I think he's some kind of word wizard," Jack said to Veronica.

"I tend the un-penned garden of words that grow all around us, Jacket. That's my stock and trade. But what I say about you and Veronica, like all good verbal blooms, grows out of the truth." Uncle Browne punctuated his statement with a wink, and then continued. "Now are you two hungry at all?" He asked the question, did not wait for their answer, and nodded yes for them.

"Good," he said, "we'll go over to The Doc's Diner. I love it there. It's the best greasy spoon on Earth."

Jack and Veronica had not had breakfast so the diner idea appealed to them. They followed Uncle Browne up from the ferry terminal parking lot and crossed the road to enter a path in the field that bordered the still sleeping town of Chimera. A pleasant sea breeze came off the water and they inhaled the briny sea air. They walked with the sun rising higher over the sound behind them, feeling generally uplifted by the fresh quality of a new day on the island. The quiet streets of Chimera were empty but for a few early risers out for breakfast or to walk their dogs. Uncle Browne, Veronica, and Jack were the only ones walking on their side of the street. They passed a series of closed shops on Chimera Way.

Chimera was the whimsical equivalent of the quaint fishing village of Cythere where Uncle Browne and his wife lived. It had become a kind of artist's colony in the last decade. And it was unusual with its gingerbread houses in as many bright colors as there are crayons in a crayon box; an antique ·but still functioning carousel; a main street loaded with esoteric boutiques. Jack hadn't been there in three years but particularly remembered one shop, a glass blowers shop that had enthralled him. He looked for it as they walked along Chimera Way.

They passed a series of other unique shops with everything and anything artistic and eclectic: a bead store, a rare book store, a medieval dress shop. Then Jack spotted the glass blower's shop. Uncle Browne and Veronica walked ahead chatting, so Jack paused by himself to look at the shop.

Through the front window he could see some pieces displayed that returned the exuberant feeling he'd had the last time he'd come to the shop. He'd gone into it then. Today, he had to settle for what he could see in the display window.

A piece containing swirls of orange suggestive of desert sand caught his eye. It was as if sunlight over the sand at dusk had been glazed for posterity and now remained forever captured in the surface of a table top. Next was a glass lampshade of silver delicacy, spun in a spiral, surrounding muted light. This shade resembled a pine tree enameled by crystals of ice shining on a winter night. Another piece, a honey-colored vase, touched by dots of glistening mica, stood out without flowers as if itself in bloom-the white-silver specks of mica rising in relief from the honey plane like pearl droplets on a suntanned hand. All of these nuances of light, these specks of gold the artist must have known and drawn upon, Jack thought, as he gazed at them. He wanted to see more. He tried entering but the door was locked. Then he heard Veronica calling, and moved quickly to catch up. At the end of Chimera Way they turned onto a short, narrow, street and walked toward a different dock. They came to a cobble-stoned alley fronting the water and there The Doc's Diner sign hung, creaking in the slight wind. The sign was dark blue and rusty around the edges. The diner faced the water, which was calm and sunlit. Above the water a swirl of small birds swept the sky in what looked like a pointillist's black hand as they flew in perfect synchronization this way and that before disappearing somewhere. Jack admired the pattern the birds made while Uncle Browne lifted his nose; nostrils flared, and took in the aroma of coffee.

"My God," he said, "I love that smell." He walked into the diner without hesitation, smiled at those he knew, and sat down on a stool at the long counter. He spun a little on the stool so that he could see Jack and Veronica entering. Then he patted the stool next to him for them to sit down.

They sat on stools at the counter of this railroad-car like diner. Bacon sizzled on a huge, grease-smeared grill. It smelled wonderful. A tall man, thin, with a pony tail tucked under his baseball cap worked the grill like a magician. His tattooed forearms moved in repeated patterns and his large hands fetched and broke and spilled what seemed like half a dozen eggs at a time onto the sizzling skillet when they weren't stirring and turning and flipping the flapjacks or eggs or grabbing slabs of bacon to separate and fry.

"What'll it be, Browne?" the cook asked.

"Whatever's most decadent, but don't tell my cardiologist," Uncle Browne retorted.

"I'll give you the artery clogger special," the cook said.

"Delightful," said Uncle Browne with a devilish smile.

"Doc," he said, addressing the cook, "I'd like you to meet my nephew, Jack, and his girlfriend, Veronica."

"Nice to know you; vacationing?" the cook asked.

"We're taking a few days, yeah," said Jack.

"You came at a good time," the cook said. "It was just announced, Illumination Night is this week."

"Is that right?" said Uncle Browne. "I thought it'd be. You two will enjoy that," Uncle Browne said earnestly. "Jack just graduated from Duke," Uncle Browne said next.

"Impressive," the cook said, "know what you're going to do?"

"I'm thinking things over," Jack said.

"Good idea," said the cook.

"He's thinking about Wall Street," Uncle Browne said, giving the cook a long contemplative expression, acting very dignified in the process.

"Are you?" the cook asked, and then softly, "I used to work on Wall Street." He moved down the counter after that, working the line of customers. He came back to them when they had finished eating.

"Enjoy your food?" the cook resumed.

"You're going to kill me," Uncle Browne said, and then like a vaudeville comedian, "I'll see you tomorrow."

"Sure, Browne," the cook said, "I'll prepare something equally deadly for you."

"What did you do on Wall Street?" Jack inquired, his interest piqued.

"I have a doctorate in economics," the cook answered.

Uncle Browne seemed delighted with this. Jack and Veronica reacted with surprise, looking at each other as if to say do you believe this?

"That's why it's The Doc's Diner," Uncle Browne said.

Once outside Jack pressed Uncle Browne. "Does that guy really have a doctorate in economics?"

"Absolutely. Next time we go in I'll get him to show you his diploma. I think it's hanging in the pantry."

"And did he really work on Wall Street?"

"For ten years, I think. Hated it. Loves this, though," Uncle Browne said.

"That's amazing," Veronica said.

"So why the diner?" Jack queried.

"Doing something he likes." Uncle Browne sounded slightly more serious.

"Wow, an economist working a diner," Jack said. "I guess he used what he'd studied on Wall Street. I guess he did what he had to."

"Uses it now, too," Uncle Browne put in. "He tells me he can figure out, way ahead of time, how many eggs the summer will eat."

# 6

Uncle Browne took the Island Road out of Chimera and headed for Cythere. The road passed through forests and then back into a clearing before ascending a hill in a serpentine pattern above the water. The water below was silvery blue in the morning light and some small boats drifted at anchor, back and forth close to shore. Along the road, wisps of long, green grass bent with graceful suppleness blown by a gentle wind. The grass bending and boats drifting and car climbing to make the hill combined into one large movement—like some silent music played in perfect rhythm with the world.

Soon Uncle Browne and Aunt Millicent's house came into view. Through a mist of light and haze of motion, Jack and Veronica saw the small cape emerge from the landscape. It was a house like in a dream with a hilly background, half-light and half-shadow. Uncle Browne stopped the car on a plateau and gazed toward his property to see if he could spot what he referred to as his mystery of affection.

"You might be able to see Millie," he said, his hand shading his eyes, "she's at her painting now, probably checking the morning light."

Aunt Millicent was an artist who had recently attained a kind of local celebrity for her seascapes. Her current project was to paint the cove near their house at different times of day to see how the light changed it. Uncle Browne pointed toward the house and hill of land it sat upon and then lowered his focus, "The light's brilliant over the cove, I'm sure she's out there."

In a moment, they drove onto the property. Jutting toward them at a bend in the driveway was a wooden placard mounted to a robust elm. It was a small, oval placard with black italicized letters that read Maison d'Etre.

"That's a cool sign," Veronica offered. "You like that?" Uncle Browne responded.

"Yes," Veronica said.

"That's one of Millie's creations. What do you think it means?" Uncle Browne asked.

"Oh no, here comes my uncle the professor," Jack said.

Veronica answered like she was asking a question, "That your home is your reason to be?"

"C'est bon," Uncle Browne said. "Jack, your girl gets an A for life." Veronica beamed with the complement.

Aunt Millicent approached the car as the others got out, coming up to them in a paint-smeared smock. She hugged Jack right away, a brush still in her hand.

"Oh dear, it's so lovely to see you," she said.

"Jack's girl's a keeper," Uncle Browne reported.

"Is she?" Aunt Millicent asked pleasantly. Then she turned to Veronica with a welcoming smile.

"Aunt Millicent," Jack said, "this is Veronica."

"Hello, Veronica," Aunt Millicent said, taking both Veronica's hands in hers and squeezing them.

After pleasantries were completed and Jack and Veronica settled in, Aunt Millicent decided to go to the Up Island market for groceries. She invited Veronica to come along. Jack and his uncle stayed behind and Uncle Browne suggested a walk.

It was close to midday when they started walking and the sun was high, bright and strong. They dressed in swim suits and T shirts and Uncle Browne suggested they walk along the shoreline in the cove out toward Smith Point.

Smith Point was a large cliff that projected out into the sound and separated the sound from the ocean. It was the most prominent land mass on the island, renowned for its red clay cliffs; high, massive, wall-like bulk, and magnificent views. It was the island's natural wonder, looming as it did above the water and holding back the land. Smith Point was two miles away and, according to Uncle Browne, perfect walking distance for stretching out his aching muscles.

Uncle Browne's hair had gone gray when he was still in his forties. Now it was silver and sometimes in the light shone bluish. He kept his full head of hair long and combed it off his forehead to the side. The long silver strands completely covered his large ears which were only visible when the wind blew or the hair was wet, and which always made Jack laugh. Jack was his only nephew and Uncle Browne looked upon him fondly and proudly, the way he might have looked upon his own son if he had one.

Uncle Browne had a nickname for Jack that came about when Jack was just five years old. Young Jack had heard his Uncle calling to his wife for his jacket and thought he was calling him. So Jack became Jacket. It was a name Uncle Browne delighted in saying. As they walked, Uncle Browne inquired about Jack's plans. "Jacket, where do you go from here?"

"I'm going home for a couple weeks, then to Montana with my parents," Jack said.

"Isn't that something you do every year?" Uncle Browne remembered.

"Yes it is," Jack said, "we usually go there around my birthday."

"Twenty-two, right?" Uncle Browne calculated. "It's hard to believe, I remember you as a baby." Uncle Browne patted Jack's shoulder. "Long range plans?"

"I have an opportunity to work in Durham," Jack said.

"What about Wall Street, isn't that the family plan?" Uncle Browne asked, gazing ahead toward Smith Point.

"No interviews yet," Jack said.

"That's surprising," said Uncle Browne.

Jack viewed the water off in the distance. He felt uneasy not telling his uncle about Sanders Brown and was relieved by the next question.

"How do your folks like Veronica?" Uncle Browne asked.

"Oh, I think Mom's just a little jealous. Dad doesn't say much.

He seems to like her. But I'm pretty sure he doesn't want me to get seriously involved. I know Mom doesn't."

"Oh, I see. They're practicing parental blindness. I see it among my friends with their children. But your parents are more astute than that. They must know what's what."

"Is it that obvious?" Jack smiled.

"Abundantly so, and from what I can glean, with good reason. She's charming and lovely, Jacket. I'm happy for you. How does she get on with them?" Uncle Browne asked.

"Veronica likes them. But she doesn't share their conviction about what's right for me and what I should do now," Jack said.

"Explain, Jacket."

"Well, she's not keen on me going to Wall Street. She thinks I should do what I really want to. She would like me to stay in Durham."

"What's the Durham offer?" Uncle Browne asked.

"To work for the Durham Nursery," Jack said.

"Interesting. Of course you'd be closer to Veronica that way," Uncle Browne said considerately.

"I'm sure that's a big part of it, but it's more than that, Uncle."

"Tell me." Uncle Browne leaned a little toward Jack so as to better hear him.

"I have a chance to work as a landscaping consultant. I've worked at the Nursery through college and the owner likes me, thinks I'm good at landscape design. He's offered me a full time job doing that."

"What kind of business is it?" Uncle Browne inquired.

"Oh, it's big in the area, doing a lot of commercial design, and high-end residential design, doing municipal planning too. It's growing all the time-three locations now and will expand," Jack said.

"And you're qualified for that?" Uncle Browne followed.

"I took courses in landscape design at Duke. My minor, I guess you could say."

"So you like it," Uncle Browne said, turning to Jack to catch his expression.

"Love it!" Jack lit up.

"So why finance?" Uncle Browne's voice rose with the question.

"Realistic, I guess. I could make a lot more money in finance than landscape design," Jack said, sounding as if he were reading a script.

"That doesn't sound entirely like you, Jacket," Uncle Browne said, peering at his nephew.

"I guess I've grown up, know my responsibilities." Jack's voice lacked the conviction it had when he'd spoken about the Durham Nursery.

"Being grown up is overrated if you ask me. Besides, Jacket, you were born grown up," Uncle Browne said. "Will you take the Durham offer?"

"I'm not sure," Jack said."

"Why not?" Uncle Browne prodded.

"It's not Wall Street!" Jack said soberly.

"No, it's not. Sounds more like Main Street. What's wrong with that?"

"It doesn't present the opportunity Wall Street does," Jack recited.

"Jack, excuse me, but you sound like your father. In a minute you're going to tell me it takes a lot of money to float the boat," Uncle Browne said, his voice sounding in gentle reproach.

"It's true, Uncle." Jack spoke as if with allegiance to a cause.

"But is it true for you, Jacket? Is Wall Street true for you?" There was a provocative tone to Uncle Browne's question. Jack thought it might be the same tone his uncle used when challenging his students to think.

"I am my father's son," Jack said, still going by the script that had directed his life until now.

"Indeed. And from the time you were young, you've been made into his image. And through it all, you've excelled. You are a testament to your father. You have his drive and pluck. Now you speak with his sense of responsibility. You're admirable in every way a young man can be. But Jacket, this idea that only by going to Wall Street, as your father did, will you be fulfilling your responsibility to yourself and the country is, perhaps, specious as it applies to you." Uncle Browne faced Jack with an earnest expression.

"What do you mean, Uncle Browne?" Jack said.

"I mean there is no rush. I mean you are not exactly your father," Uncle Browne returned.

"I'm enough like him that going to Wall Street would not be a mistake." Again, Jack's answer sounded in self-debate.

"Perhaps, Jacket, but what's the rush? You should take time to explore your options. Wall Street is not going anywhere. Ever since you were a young boy, you loved being outdoors. You thrive in the open air. Now I hear about your talent in landscape, a talent that's worth considering before you plunge into your father's dream."

"It's not just his dream," Jack said. "It's what I've talked about forever."

"Then it can wait a little longer, it will be there if it's real," Uncle Browne said. Uncle Browne walked over to the shoreline and bent down and dipped his hands into the water. With both hands he wet his face then returned to Jack. He gazed at Jack with as accepting a look as any man could give another.

"Jack," he said warmly, "it's okay to be confused." In Uncle Browne's tone was a kind of permission, conveyed to his nephew like a release. Then, as though something had just occurred to him, Uncle Browne added, "But I'm putting the cart before the horse. You don't have an interview anyway."

Jack wanted to open up. He was acutely aware of being dishonest. He blurted out, "But I know I'll get one." The force of his remark caused Uncle Browne to raise an eyebrow. Uncle Browne addressed Jack with an expression of serious consideration, "When it comes down to it, Jacket, do what makes you happy."

Jack's eyes filled with gratitude. But then he paused, reflecting about Sanders Brown, Wall Street, and the Durham Nursery. He became subdued. He needed to air his dilemma but couldn't, so he put into words the heavy question he'd lugged around too long without help.

"Uncle, what if I don't really know what I should do?"

"Give yourself some time, you'll figure it out."

"Uncle Browne," Jack inquired, "do you think it'd be wrong if l didn't go to Wall Street?"

Uncle Browne's answer rang with the clarity of a bell at midnight. "No! You must be true to yourself, Jacket. That's what the Greeks said: Know thyself and nothing in excess." Jack needed to hear that but had more to get off his chest. He was thinking about Duke and Phil Dayton, and about his parents.

"You don't think I'd be shirking my responsibility by not going?" he asked timidly.

"Absolutely not," Uncle Browne insisted.

"You see, Uncle, I've always been responsible." Jack said, questioning himself out loud.

"I know your qualities, Jacket," Uncle Browne said, "they won't change."

"But shouldn't I do what I have to first. I can do the rest later?"

"Jacket, you'd be no less a man for adding local color to a region's growing possibilities, than you'd be by launching a business in the markets and seeing to it that the yearly yield beats the averages."

Jack looked at his Uncle, his eyes nearly closed in a squint from the bright sun.

"It's important."

"What?"

"Beating the average."

"Whatever you decide to do, Jacket, you'll beat the average. All I'm saying is take your time-don't let it take you."

They were at the summit of their walk now, at the top of Smith Point. They walked up to a railing positioned on the cliff side and looked out and down. Below the cliff on the eastern side was a long stretch of smooth white sand. The beach there faced the Atlantic and at that moment the water was exceptionally calm.

"That's inviting," Jack said.

"Liberating too," Uncle Brown said wryly. "Is it, really?" Jack grinned in understanding.

"Oh, certainly, that's probably the most liberating beach on the island."

"Do you and Aunt Millicent ever go there?"

"We're liberated at least once a week," Uncle Browne said, casting a mischievous stare down at the beach.

"God, Uncle, you crack me up. You and Aunt Millicent have always been so . . . I don't know what the word is . . . Liberated!"

"Should we have a go at liberation?" Uncle Brown queried with a double jump of his eyebrows.

Jack paused at his uncle's suggestion, but loved it. That's always how it was with his uncle. It was like being with a close friend who knew you better than you did yourself and with whom you always enjoyed doing things you'd never thought of trying.

"What the hell, Uncle, you only live once!" Jack said.

They descended a weather bleached set of wooden steps down the side of the cliff to the soft sand of the shore. In a flash, Uncle Browne was out on the sand as naked as a newborn, running like a teenager toward the water, his silver hair waving in the light breeze like a freedom flag and his big ears clearly visible in the sunlight. In an instant, he dove into the water.

Jack followed, laughing hysterically at his Uncle's boldness, smiling at the other sun-worshippers on the beach whom he passed going out to his Uncle. Then at the edge of the sand and the sea, he stopped and stood tall. His golden hair shone. The only thing he had on was his Duke ring. He heard Uncle Browne calling him to jump in. He waved, laughed, and all at once, dove in. Into the ebb and flow he shot yelling at the top of his lungs: "Liberation!"

# 7

In their last night on Taylor Island, Aunt Millicent prepared a special dinner for Jack and Veronica. She'd made a bouillabaisse that she'd served with a crusty French loaf and well-chilled Chablis. Everyone loved the dinner with Uncle Browne the most vociferous admirer of his wife's work. He extolled the virtues of saffron and fennel, proclaiming the bouillabaisse perfect because the cook had mastered the broth rather than overwhelming the dish with a surfeit of seafood. "You're an artist through and through, Millie," he toasted his wife.

Coincidentally, it was also Illumination Night in Chimera, so the pleasant lingering around the table after a meal had to be curtailed. Uncle Browne, excited about the prospect of Illumination Night, nevertheless seemed least inclined to move. "I could use some more of that Chablis," he announced, holding up a crystal goblet.

"Shall I open another bottle?" Jack offered.

"Please," Uncle Browne said.

"Do you think you should, Browne?" Aunt Millicent cautioned. "Parking is atrocious on Illumination Night."

"I know exactly where to park," Uncle Browne said assuredly. "It won't be a problem."

"On Illumination Night?" Aunt Millicent asked incredulously. "Browne, I think the Chablis has gone to your head."

Jack gave Veronica a quizzical look. He didn't know whether to get the wine or not. Veronica returned the puzzled glance with a half-smile and shoulder shrug, sorry she couldn't help.

"Chablis," Uncle Browne exclaimed, putting an end to Jack's dilemma. Jack left to retrieve the wine which was stored in the butler's pantry off the kitchen. On his way through the house, he took in what he saw: There was a small television in the great room. Books were scattered everywhere as were the paraphernalia of art: easels, brushes, paints, frames, cameras. That stuff filled a side room that must have served as Aunt Millicent's studio. The whole house apparently served as Uncle Browne's reading room.

In the kitchen, he glimpsed framed photos of children mounted on the walls. All the photos had accompanying acknowledgments and were of children that Uncle Browne and Aunt Millicent had evidently helped to feed. Jack felt admiration for his aunt and uncle and some sadness as well that they'd never had their own children. But they seemed happy to him.

Momentarily, he was back with the wine. He poured a glass for Uncle Browne who took a long drink then rose up all of a sudden. Pacing the room with a sort of magisterial grace, he stopped suddenly to address the others.

"Everyone," he said briskly, "I hear the lanterns calling.

Illumination Night is upon us!"

"You're looking illuminated already, if you ask me, dear," Aunt Millicent said.

"And you, radiant," Uncle Browne returned.

After a perfunctory clean up, they were off to Chimera. By the time they arrived, night had fallen. The streets were lined with cars and teeming with people. Uncle Browne parked far away, finding a spot with only a little trouble near the bluffs opposite the Chimera police station.

"My beauty should be safe here," he said, patting the Coup as he got out.

"Oh thank you dear," said Aunt Millicent, "I feel quite safe indeed."

"Wonderful," said Uncle Browne.

"Jacket, you and your Inamorata don't have to stay with us if you want to look around. We're headed over to the Tabernacle. We'll be at the community sing. I love to show off your aunt at such things." Aunt Millicent let out an operatic, "Ah..ah..ah..Ah!"

"Isn't she divine?" Uncle Brown said wryly.

"Out of this world," Jack said, raising his eyebrows and tightening his face as if he'd just heard chalk scratching a chalkboard. He and Veronica accepted the offer to wander off.

The Tabernacle was a large open-air structure built in the mid-nineteenth century for prayer meetings and spiritual revivals. It was now used for things such as the community sing. It had a large stage with wooden pews below the stage that spread back to an open exit. The tabernacle could hold five hundred people at a time. Its wooden roof was octagonal and pitched in such a way as to allow in light while keeping the congregation dry. When Jack was young, he'd attended summer day camp at the Tabernacle. He remembered hiding in its nooks.

"We'll see you at the Tabernacle," he said.

Uncle Browne and Aunt Millicent walked away arm in arm. A big orange moon filled the sky above Taylor Sound casting an orange glow over the nighttime water. Jack and Veronica walked along the top of the bluff across from where the car had been parked watching the calm water of the Sound shining in the moonlight. They walked down some stairs to a beach under the moonlight. Holding hands, they strolled.

"Your aunt and uncle are something," Veronica said.

"I know," said Jack.

"They really enjoy each other," she commented.

"Always have," Jack confirmed.

"How do you think they've stayed so close?" Veronica asked.

"Love and honesty," Jack declared.

"Love and honesty." Veronica sounded out the words. "They seem like perfect names for a couple. Let's call your aunt and uncle Love and Honesty, Jack," she said, "May we?"

Jack made a face that suggested he thought the names too cute.

"Oh all right, Jack. They'll remain Browne and Millicent. I know how much those names mean to you."

"You're considerate," Jack said.

Then Veronica added, "But what about us. We're Love and Honesty, too," she said. Jack gave her an odd look that made Veronica uneasy. She immediately spun a strand of hair around a finger.

"Is something the matter?" she asked.

"No, nothing's the matter." Jack seemed suddenly too serious. Veronica's word games had upset him, made him think of the Sanders Brown letter. She knew he was thinking about something, read it in his face. She asked again, more seriously, about Love and Honesty.

"You do see us like that, don't you? We love each other; we're honest with each other. That's all I meant." Veronica worried. Provoked by her entreating eyes, Jack wanted to allay her concern.

"Veronica, I couldn't love anyone more," he said fervidly That remark uplifted her. She held his hand tightly and they walked on. Veronica talked some more about Aunt Millicent and Uncle Browne.

"Your aunt and uncle prove you don't need that much to be happy."

"They've got a lot," Jack said.

"They've got the right things. We could learn from them, don't you think?" Veronica wasn't suggesting anything. She was merely stating her belief. There was no doubt in her mind that Jack loved her and was honest with her. But Jack's guilt added to Veronica's words an element of moral instruction that wasn't intended.

He became quiet. Again, he thought about having left Veronica out of the loop concerning something important to both of them. It didn't matter that he'd torn up the Sanders Brown letter, at least partly, to spare Veronica the burden of his indecision. Tearing the letter up made things easier for them is what he'd thought. It removed the conflict. He'd thought that, too. But then he wondered about the wisdom of avoiding conflict. Difficult things had to be shared perhaps more than happy ones in a relationship. He knew that. Perhaps by tearing the letter up, all he'd done was bury the conflict. Perhaps it would return to torment him. He felt that, in some way, it already had. It would have been better to get it out in the open, to decide things together. And here was Veronica, holding up his aunt and uncle's life as a model. When she said, we are like them, because he felt badly what he heard is, we need to be like them. He heard admonishment when none was given.

He felt remorseful and ashamed. He watched Veronica as she moved. She was innocent, faultless, undeserving of the backlash his compunction returned for not confiding in her. He checked his mood and saw through her eyes, the sweet wisdom she'd intended.

"V, I hear what you're saying about Uncle Browne and Aunt Millicent. They lead a good life."

They walked back up the stairs. At the top, looking over the bluff down to the water and then up at the moon, Jack paused and put his arm around Veronica. He appeared somewhat burdened.

"I just don't know," he said. "I've always been sure about things and now I'm not. I'm sure about you. I'm sure about us. But about the rest . . . I just don't know."

Veronica heard Jack's torment. "Let's go enjoy the celebration," she said. "Let's not worry right now."

Across the road, the paths of a wide field were filled with people. They walked in lines, many two by two, quietly, almost reverently, toward the Tabernacle. The Tabernacle was beyond the field behind a row of houses, nestled in a space all by itself. The field was well lit both from moonlight and the glow of lanterns hung on porches all around.

The houses around the field looked like giant gingerbread houses. All wore their Illumination Night decorations lanterns hung from their spacious porches-throwing off light like beacons. Lanterns made of paper shades, hung from porch ceilings-strung up, spread out, wrapped around in spectacular radiance, like glowing necklaces. Paper shades of myriad colors casting myriad colored light: blue, green, lemon yellow, salmon, teal and pink, a panoply of magical, enchanting light that touched the field from every direction. People moved out of darkness in streams of light into color. Then they passed again into darkness and were lost, headed toward the Tabernacle. They moved like ghostly pilgrims toward the Tabernacle, like shadows seeking light. One by one and two by two, people moved as shadows first, then in illuminated jubilance.

At one point all paths in the field converged and everyone coming out of the field had to use the same path to exit and pass on toward the Tabernacle. In this milling procession, Jack lost Veronica. She'd gone ahead. He walked off the path into an unlit area of field. He was just at the edge of the road that came after the field and before the houses around the field. But he could not tell where he was. He could not see in the dark. He could not see with the light from the nearby lanterns flooding his vision. At last, he exited the field only to pass into a profusion of orange light.

A grand Victorian house immediately in front of him had its huge porch bedecked with ten globes of light-all orange. At first, in the dark and not being able to see, Jack felt lost. Now, engulfed by orange light, he felt blind. In each instance, it was too much of the same thing, too much darkness, and then too much orange light. He felt twice lost. Orange, orange, all around—it was too much orange light. It surrounded him, entrapped him. Everything glowed orange, even his own skin glowed orange. No shapes were discernible, no borders could be made out, and nothing was defined. Only orange light, incessant.

Jack yearned for certainty: shape, one choice, Veronica. She defined the colors. His confusion gave way to agitation. He wanted to get out of the excess of light to where light was defined. He wanted the shadow that brought form and the form that made color real. Above all else, he wanted Veronica. With her, I am more than just my father's son. I am more than just my uncle's nephew. I am more than just one color, one choice, one way. With her, I will have all the choices I will ever need. I will live fully. I am not a score. Not one moment, one way, one preconceived notion. I am more than just my father's son. And then he thought about Wall Street and about what Uncle Browne had said about time.

He wanted desperately to see Veronica. When he finally groped his way out of the lanterns flame, Veronica was next to him.

"I found you," she said.

"Veronica," Jack said. He pulled her to him and held her tightly. He smelled her hair and held her as if she were what gave him life.

They walked on to the Tabernacle and met Aunt Millicent and Uncle Browne. Aunt Millicent sang loudly, her voice going forward. Jack and Veronica sang softly. Their voices stayed back. Uncle Browne's voice, increasingly distinct, reached up toward his wife's and they sang together. Eventually, they all sang together. When the singing was over, they went home to Uncle Browne's.

Jack and Veronica took a walk after Aunt Millicent and Uncle Browne went to bed. The moon, still bright, lit the wooden catwalk in the woods. They took the walkway toward the cove. It was cool in the woods. There were hushed sounds of wind stirred leaves. Crickets sang. They heard the lapping of the waves on the shore at the cove. They reached the sand and walked along the sand to the lush sea grass. Tenderly, Jack took Veronica's hand.

They lay down in the soft grasses. Jack held Veronica's hand as he kissed her. He kissed her hand, too. He opened her mouth with his and they kissed deeply. Her lips were soft on his and he felt her lips and their moisture with his own. He kissed her lips, separately and together. He held her close to him, tightly. He combed back her midnight hair with a gentle hand and slipped a band from off her hair so that it could drop down over him and onto her shoulders. Her shoulders were bare and her soft hair fell over them. In his arms, he folded her and in his arms Veronica felt his love. His love held her closely. And it was as if in holding her, all love was held for all time. The moon was lower in the sky now. It cast a soft light on them and in the background the only sound besides the sound of their breathing was the sound of the water lapping the shore-coming into the shore and washing the beach, then receding. They breathed together, in unison, with the sound of the lapping water. No light could ever be as sacred as that soft luminescence that fell over them-no light except the light in Veronica's eyes and in Jack's.

When it came time for them to go, Jack and Veronica did not want to leave Taylor Island. Everything seemed right there, seemed possible. Time spent with Aunt Millicent and Uncle Browne was uncomplicated. Parting from them had always been hard for Jack. Now it felt even harder. It wasn't just that Uncle Browne and Aunt Millicent were getting older. That was part of it and Jack thought about that. And he thought about how quickly time passes as he thought about leaving the island. He thought, too, about all the times he'd been there before as a boy and his time there with Veronica now. But now, time seemed to be pushing more than usual, pushing his aunt and uncle on in life and pushing him off the island.

"What if we were to just stay here," Jack said to Veronica, his eyes checking hers for the same reluctance to leave that he now felt.

"Somehow, I don't think I'd mind," Veronica said.

"We could live simply," Jack said.

"Happily," Veronica added.

"It could be fine," said Jack.

"It could be lovely," Veronica said.

When they were on the ferry leaving the island after good byes with Aunt Millicent and Uncle Browne, Jack and Veronica held each other standing at the stern of the boat looking back. The island slowly disappeared behind a mist of fog. Even when the sun came out the fog remained and all they saw was a golden mist-no sign of Taylor Island.

# 8

Following Jack's graduation his parents went to Hilton Head Island, South Carolina to visit friends. They'd stayed a little over a week and returned to Claremont Hills late the night before Jack was to return home. They went to bed tired from their long drive and awoke mid-morning the next day to the sound of the doorbell. Their mail had been held for two weeks and was now being delivered. Catherine collected the mail and set it on a table in the living room, and then she went to the kitchen, made coffee and placed the pot down on a spotless gray Corian counter. She had a quick cup. With business at their country club finalizing plans for the Tennis Ball she'd agreed to chair, she was in a hurry.

Alexander showered, stepped out onto the heated tiles of the bathroom floor, dried himself under the orange glow of a heat lamp, brushed back his full head of sandy hair, and then went into his dressing room and got dressed. He came out into the bright lights of the spacious kitchen, looking put together and polished, gave his wife a peck on the cheek before she left, and then strode into the living room with a large cup of coffee. On his way in, he flicked a switch that piped classical music into the room in quadraphonic splendor, adjusting the volume to comport with his morning mood. Then he walked across the room to a plush looking, brown, suede ottoman. On a wall near the ottoman, he pushed another button and the blinds of the living room windows automatically adjusted to a setting Alexander had determined optimal for reading. He sat down on the couch before a rosewood table where Catherine had placed the mail. He set a velvet green, circular, coaster on the table top for his coffee cup and then took in the interior of his townhouse with satisfaction.

The Conroy's were wealthy, Alexander being a semi-retired Senior Vice President for Fiduciary Capital in New York City. When Jack lived with them, they'd occupied an old Victorian home close to town but after Jack left for Duke they had sold the old Victorian and moved to this gated community of luxurious townhouses, close to their country club in the hills above town.

Claremont Hills, New Jersey, had a distinct social configuration reflected in the pattern of its residential arrangement. The higher up the hill you lived, the more prestigious your home. On this scale, the Conroy's lived on the penultimate rung of the social ladder, just below the outrageously rich. Jack had liked living close to town and had always objected to the idea of moving up into the hills. He disdained the opulence of the new townhouse. But he had a room there where he stayed when home.

Alexander came from modest beginnings. His father died when he was very young. His mother, who'd never remarried, worked for years serving food in a public school cafeteria. From the time Alexander was ten years old he worked part time in addition to attending school. He worked hard and studied hard and did well. Along the way he developed a work ethic that paid off, as well as a set of principles to live by: make money because money matters; take good care of those you love because they matter most; give back to your community and country for what it has given you. He was also fond of saying "it takes a lot of money to float the boat of our freedom." By adhering to those principles he was satisfied that he did what he needed to keep the boat afloat.

To Alexander, the sumptuous elegance of the townhouse exemplified success in adhering to his principles. It signified a level of attainment available only to those who made it to the top. He had worked hard and made his way up the hill and this house mirrored that.

In the mail before him, the Claremont Hills News stuck out. Alexander pulled it from the pile and perused the headlines of the first page. Nothing interested him until he noticed a blurb in the lower right hand corner: Happenings in the Hills: Recent Graduates.

He turned the pages rapidly, looking for the section that interested him. He sipped his coffee absent mindedly. When he came to the page he wanted, he read the paragraph about his son. Then he read it again, out loud:

> Jack Conroy graduated from Duke University Magna Cum Laude in the Class of 2001. At Duke, he majored in finance and was a varsity swimmer all four years. He was captain of the Duke Swim Team in his senior year. Jack will follow in his father's footsteps and go to work on Wall Street. Jack Conroy is the son of Catherine and Alexander Conroy of Claremont Hills and Nantucket, Massachusetts.

Alexander read this several times. That's my Son; that's my boy.

He will follow in his father's footsteps . . . There was no question about that in Alexander's mind.

He glanced at the rest of the mail which he didn't feel like going through now. He wanted to go show Catherine the article. But he noticed a green sticker. He picked it up, still eyeing the article about Jack. The sticker read Sanders Brown. Alexander understood immediately what it meant. He wondered if Jack got the letter. He knew Jack was on his way to Claremont Hills but he called Uncle Browne to be sure. Aunt Millicent answered. She said that Jack had left. Uncle Browne had taken him to the airport in Boston and he was probably in the air.

Alexander went into the bedroom and looked for the keys to his new Lexus. Catherine must have taken it. He'd use the BMW. He located the keys and drove to the post office, got the certified letter, and quickly opened and read it. June 15th, that's today, he thought. Jack has to call by today to get an interview. Jack had asked him not to involve himself, knowing his father had connections on Wall Street. But this was different. Alexander wasn't sure whether Jack had gotten the mail. He could wait for Jack to get in and tell him about the letter and deadline, but why push it. Paul Brown of Sanders Brown belonged to Claremont Hills Country Club and was an acquaintance. Alexander hesitated thinking he should wait for Jack. He looked at the date of the letter. It was dated May 31st. Jack had probably received it at school and taken care of it. So this would probably be a follow up call, it wouldn't really be interfering. It would just be to make sure.

Alexander went back home, got the club directory, and called Paul Brown. He explained the situation and was assured of an interview. Paul Brown would check to see if one had already been set up. He'd be at the club later and tell Alexander. Either way, the interview was now set. Alexander hung up the phone feeling delighted with himself as a father.

# 9

Jack and Veronica flew into Newark and took a taxi to Claremont Hills in the late afternoon. As the taxi made its way through the center of town, Jack peered out the window, complaining to Veronica, "Each time I come home, I feel like I know this place a little less."

Veronica asked why.

"I hardly recognize my old town. It never had all this." Jack pointed to stores whose display windows used green and gold colors uniformly to advertise their wares. "All these shops look the same," he said.

"But they are elegant," Veronica expressed.

"Elegant sells," Jack said skeptically. "It wasn't like this when I grew up here. The town used to have genuine character. I don't know what happened, where it went?" He sneered when the taxi stopped for a light at a four way intersection. All around the intersection, on each corner, were different salons calling themselves Day Spas. "My God," Jack said scornfully, "we've become Vanity Fair."

He continued to search for the town he'd known but, disappointed at every turn, shook his head. "The town's gone gold," he said, "as gold as a lousy singer's trite song. But at least those songs I hate, the ones that sell ten million copies of nothing much have an edge to them. All I can glean here is a kind of dumb complacency. It's preciously empty."

Veronica didn't care for what she saw either, but said nothing. She listened and stared out the window and began curling a strand of hair around her index finger. Claremont Hills was not Taylor Island. Nor was it Durham, which is where she wished she were now. This town was extravagantly upscale, flaunting its affluence. Car horns blaring outside the taxi now distracted her from further comparisons.

Approaching an intersection, two Range Rovers going in opposite directions tried to turn onto the same street at the same time. Each driver attempted to enter the street first, with the result that they met in a V and neither wanted to yield. Traffic backed up behind them. With loud, angry honks the Rovers blasted each other. Jack had heard enough. He called to the taxi driver, "Get us out of here." In an instant the cab escaped the ruckus and made its way into the hills.

Once past the gates of his parents' community, Veronica gasped, "Jack, I'm feeling a little intimidated." With eyes wide she spied the manicured yards and superabundant prosperity of the marvelous residences.

"Take it easy, Veronica. It'll be alright," Jack assured her. At last they were at the Conroy's' driveway. They got out and Jack tipped the driver and the taxi left. Jack walked Veronica to the front door where they found a note taped. Jack, please join us at the club. Take the Ford; keys are in the kitchen drawer. Jack opened his duffel bag and took out a small, black leather travel folder. From a tiny pocket inside the folder he withdrew a key to his parents' home and opened the door.

Inside, the townhouse did nothing to lessen Veronica's apprehension about how the Conroy's lived. She'd met Jack's parents before but had never visited their home.

The art on the interior walls might have been hung in a gallery. Beautiful vases filled with fresh flowers sat upon fine tables. The decor was cloyingly elegant, and Veronica shrank before the overwhelming wealth. She comprehended just how differently Jack's growing up had been from hers. Jack read the fear in her eyes and approached her.

"Veronica," he whispered, "I'm not sure what's going through your mind, or how you feel exactly, but I want you to know this isn't me."

Veronica absorbed Jack's words and clung to them. Even so, she couldn't relax and panicked when Jack told her they were going to his parents' club.

"Do we have to?" she pled.

"You'll be with me and you'll be all right," Jack said.

The old Ford wagon looked neglected. It was a car the Conroy's hardly used. A very basic car, Alexander called it, that he had held onto for some sentimental reason because it reminded him of where he'd come from. It was the first car the Conroy's had in Claremont Hills. Jack used it when at home if he hadn't driven home. Jack liked it, preferred it. He got in, turned the key, and cheered praise when it started.

When they parked in the main lot across from the clubhouse, several members stared at them as if to say the employee parking lot is up behind the tennis courts. Jack enjoyed the reaction, but Veronica was put off by it.

"Are you sure we can park here?" she asked anxiously, aware of the looks and checking out the parking lot. The cars around theirs shined like gold bricks laid out in rows. New Mercedes, BMW, Lexus's. For variety, a few Range Rovers, a silver Bentley, a contingent of Jaguars mixed in. Reviewing the cars, Jack bragged, "The Ford looks great here."

Veronica was not comfortable with Jack's boisterous claim. She moved closer to him. She noticed a few women had stopped just beyond the parking lot to discuss something. Veronica felt certain they were the subject of discussion as the women fixed on them.

"Why are those women staring at us?" she asked, digging her fingers into Jack's hand.

"I have no idea but wouldn't worry about it. You have to understand, V, these women live up on this hill and their only contact with other people is here at the club." Jack spoke of the women in clinical terms as if he were talking about handicapped people. He concluded his assessment with a broad grin that made Veronica chuckle.

"So you're telling me they don't get out much, in a way, right?"

"Yeah, kind of, but it's more like they don't get down much," he said.

"Down?" Veronica said.

"Yeah," Jack said facetiously, "down from the mountain, down to earth. I mean they live up here in their own world. To them, a world crisis might be whether or not they make the women's A Team in their sport of the moment."

"You understand them pretty well," Veronica said, more composed.

"Yeah," Jack asserted, focusing on the group of women again, then he stopped.

"There's mother."

Catherine Conroy had just finished a round of golf and stopped momentarily to speak with the same group of women Jack and Veronica had been talking about. She saw Jack and waved casually. She spoke another moment with the women, and then walked toward Jack and Veronica.

"Looks like she's just finished golf," Jack told Veronica. "She's captain of the women's A team," he said wryly.

Catherine Conroy was still pretty at fifty-seven. Her silver hair was cut short and neatly combed to the side disclosing an attractive face: full, rounded lips, smooth skin, a sculpted nose that was rather long, but narrow, and terminated in a refined, upward, point. She still had her Hilton Head tan and her eyes were clear blue and fetching. She spoke in a modulated tone of gentility, assured of her position in the world and certain of her place at the club.

"Hello, Mother," Jack greeted her.

"Hello, dear," Catherine Conroy replied in a voice of restrained affection.

"We were just discussing, Veronica and I," Jack said, "the country club mentality." Jack glanced over toward the women Catherine had just left. Catherine did not look at the women but turned to greet Veronica.

"Hello, Veronica," Her welcome was an assessment. She took in the girl before her fully, as if immediately thereafter a summary of Veronica's entire being might come printed out of Catherine Conroy's eyes. Veronica, aware of being considered, turned to Jack with inquiring eyes.

"You were wondering why those women were discussing you," Catherine Conroy said in a matter of fact tone. Before Veronica could respond, Catherine continued, "It's because you're wearing blue jeans. My son must have forgotten our club rules. Blue jeans aren't allowed."

Perturbed by his mother's effrontery, Jack retorted, "I don't know how something so important could have escaped me." Veronica reacted differently than Jack expected her to. Rather than shrinking into an apology, uncalled for under the circumstances, she simply said she regretted not having known the dress code.

"Of course you wouldn't know the rules, Veronica, and it's not a problem," Catherine said with finality, then continued, "We're to meet your father on the terrace."

Jack and Veronica followed Catherine through the clubhouse and then out back onto a fieldstone terrace where numerous circular tables sat dressed up for outdoor serving.

Observing the tables as he walked by, Jack fancied a fleet of martini glasses scattered over their tops. Sunlight skimmed the surface of the martinis, making them glimmer. Their submerged olives resembled faint, green jewels. The sunken treasures of Cocktail hour, he thought.

In her pale blue blouse Veronica, with her swarthy complexion stood out among the waspish crowd. Nor did her distinctive appearance go unnoticed. Several times she was greeted by looks of aloof consideration. Her chestnut hair hung long, almost to her waist. She wore open-toed sandals. When looked upon, her dark eyes met the eyes of those observing her with polite tolerance. But it was clear to Jack that Veronica did not feel at home. He made a point of staying close by and Catherine Conroy wasted no time ushering them to their table. They sat in a nook at the end of the terrace, apart from other members. Catherine immediately ordered a martini and invited Jack and Veronica to order as well. Jack had begun to regret bringing Veronica. He could tell by her reticence in ordering that she felt uncomfortable doing so. She wanted this ordeal to be through. She'd been injured by the looks, the admonition about the dress code, and the condescension of Catherine Conroy. His mother had been much friendlier at Duke. Jack concluded that his mother hadn't really understood then how involved he was with Veronica, perhaps thinking he'd graduate from her as well as from Duke, but his mother's altered attitude now indicated a revised understanding.

His dad approached and greeted them with a moment of genuine welcome. But his mother's continued coolness toward Veronica curtailed its effects. Then Alexander imparted information to Jack that changed the meeting utterly.

Alexander didn't seat himself right away. He stood erect and formal. His sandy hair, catching the sunlight coming over an ivy covered wall, glowed. He wore salmon pants, polished penny loafers, and a green club blazer over a bright yellow, silk golf shirt. As he stood there, appearing to be about to give a speech, he gave a quick wave to one of the white-jacketed servers and in an instant a bottle of champagne popped open at the table. Glasses were passed around while Catherine, Jack, and Veronica looked on bemused. With his glass full, Alexander raised it toward Jack.

"Congratulations, son, you have an interview with Sanders Brown."

"Congratulations, dear," Catherine Conroy exclaimed, instantly delighted. Jack stared at his father in disbelief. Veronica turned to him in confusion.

"What do you mean, Dad?" Jack's voice rung in anguish instead of delight.

"You didn't get their letter at Duke, did you?" Alexander asked knowingly, and then continued in a triumphant tone. "It's because it came to you on the 5th. You'd already left by then, right? But that's where our planning paid off. Remember, I suggested adding your home address. Well, we got the letter too. We got it late, just today, but it worked." Alexander looked at his wife, relieved. "Boy, if we had stayed in Hilton Head another day you mightn't have gotten this chance."

Stunned, Jack struggled to understand. He remembered adding the home address. The regret which covered his face Alexander misread. He held up his hand. "Jack, I'm sorry for getting involved. But you were on your way from your uncle's and I had no way of reaching you. You should get a cell phone. I had to set up the interview for you. I did so as soon as I heard from Paul Brown that you hadn't done so yourself. The safety net worked, Jack. Don't be disappointed you didn't handle it yourself. You couldn't have."

"Alexander, how could he be disappointed that you saved this opportunity from passing," Catherine Conroy interjected.

Catherine cocked her head and stretched her lips in an expression that suggested Alexander was being absurd.

Alexander and Catherine, together now fixed their eyes upon Jack, waiting for him to react to the good news. Jack's head was down. He didn't look at them. Nor did he look at Veronica. Veronica sat quietly trying to piece it together, waiting for his response and not sure whether to congratulate Jack.

Catherine spoke first. "Is something wrong, dear?" Her bewildered look landed on Alexander.

Jack gazed at Veronica, and then turned intently to his father, "Dad, I've already taken a job."

Alexander's mouth dropped. He tilted his head as if to better hear. His eyes showed confusion. "I don't understand."

"What do you mean, you've taken a job?" Catherine Conroy asked.

"I mean when I didn't hear from Wall Street I worked it out with Mr. Bellini at the Durham Nursery that I'd work for him."

"That's a summer vacation job. What your father is talking about is a career opportunity," Catherine said.

"Surely Mr. Bellini will understand if you keep the interview," Alexander said vehemently.

"He would, but I don't intend to," Jack said.

"Don't intend to?" Catherine announced perturbed.

"No, I don't intend to. I want to work for Mr. Bellini." Jack stared into his mother's eyes with dead certainty.

"What?" Catherine said with outraged disbelief. "Jack, that's not what we brought you up to do. I can only assume you're under the influence of someone else's desire, not your own."

"Mother, Veronica has absolutely nothing to do with my decision. It's my decision. I made it myself. I had the opportunity to answer Wall Street. I chose not to," Jack said strongly.

"What do you mean, Jack?" his father inquired. "What do you mean, you had the chance?"

"I mean I got the Sanders letter. I never told Veronica about it.

I simply tore it up." Jack said.

All three with him were in their own way devastated. Veronica had been confused, then angered by Catherine; now she felt betrayed. Jack had excluded her from his confidence, decided without her.

Catherine and Alexander sat shaking their heads.

"Jack," Veronica pleaded, "I want to go."

"Veronica, I'm sorry," Jack said. She got up from the table trembling.

"Please," she said.

# 10

Finally, late in the evening after spending hours by herself in the guest room Veronica sat down with Jack. He suggested they go elsewhere and avoid further contact with his parents, but Veronica disagreed.

"No, let's deal with it now;" she said resolutely, "avoiding the question doesn't work."

"If you mean the question of whether I want to keep the interview, I think I've already answered that." Jack's sounded conciliatory.

"Maybe," Veronica replied, "but why did you hide getting the letter?" She sat next to him on a love seat in his parents' den and turned to face him with her question.

He saw her injured eyes and answered apologetically, "I didn't want to complicate things."

"This is complicated," Veronica responded. "Telling me wouldn't have been. Are you under my influence?" She appealed for honesty. "That's what your mother thinks."

"Not in a bad way," Jack said.

"Then how?" Veronica searched Jack's eyes, compressed her lips and looked as if she might cry. She turned away from Jack, put her head down and waited for his answer. Jack placed his hand under her chin and lifted her head with a finger so that she looked at him.

"Veronica, I've never been truer to myself than with you in my life. I should have told you about the letter. I will never leave you out of anything again. But when I got the letter, I knew in my gut I didn't want to go to Wall Street. I want to be near you." Veronica smiled through tears and placed her head against Jack's chest. "Oh, Jack. I do love you so much."

"I love you, too," he whispered.

Then Veronica collected herself, pulled away and spoke deliberately, "I know you told me the truth just now. But Jack, I think I may have influenced you too much about Wall Street. You said you want to be near me. You didn't say you want to work for Mr. Bellini."

Jack interrupted her. "You know I do," he said.

"Yes, but why, so that you can be near me?" Her question sounded like a conclusion. She went on, "I believe you want to work for Mr. Bellini. I believe you would love that work. I also know, and cherish, the fact you want to be with me. But I know you completely, Jack. How competitive you are. How you like to prove yourself. I know that Wall Street means something to you as far as that goes and I don't want to think, ever, that by loving me you failed to live up to your expectations." When she stopped speaking, Jack kissed her.

"What on God's wonderful Earth could I ever ask for beyond what I have with you, V?" he said.

"Oh dearest, Jack," Veronica sighed, and then animatedly she continued, "Since I'm going back tomorrow I want to give you your birthday present." As she exited the den she thought she saw someone in the hallway shadows but, hearing nothing, went on to the guestroom to get something out of a travel bag. Jack sat still, charmed by her movements. He gazed lovingly at her leave then room and comeback. When she came back into the room she sat down closely to him and handed him a small square box. It was a silver jeweler's box closed tight by a violet ribbon. Jack took the box in his hands and while opening it, thanked Veronica with his eyes. He withdrew a gold cross on a gold chain. Veronica asked excitedly, "Do you like it?"

"Love it," Jack said.

"I hoped it would remind you of the lake and, well, of . . . me," she said.

"It means the world to me, V, please put it on me." Veronica placed the chain around Jack's neck so that the gold cross dropped over his heart. She looked at him with it on, great affection in her eyes. He looked back and they kissed.

"I wish you didn't have to go back," Jack said.

"These summer courses will get me out faster," Veronica replied.

"There's no rush," Jack said.

Veronica thought about it and laughed. "No, I guess not." Shortly after that they went to bed.

In the morning Jack was up and out for a jog. Veronica was in her room getting her things together when she heard a soft tap on the door. It was Catherine Conroy.

"May I come in," Catherine asked. Veronica felt uncomfortable but wishing to be courteous allowed Catherine in. Catherine sat down on a chair in a corner of the room.

"We have breakfast ready for you, Veronica," she said.

"Thank you, Mrs. Conroy, but I'm not really hungry."

Veronica couldn't be still and began hurriedly checking her travel folder, diverting her eyes from Catherine all the while. She took things out and then placed them back into the folder, hardly looking at them before they were returned. More than once she looked toward the doorway anxious for Jack to return. Catherine could tell her presence made Veronica uneasy.

"Veronica," she said, "I want to apologize. I shouldn't have suggested you are the reason Jack decided against interviewing for Wall Street. You see, last night, although I didn't mean to, I overheard your conversation with Jack. Against my better judgment, I listened at the door." Veronica recalled thinking she'd seen someone and knew now she had.

"I know you knew nothing about the Sanders Brown letter. I'm sorry for what I said," Catherine said. Her voice was flat, almost official. Veronica was glad for the apology though surprised by Catherine's admission of eavesdropping even though it might, however, end up being for the best.

"I accept your apology, Mrs. Conroy. I'm sure you just want the best for your son."

"That's exactly right, Veronica," said Catherine, standing up and placing her right thumb and index finger on her lower lip. Catherine looked reflectively about the room. She stared down at the floor of the room, looking at nothing, but apparently considering Jack's future. She said frankly, "How does a mother know for certain what is best for her child?"

"I'm sure you must worry about Jack's decisions, Mrs. Conroy," Veronica said empathetically, "but I don't think you should."

"You don't?" Catherine replied.

"No, I don't. Jack has good judgment and knows himself. If I were you, I'd trust his judgment," Veronica urged.

Catherine resented this advice. She turned away and came back to face Veronica.

"That's just it, Veronica, you're not me. We are from different worlds. I hope you don't think me condescending for saying so. It's simply a matter of fact. So, I don't think you can say, especially at your age and with your life experience, what is best for Jack. I don't even think Jack knows that."

An expression of injured surprise showed in Veronica's eyes. She drew away from Catherine regretting having opened up to her as Catherine Conroy continued, "Jack is extraordinary. His father and I raised him believing that. He did so much, so well, growing up," Catherine reflected, her eyes unfocused, as if considering her thoughts. "Some people in this world seem destined for great things, for great individual accomplishment. My father was that kind of man. I think Jack's father, my husband, is too. But Jack, he surpasses both of them."

Veronica considered Catherine's opinion. In her heart, she agreed Jack was truly special. Indeed, she'd thought the same thing herself numerous times. She knew exactly what Catherine meant.

"Mrs. Conroy, I appreciate what you say about Jack. Honestly, I think it myself," Veronica admitted.

"Then don't you think he should at least see what that Sanders Brown position is?" Catherine asked the question in a tone that suggested the conclusion was indisputable.

"I think Jack will be exceptional no matter what he chooses to do," Veronica replied.

"But Jack's history points to Wall Street. His father went to Wall Street. He grew up thinking that he would. And I know his being on Wall Street would make a difference. I just know it," Catherine concluded.

Catherine rendered her opinion with such force that Veronica felt confused. Of course she didn't want to limit Jack.

"But, Mrs. Conroy, it's up to Jack," she said.

"Veronica," Catherine Conroy countered immediately, "I heard you and Jack last night. He'd never consider going for the interview without some prompting from you."

Veronica couldn't think. She wanted to say something smart to support her fundamental belief that Jack would thrive in Durham and didn't need to go to Wall Street. She wanted to be able to precisely describe and define Jack as the person he'd developed into in such a way that Catherine Conroy would understand and acquiesce. But she couldn't. All she could think of saying was, "But, I don't want him to go to Wall Street."

Catherine stared at Veronica with a confirmatory expression, one that said of course you don't. Then, before leaving Veronica, Catherine asked her to consider one question: If she were not in Jack's life, would Jack remain in Durham and work for the nursery or would he go to Wall Street? That question asked, Catherine left Veronica alone. Alone now, Veronica had the distasteful sense that what had begun as an apology concluded as an indictment. She was holding Jack back.

# 11

Earlier that morning, after Jack had gone running and before she'd spoken to Veronica, Catherine Conroy had placed a scrapbook on her son's bed. Knowing Jack would shower after his run, Catherine made his bed and left a fresh, white towel on the bedspread. Next to the towel she'd conspicuously placed the scrapbook, opened to the first page and a report her husband had read to her several times the night before.

Alexander Conroy hadn't understood Jack's revelation at the country club at all. He'd spent a restless evening upset by it. He pulled out the scrapbook and read through the entire thing to validate his frustration.

The scrapbook documented Jack's accomplishments grow ing up. A chronicle of his development, the book also served as a testament to his parents' steadfast support of their son. They were the editors of this book, just as they had been, largely the editors of Jack's life. They chose what went into the book. They preserved what needed to be remembered. For Alexander, the scrapbook spoke the truth.

To accentuate the extent of their son's progress, they'd begun the scrapbook with an early, troubling, assessment of Jack's abilities. Placed as it was at the beginning, then followed by countless contradictory results, that first alarming report now seemed mere casuistry. It hadn't approached the truth. The truth had always been that Jack was exceptional. The scrapbook recorded that truth in abundance after that first page, like a song where a beautiful melody follows an opening discord.

Alexander treasured the scrapbook and sought within its pages a comfort Jack's revelation had taken away. He couldn't relinquish his conviction that Jack was meant to be a leader of men, a steward of the nation's resources, responsible in his time for keeping the country sound, the economic boat afloat. Nor could he accept that Jack wanted to remain in Durham and work at a garden nursery. He'd read the entire scrapbook, from beginning to end appealing to God for the understanding he lacked about his son's decision.

To him, the book was much truer than Jack's altered direction. And he still firmly believed his son would come around and decide on Wall Street.

Catherine, upset by Jack's news as well hadn't bothered to review the scrapbook, although she listened to Alexander read from it. But she wanted Jack to go through it and remember how he'd been raised. Once he'd read the entries his interest in Wall Street would be rekindled she hoped.

In the shower Jack went over his decision to stay in Durham, rationalizing that to work there was justified. His parents had become blind to their own decadence, had lost perspective, cashed in their chips in the game of life in order to spend the rest of their time in dumb indulgence. That conjecture aroused a divisive impulse in him. If he could somehow use what he'd seen as a vapid life style to reject their expectations of him, remaining in Durham would be reasonable. He could say, rightly, that he stayed in Durham to make a difference they hadn't: from the ground up, by the grass roots, and not aspiring to the false grandeur of the Hill. That assessment buffered Jack from the harsh reaction of his parents. Knowing he'd still be with Veronica just increased the vehemence of his conviction.

But when he saw the scrapbook on the bed after showering, he didn't ignore it. He'd guessed it was put out for him and read it anyway. But he didn't begin where his mother wanted him to, with that first report, the one his father had read to his mother the night before. He read everything else but that, ten years' worth of positive results. And in reading, his attitude toward his parents gradually softened. This was no incidental collection, no real scrap book. Effort and thought had gone into making the book. None of it was immaterial. All of it spoke of purpose. All of it, carefully selected, contributed to the whole as it revealed the individual: Him. And perhaps more importantly, it documented his parents love. He read out loud:

> Alexander and Catherine Conroy are happy to report the birth of their son John Conroy. Born July 3rd, John Conroy weighed 9 lbs.4 oz. He is the first child of the Conroy's and the most blessed event of their ten year marriage.

He read most blessed over and over. He felt the love that went into those words. His parents had always said he was their miracle. There was never any question of their love for him, although at times that love had overwhelmed him. He'd always known how they felt. He'd always wanted to return their love to please them.

Having read the good parts, he went back to the first page. He went to Dr. Jacobsen's report as if he'd been inoculated against it by all that followed.

That report had been his nemesis growing up. His parents kept it to defy the doctor. And because of what followed in his life, Jacobsen's report took on an unintended significance for Jack. It'd become key by reason of its inaccuracy, prominent because it was so wrong. It'd served continually as the unwitting catalyst for his success.

From time to time throughout his development, his parents considered sending Dr. Jacobsen back the report. They'd wanted to attach copies of Honor Roll report cards and clippings of swimming triumphs. They'd wanted that doctor to know how utterly wrong he'd been. They had discussed their intentions numerous times. So much so, Jack knew what they said by heart. He fondly recalled their discussion:

Remember what that doctor said. Specialized education for the rest of his life! He looked at us gravely, his tidy professionalism showing all around him in degrees mounted neatly on the wall and his Best Doctor announcement framed and hung so visibly. He had those manicured fingernails that shone in the light of his office. Then he said with absolute certainty: Specialized education for the rest of his life-all those accolades and not a clue.

His parents always spoke those last words triumphantly. Jack smiled thinking about it. But the report itself still ignited anger in him. And it still made him want to prove the doctor wrong, the report worthless. Again, he checked the results in the scrapbook against the opinion of the doctor with contempt for the misjudgment and the man who'd made it.

There was the letter from Mrs. Donogan, his kindergarten teacher. She'd gotten it right. She'd said Jacobsen's report was "hogwash," said Jack should be "mainstreamed." So, he had been. And he did well.

There was another letter, written to Jack's principal in sixth grade. It came from a prominent lawyer in town. Jack had served in a program at the local YMCA to assist children with cerebral palsy. The lawyer said Jack was the kind of kid who made a favorable difference in the world: a talented, intelligent, and caring young man. These documents buoyed Jack as he reviewed them. He'd proven himself again and again.

To beat the doctor, Jack had developed a fierce competitiveness, a tenacious inner resolve, competing always against himself and that report, winning all the way. I can do it he'd say and that became I will do it. Fear of failure propelled him. He never spoke about it, didn't really articulate it. Veronica, aware of his history, had sensed it though. But his parents didn't, and their certainty about his ability didn't always comfort him although he did appreciate it.

He looked at the scrapbook once more. There was no question that he'd proved himself. He thought about it as he thought about the Durham Nursery wondering if that was the right choice.

Later that morning, on the way to the airport with Veronica her question to him was a surprise. It was the same question Mrs. Conroy had asked her. She felt compelled to ask Jack:

"Jack, if I wasn't in Durham would you still go to work for Mr. Bellini?"

Jack didn't know how to answer. He said he thought the question was absurd but he didn't answer it. Veronica wasn't upset with him. She hadn't been able to answer it either. But she didn't want to be responsible for him making the wrong decision. And Jack still wasn't absolutely sure what the right thing to do was. Having reviewed the scrapbook confused him. Veronica looked at him caringly, uncertainty in her eyes.

"I don't want you to ever have any regrets," Veronica said.

"We're too young for regrets," Jack answered.

"Don't hold it against me for influencing you," Veronica continued.

"Hold it against you for loving me?" Jack said. "Never. Besides, I love you as much."

"Perhaps," Veronica offered, "you shouldn't start out your adult life by closing doors." She meant what she said, and she didn't mean it at all. But Jack listened.

"I can keep the interview, I guess," he said, "just to see." Jack sounded and looked resigned.

"Just to see," Veronica echoed, and she felt happy with her very mature attitude and she felt tremendously disheartened.

# 12

He took the same train from Claremont Hills that his father did every day when he worked: The 6:50 Express. It would get him into Lower Manhattan by 8:30. The Express made only two stops as it barreled down the Gladstone line, passing through the suburbs between Claremont Hills and Hoboken on its way toward New York City.

After Summit, town followed town with indiscriminate rapidity. Increasingly, buildings took over the landscape. Homes crowded into the residential areas, and every town seemed to have more people. Highways, strip malls, super malls and town centers, hectic with activity, blurred together, all looking the same. Jack peered out the window at this indistinguishable jumble as the train sped by. The ride seemed dead to him.

Just outside Newark, both rural charm and suburban sophistication disappeared. He looked on ramshackle dwellings, many of which appeared abandoned. Numerous others had broken windows and doors. Some, partially scorched, still had people living in them judging by the fatigued looking clothes lines strung from their unscreened windows. Junk strewn back yards looked hopelessly soiled, as if dirt and grime had accumulated for years and was now part of everything it touched. A soot and grease stained world is how Jack saw it. He winced, wondering how people could live that way and why society didn't help them. Why do people still live in such squalor he questioned?

He thought he could see exactly where money stopped and poverty began, where people cared and then couldn't possibly, and where a dream was a luxury no one could afford. To live without hope, he thought, dismayed by the idea. It would be nice, he said to himself, if kids here could look at flowers instead of rusty junk, old tires, and charred wood.

Jack was never one to say that someone else should do something. He thought he should. How could he make a difference? He scanned the mess outside the train as it came into Newark.

Newark: replete with skyscrapers, trains, and taxis, teemed with people, palpitated with noise. Despite his grandiose imaginings of revitalizing what he'd seen, Jack remained uncomfortable. He didn't like being on a crowded, stuffy train. The windows of the train car were streaked with dirt, just as the junky backyards had been. What was worse, no one seemed to notice or care. And east of Newark the seedy picture of things continued, spreading in all directions over the land. Even the water appeared filthy.

The Meadowlands were the natural equivalent of the grimy city. Tall grasses and wetlands sat like dirty mops and dirty mop water. Here, the outside world seemed like the vacuum bag of industry to Jack. Progress, he said facetiously to himself.

Soon a marsh along the tracks came into view. High voltage lines surrounded the marsh. Behind the lines was a cement factory, dusty and dirty. Even so, sitting by itself in the morning light, the marsh had a natural beauty. Purple grasses, perhaps four foot high, swayed in a slow motion—indifferent to the pulsing thrust of the train, separate from the high voltage lines and cement mill. Encircled by the grass, a small pond rested. Its placid water shone silver. Waterfowl floated on the water's surface. Jack sighed. He felt suddenly optimistic, awed by nature's persistent possibility.

The train stopped in Hoboken. He got off and found the ferry that would take him to Lower Manhattan. It was a ten minute ride across the water. He couldn't stop thinking of Taylor Island and Veronica. He felt a homesick feeling thinking about V and their trip.

His appointment was for nine o'clock. It was only eight-thirty when he got off the ferry so he walked along the Esplanade toward Battery Park. Along the way, he checked the time periodically by looking across the river at a giant clock that stood out on the Jersey side. He marveled at the scalloped waves of the river, glistening in the morning sunlight. He felt uplifted by the trees and flowers and plants along the Esplanade. Before long, he was in Battery Park.

There, with flowers in bloom and trees all around, Jack felt at home. He thought of Duke and, again, of Veronica and felt happy and sad at the same time.

He continued walking until he came to the East River. Near Pier Thirteen, he stopped. A congregation of different types of sea gull covered the dock in such a multitude he couldn't see between them. Some of the gulls were large, some small. They all sat together, gray and white, above Pier Thirteen. Other gulls flew in super abundance-filling the sky: soaring, gliding, and drifting on breezes, like floating dreams. Then the birds in the sky began to descend, landing on the dock at Pier 13. They fell lightly from heaven to earth, like natural confetti. And others still soared, way up above him in the sky. If he could, Jack would have flown with them. He felt the impulse to fly away. Then he checked the time again. It was eight forty-five, time to head to the interview.

He located Wall Street and started up. He walked among a throng going to work, on a street that seemed small below the monstrous buildings on either side. The buildings were so enormous they blocked out light. In this concrete canyon, dimly lit, he felt disoriented. He didn't like the closed space or the urgency with which people walked. He felt somewhat nauseous. He continued walking and came to Broad Street where he turned left. He walked about a block to 30 Broad.

Grand Thirty Broad's interior was brightly lit. Its walls and floors were made of an orange-brown, polished looking marble that reminded Jack of caramel candy. A large security desk in the center of the lobby had a sign requesting visitors sign in. A bank of shiny silver, ornate looking, elevators sat opposite the security desk. Jack signed in and then proceeded to the elevator bank, the vest pocket of his new blue suit tagged with a visitor badge.

Jack looked sparkling and handsome, like a newly minted gold coin. He wore a navy blue, pin-striped, suit with a crisp white shirt and red tie. The tie had dark blue and gold stripes running across its surface, the blue stripes wide, gold stripes thin. His hair, golden with tints of red, bright blue eyes, and tall athletic build impressively accentuated his appearance. Young, handsome and put together, he stood out. And then, too, his manner of speaking and way of making eye contact instantly charmed whomever he met. The security people, for example, acted happy to help him.

He came off the elevator at the eighteenth floor and saw Sanders Brown on the glass office door. He pressed a button beside the closed doors, heard a click and entered. The receptionist, smiling, inquired how she could help him.

"Good morning, I'm Jack Conroy, here to see Mr. Sutton."

The receptionist handed Jack an application clipped to a hard brown clipboard.

"Please fill this out while you wait. I'll buzz Mr. Sutton, "she said.

Jack sat in a red leather, straight-backed, chair beside a cherry table and completed the application. Soon, the pleasant receptionist returned and announced that Mr. Sutton would see him now. Jack held up an incomplete application.

"It doesn't matter, he'll see you now," the receptionist said cordially.

Jack rose, buttoned his suit coat, and followed the receptionist. He liked the look of the office. It had plenty of light. Its walls were of golden oak wood. The offices were spacious and well illuminated, and attractive art hung at regular intervals along the hall. There was a cultivated feel to the office, as if it might be an academic department at an Ivy League college rather than a brokerage house. Without thinking, Jack became invigorated.

He passed a few offices on his way. Some had their doors shut, others open. The people in the offices were invariably young. All were busy. A couple of them looked up with friendly smiles as he passed. Jack perked up with the friendliness and youthful energy coming his way. Instinctively, he felt competitive. These people were his peers. If they could do this, he could. A passing thought that he'd beat Dayton to Wall Street exhilarated him. He and the receptionist reached the end of the hall and stood at the open door to the corner office.

"Here we are," she said. "Good luck!"

Jack watched her walk away until she disappeared around a corner. A tall man, perhaps fifty, in a blue suit, white shirt, and gold tie, approached Jack. He wore steel rim glasses with circular lenses. The lenses looked thick. As the man extended a hand, Jack noticed his serious pale blue eyes studying him from behind the lenses.

"Good morning, Jack, I'm Cliff Sutton. How was your trip in?" As Sutton's hand extended toward him, Jack noticed the cuffs of his starched shirt fastened with gold cuff links.

"It was a fine trip in, thank you," Jack said.

"Let's have a seat so we can chat," Sutton said.

Sutton moved his chair out from behind his desk and brought it over to where Jack sat on a brown leather couch. They sat facing each other. Sutton turned and reached behind to take something from his desk. Before addressing Jack, he quickly reviewed what he'd removed. Then he spoke to Jack in a professional tone, business in his eyes. "You have an impressive record, Jack."

"Thank you," Jack said.

Sutton folded his hands, resting them on his lap, then raised both thumbs of the interlocked hands and tilted them toward Jack: "So why Wall Street?"

Jack paused, and then answered. "I've wanted to work on Wall Street my whole life. My father worked on Wall Street still does part time-and from the time I was young I've wanted to, also."

"Why?" Sutton inquired. After he asked the question Sutton straightened up in his chair and studied Jack.

"Because, I think with a job on Wall Street you can make a difference, have a positive impact on the country. Plus, you can have a good life. I know that firsthand."

"Why Sanders Brown?" Sutton asked.

"My father knows of your firm and recommended it to me. He said Sanders Brown is one of the best places to learn this business and that you treat your people well." Jack directed his eyes at Sutton's and kept them there as he responded.

"It sounds like you value your father's opinion," Sutton said.

"I do. He knows Wall Street," Jack said.

"He's right about this company, I can tell you that. Those who know, say we have the best mentoring program in the business," Sutton said. "Do you know about it, Jack?"

"No, sir, I don't," Jack admitted.

"Well, I won't go into all the details now. Suffice it to say, we pride ourselves upon selecting the right people and then spare no effort in their development," Sutton said, as he conveyed the information to Jack. Then Sutton scanned his notepad for a moment and tapped his right index finger on the bottom of the page he was looking at and then raised his head to look at Jack and asked:

"Tell me Jack, how much do you know about the actual work?"

"I know you're plugged in, doing this work-highly automated. I know the field is competitive. I know selling matters. And I know you expect results right away."

"Do you like getting results right away?" Sutton asked.

"Good results," Jack said.

In his preparedness Jack gave the impression that he was older than he was.

"And competition, you're okay with that?" asked Sutton as he returned his noted pad to the desk behind him.

"I thrive on it," Jack said immediately, and continued," I've competed all my life, in sports, school—in just about every way a young man can."

"Do you consider yourself a team player" Sutton emphasized.

"Definitely, I was captain of the Duke Swim Team, But, I'm also independent enough not to go with something just because it's the consensus. You have to be discriminating." Jack said.

"That's true," Sutton said, following with, "You said selling matters, explain."

"I mean you have to get accounts and keep them. It's a money business even more than most. So to succeed at it, you have to bring in the money," Jack said.

"Is that something you got from your father?" Sutton asked.

"My father's pragmatic. His favorite saying is: 'it takes a lot of money to float the boat." said Jack.

"What do you think he means by that?" Sutton asked.

"I think he's saying we have a lot and we do a lot in this country and much of it depends on money. Certainly a good business does," Jack said.

Sutton moved on to his next question, "Do you have any sales experience, Jack?"

"Yes, for the last three years I've worked for an expanding landscape business in Durham. I came up with some design ideas that landed accounts for that business. In fact, the owner offered me a full time job because of it."

"Sounds interesting, why not take it?" Sutton asked seriously.

"Because I think I can do more on Wall Street," said Jack.

"Jack I don't know your father but it seems to me he's raised a winner. I have to say looking at you and listening to you, I'm impressed. I'd like you to meet with a couple more people if you don't mind. Do you have time?"

"My time is yours," Jack said.

The rest of the interview went well. Jack had to meet a manager and the Regional V.P. The only one with apparent reservations was the Regional V.P., although even he agreed that Jack made an excellent appearance. Cliff Sutton saw Jack out at the end of the interview.

"I enjoyed meeting with you, Jack, and I think we'll have an answer for you soon. We're talking to a few more candidates but I like your record and attitude."

Once outside, Jack gazed up at the walls of buildings all around him. He'd done well; he knew it and thought he'd be offered the job. He looked around the busy street and at the Stock Exchange. He felt odd . . . very odd. His father would be happy but Veronica. She seemed so far away. He didn't quite understand what had happened. Part of him had surfaced inside those offices, came up and out stronger than he would have predicted.

It was in him to want the job. It was as if he couldn't deny his father, as if then he would have been denying himself. Before getting back on the ferry he sat on a bench facing the Hudson to think about the interview and more.

Watching the sunlight brightening the water's surface and following the light across the river to where it reflected from the skyscrapers in Jersey City, he worried. Wall Street pulsated with a stimulating intensity. It was the heart of world moneywise, where the action was, and yet in a visceral way it repelled him. But could he walk away from the challenge?

Leave the future in the hands of others like Dayton? Much of him wanted to but he also wanted to accomplish a lot, to help set the course, pave the way for the country, and lead. The thought occurred to him that he must first make his mark in the business world of Wall Street, grow fortunes, and make his own. Then he'd make time to devote himself to his dream of transforming urban landscapes. With the type of designs Mr. Bellini said he did so well, he'd add a depth of grace to industrial settings he thought were devoid of it. But when would he go to Wall Street? Being with Veronica during her last year had grown from a preference to an assumption. His thoughts remained perplexing until he gazed at the giant clock across the water.

*Time, time, time, he thought. What time? A clock as big as that* should tell me time's always involved. I know at some point in my life I will have to test Wall Street. I have to find out if I can do that work and contribute to floating the boat, as my father says.

Jack kept staring at the giant clock, now with greater intensity. He considered the position of the clock's hands.

> *11 o'clock. The hands look like a V. I guess I see V in everything. Would I have accepted Mr. Bellini's offer if V wasn't in my life. But that's stupid. She is. At 12, the hands come together. V and I will be together soon. It's not long from 11 to 12.*
>
> *It wouldn't be a full year we'd be apart if I take the job here. School's less than nine months. Plus, she has a month break in winter and a Spring Break. I could come down on weekends. If they offer it to me, I think I might as well face the music and find out. It would be a short time, really, like the time from eleven to twelve. Hell, I know I could do that job. I could do what my father did; better than any Dayton ever could. I'll see if they make me an offer, present my plan to V. She suggested I keep the interview. I think she'd be proud of me, too, being my own man.*

# 13

July 3, 2001

The Conroy's always celebrated Jack's birthday out west. They had a cabin on a ranch below Big Sky, Montana, and that's where they were when Jack got the news from Sanders Brown. The call came early and rang so loudly it seemed the only sound in the world and usurped the serenity of the new day. Jack walked into the cabin with reluctant assurance, picked up the phone, and brought it with him back outside. His parents sat nearby, two figures of earnest hope.

He listened intently for a while, and then a grin covered his face. "I've been offered the job!" he whispered triumphantly to his parents. They rejoiced. He walked with authority across the porch, looking victorious, as if he'd finished first in another big race. This was more than just a single victory, though. It was a constellation of victories. When he hung up the phone, he turned to his parents.

"I did it!"

He paced the porch as if doing a victory lap. All he could think was Wall Street chose me. After a time, he sat down. No one spoke. All three of them just sat there and absorbed the news and watched, silently, as the morning sun crowned the mountains that faced them.

Jack got up and looked out over the porch railing. With the mountain behind him, he seemed to be part of the mountain. And the sun that crowned the mountain seemed also to crown him, so distinctly did his hair shine in the sunlight. His clear blue eyes held a look of destiny. Everything about the morning had the quality of a decisive turn.

He'd start in the same field his father had but in a bigger way. His dad had to work his way to New York. He'd be there to begin with. And, as proof he could match his father's accomplishments, this offer bode well.

Jack hadn't accepted the job yet, though. He'd told them he had another offer and needed to weigh everything. The Sanders Brown man was not surprised; a day would be all right. It wasn't a ploy on Jack's part either.

It gave him time. Durham and Veronica had flashed through his mind during the call, and then he'd recalled Uncle Browne's advice-not to rush into anything. Finally, he wanted to talk it over with his father. He still wasn't sure.

Alexander and Catherine were delighted, though. The morning news had crowned their life's achievement.

"How should we celebrate the news?" Catherine asked.

Celebration felt in order to Jack. He'd done it, cleared another hurdle. Still, he paused. Any big celebration presumed he'd take the job. Nevertheless, he wanted to enjoy the moment.

"I'm going to do it all today," Jack answered, "ride Buffalo Ridge Trail to its summit and look over the rim across the valley, all the way to the plains of Wyoming. It's so clear today; I bet I can see to Heaven.

"After that, I'm going to fish the gorge like never before . . . like never again. Bring out the best of the cutthroat. Mom, you can meet us there for lunch."

"Well, I did want to go to Big Sky and get my nails done." Catherine Conroy shot a facetious glance toward her son, lowering her chin and widening her eyes to pretend disappointment.

"Oh, well, that's more important," Jack said. "I don't want to see you near the gorge without a couple of inches of red lacquer on your fingers and toes."

Catherine looked down at her fingers and sighed, then gazed at Jack happily. "I guess I can forego the parlor and meet you at the Gorge sans paint."

"Dad, are you up for it?" Jack exhorted his father.

Alexander stood up. He beheld his son the way he might have when he was born twenty-two years ago, lovingly, jubilantly.

"Today is yours!" Alexander said, holding up his palms to the sky as if presenting Jack the world.

After plans were made, the family trinity sat delighting in the afterglow of fulfillment. They looked at the mountains-feeling the day begin-the fortunate day. The day promise came.

The Montana morning enveloped them—cradled their mutual joy and rocked it in a gentle sunlight. The mountains, bathed in that new day's light rose so high they seemed to touch the clouds. And the day was so clear and flawless; they could follow the mountains ascent with vivid clarity from their foothills to their crowned peaks-shimmering morning.

Between the mountain range to the north and another to the south, a valley spread in a yellow sweep of grass. It spread in a dull yellow roughness up to the river where the dried, sun baked, grass gave way to a soft, luxurious, green fringe. More than three miles of winding Gallatin River crossed through Big Gorge Ranch and today, in the early light, it looked like a blue stained-glass, reflecting and illuminating a Montana mountain cathedral.

On the facing mountainside, sprawled in lazy indifference to all around them, horses grazed on dewy grasses.

"God, it's a marvelous day!" Jack exclaimed.

"Why don't we stop by the barn before breakfast and tell the wranglers to get the horses ready for us," Alexander suggested.

"I'll do that, Dad. But first let me call Veronica. Then, I'll meet you two at the dining hall."

Jack went into the cabin. His parents got up and started for the dining hall. They were reluctant for him to phone Veronica but convinced, by the way he'd reacted to the job offer that it wouldn't matter.

"He seems like his old self today," Catherine said.

"He does, doesn't he? Maybe all that stuff back home will disappear now that he knows he's made the cut," Alexander said hopefully.

"You think he's happy about it?" Catherine wondered.

"Oh sure," Alexander said. They went off to breakfast contentedly. In the cabin, Jack couldn't reach Veronica by phone so he sent an email:

*Dear V,*

*I was offered the job. I have to admit, I'm proud. So now I'm proud and confused. But it is a great opportunity. The intern aspect seems like a no lose situation. I'm inclined to give it a try. But then, I miss you so much already. Wish you were here. I'm going to tell my dad exactly how I feel, his judgment's sound. Of course, I'm not forgetting how you feel. I will not make a final decision without you. Going to be out most of the day, I'll call later. I have to call Sanders Brown back by tomorrow. Love You Big Time, J*

After breakfast, Alexander and Jack went to the barn and mounted horses. They trotted off, up a mile long dirt trail to the beginning of Buffalo Ridge Trail, a trail that went up the mountain some nine thousand feet to the top.

The mountain gleamed in the morning sunlight as they worked their way up the winding trail through coves of pine and open meadows, past wide stretches of scree, and along a rumbling mountain stream. The stream poured down from the mountain in gushes of icy water, over fallen trees and slick-looking stones. An eagle soared. A baby mule deer slept, trying to hide, pressed up against a downed tree in high grass where only its large, tawny ears, gave it away.

Jack and Alexander gradually moved the horses up the face of the mountain, stopping only a few times to let the horses drink. Jack led. It took about two hours to make it to the mountaintop.

There the earth leveled off, extending for about a hundred yards to the steep cliff called Buffalo Ridge. That was the place Jack had in mind for a vista. They worked the horses slowly toward the ridge, dismounted and tied them to a large pine tree. Then, together, they walked to the edge of the ridge and sat on some prominent rocks projecting out from the cliff's face, resting and looking out across the wide valley. The panoramic view dazzled-it was so wide, sunlit, and clear.

The unequaled spectacle of the valley from that position at Buffalo Ridge never failed to please. And today there was an almost luminous quality to it: the mountains burnished gold, the river icy-blue, and the forests extravagantly lush and dark green. Through pellucid skies, Jack imagined he could see Colorado and as he gazed out, everything about his life seemed astounding, everything about his future, limitless.

"Dad, I think it's all there waiting for me." Jack's gaze took in the vast panorama before him.

"That's because it is," Alexander said, admiring his son. Quiet for a while, Jack then looked quizzically at his father. "What's it really like?"

"What?"

"Wall Street."

Alexander sensed trepidation on his son's part and spoke firmly. "Like life, it's challenging. It can be damn hard and indifferent. But, there's plenty of possibility." When Alexander spoke about Wall Street it was as if he lit up from inside. A surge of vitality showed in the ruddy glow of his face as he spoke, and he spoke energetically. Wall Street seemed to keep Alexander young. Jack wondered to himself at such times whether his father really ever wanted anything else.

They walked carefully now, farther out on the edge of the ridge and looked down into the gorge. The Gallatin pounded against the red walls of the gorge, careening off the walls in a white, furious, spray down into the river that rolled powerfully on. Jack followed the river with his eyes as it winded and turned out across the long plain before them.

"Dad, I'm not certain I want this job."

"What do you mean?" Alexander said.

"I don't know. I'm just not sure."

"What's bothering you, Jack? Something's been bothering you ever since you got home." Alexander relaxed his upper body and leaned slightly backward wanting Jack to confide in him.

"My uncertainty for one thing." Jack did not look at his father at this moment but quickly all over the place.

"What is it you're not sure of?"

"I feel a little anxious that all this," Jack spread his hand out before him and passed it across their view, "won't be available to me anymore. That's one thing."

"You don't lose this just because you go to work, Jack."

"This time and this feeling, Dad, can it last? I feel like I'm at the edge of our time together as much as I'm at this cliff's edge."

"Don't worry, son. You'll have it. We will have it. Work is not the end of your life. It's just the beginning of another part of it."

"But don't you think I should be sure about the work? I mean, know that I want to do it?" Jack groped for fatherly understanding but Alexander brushed it off, nodding no before responding.

"It's normal to have questions, but you'll like it once you start because you'll be good at it."

Jack shook his head at his father, unconvinced. "How?" Jack pled.

"How, what?"

"How do you know I'll be good at it?" Jack challenged. "Because you're my son. I know you, and what you're capable of." Alexander answered Jack's trepidation with assurance, like a wall of certainty. There was confidence in his gaze.

"I'm your son, but I'm not you, Dad," Jack asserted.

"No, you're not. You're better than me. I think you're capable of great things, Jack."

"Thanks, Dad. But, I still wish I were certain about Wall Street. Uncle Browne said I should not rush into things, and Veronica wants me to take the job in Durham. I know I'd love that work." Jack's expression underscored his imagined delight at working for Mr. Bellini.

"Your Uncle Browne's a good man," Alexander responded, "but you shouldn't make him your role model if you want to accomplish what you're capable of. He's never had your drive."

"He has a good life, an admirable life," Jack said.

"He's true to himself, I'll give you that. But, let's face it, Jack. Not a whole lot would be accomplished in this country if it was left up to men like your Uncle Browne. There's very little progress in reading Shakespeare year after year." Alexander's response had the tidy conclusiveness of a problem solved mathematically.

"Come on, Dad, you're being unfair. Uncle Browne's given his students a lot over the years-a moral compass, perhaps. And you always said it takes all kinds."

"It does. And, yes, maybe I'm being unfair. But the strength of this nation depends on much more than reading literature."

"I know, Dad, I know-it takes a lot to float the boat," Jack said, with the rote conviction of a child's Pledge of Allegiance.

"Right, Jack. It takes building wealth, financing new ideas, hard driving men and men with vision, who know how to build wealth from all of that. That's where I see you shining."

"Well, Veronica thinks I could do well at the job in Durham," Jack said in rebuttal.

"Doing what?" Alexander said with peremptory doubt.

"Landscape design," Jack declared.

"What do you think about that; don't you think she just wants you nearby?" Alexander's tone was that of dismissal.

"I know she does. But she knows me, too, probably better than anyone," Jack said.

"And she sees you blooming in the Landscape business?" Alexander made it sound absurd. "It sounds like an avocation, Jack. You have the talent and brains to do more. Build your wealth first, on Wall Street. After that, you can branch out. And in the meantime, to keep your hand in Landscape design, I can connect you with some estates back home," Alexander offered. "You'd do that?" Jack sounded like he'd somehow been rescued. He looked at his father appreciatively but then appeared hesitant again.

"What else, Jack?" Alexander asked.

"Veronica." The way he said it, Veronica sounded like love.

Alexander shook his head slowly from side to side in a negative response then raised his lower lip up to seal his reaction, still moving his head slightly to shake off the idea.

"Jack," he said automatically, "set yourself up first. Veronica can wait. If what you have with her is real-you'll want to give her a good life. That means money."

Jack looked at his father quizzically.

"Dad, did you wait? I remember Mom saying how you'd gone after her like a bull dog."

Alexander paused. "I pursued your mother, that's true. But I never took my eye off the ball about work doing it."

Jack felt that his father's objectivity had been somewhat overcome by the zeal with which he tried to convince his son of the better course of action. He let that line of inquiry go to ask something that had been on his mind all day. "Dad, you keep saying I'll do well on Wall Street. What makes you so sure?"

"Look at all you've accomplished," his father declared. Alexander was animated again. Talking about his boy brought back the vitality of his convictions.

"Am I smart enough?" Jack's eyes released a weight of doubt.

"Absolutely," Alexander confirmed.

"Sometimes, it still bothers me, Dad."

"What does?"

"What that doctor said."

"He was just plain wrong; you've proved that a thousand times," Alexander said, his eyes steadily directed toward Jack.

"And you're sure about me, right, Dad? That Wall Street is where I belong?" Jack sounded like a child, seeking the truth from his father.

"I know you've got what it takes, Jack. So do you." Alexander was next to Jack and made sure he met Jack's eyes with his own before giving a confirmatory look to his son.

Jack accepted his father's offering then focused on that part of the river just beyond the gorge where a curtain of lush grass fringed its banks. He smiled at his father, his seriousness gone, and then pointed down to the river.

"That's where I always see doe elk and their calves," he said, pointing to velour-like grass.

"And that," he went on, his voice pitched in anticipation, "is where I'm landing the biggest cutthroat trout in Montana!"

"Lead on, Gad-about-Gaddis," Alexander exclaimed as they started their descent to the river. Alexander knew that Jack had listened to him and believed him.

At the river they got on their gear. Catherine had joined them and stood on the bank holding a camera.

"It's your Outdoor Magazine photo shoot," she said.

Alexander and Jack turned to her at the same time and she quickly snapped their photo. Everything was right in the shot: the light, the background of dark green pines densely crowding together and making a backdrop like a photographer's studio canvas, everything.

The bright light of near-noon softened against the dark wall of trees and Jack's golden hair stood out in relief. The river moved swiftly before them in a crystalline roll, silver and mist filled and blue against the red rocks. It flowed and rolled and surged and gurgled and broke. And in its streaming fury or its lolling ease seemed to transport all time and history, as if natural purpose crowned each rising rivulet and pushed all process on. Jack held the foreground, Alexander backed him up. And the sky overhead and sunlight throughout gave the scene a resonance of natural calm.

Catherine swung backward and got up. Moving toward the place where her tablecloth laid spread out for a picnic, she walked across a line of rocks to get from the vantage point she had chosen, a promontory in the river, to the solid earth of the shore.

And Jack moved farther out into the river. He cast a fly. The line and fly glided out as if in suspended animation, up into the sunlight that lit the red thread of the fly, before dreamily falling back down where it lightly touched the river's surface. In the air it was a dimensionless flight of the fly and seemed more like an imagined essence of fly casting than an actual fly cast. Everything about the day had that quality of effortless suspension-of being up in midair-of rising without descent but landing, finally, nonetheless.

On the shore of the river Catherine shot more photos. She filmed Jack standing in the river, turning his head toward her with his body facing upstream-a momentary freeze of the evanescent, the river rolling, light on the far shore, Jack's gaze fixed on the camera or on Catherine. He had an interrupted look, as if he were involved in something and had quickly turned to please his mother whose insistence at his turning was not spoken but clear. He stood in the shallows of rapids in line with two large rocks, in between them. White water broke around the rocks, splashing his left calf muscle. His white T-shirt looked exceptionally white, his face and eyes somewhat shadowed by the dark green wall of trees on the far bank, his hair a golden halo atop his tall and solid frame.

They fished all day. Catherine read and took loads of pictures. On the shore while Jack was still in the river, Alexander and Catherine talked about their son.

"I had a good talk with him," Alexander said.

"About what?" Catherine asked.

"Taking the job; he wanted reassurance. He wanted to know he could handle Wall Street."

"And you told him?"

"That he can handle it."

"Can he?"

"Yes, he's good with people; competitive. He'll do well."

As Catherine watched Jack start to come in, Alexander saw confusion in her expression.

"What is it, Catherine?"

"Nothing, I just want him to be happy. I want him to succeed, but I want him to be happy, as well. He loves the outdoors. He mentioned working in Landscape design, and I guess, in some ways, I can't see him on Wall Street."

"I told him I could get him some clients around Claremont Hills if he wanted to do that part time. But he'll do well on Wall Street and then he can do what he wants. We should be glad he's got this opportunity."

"You're right," Catherine said, withdrawing her doubt.

Now Jack was on shore, next to them and they sat together looking out at the water.

"Did you have a nice day?" Catherine asked.

"A great day," Jack said.

At last when the sunlight dimmed and the purple sky of evening spread across the heavens, the sun sank below the mountains and it got dark. But the three of them still sat together at the river watching the fading sun go down -seeming to cling to the moment, before the moment went. Then like an afterthought, Alexander spoke.

"Jack," he asked, "if you take the job, where will you be working, 30 Broad?"

"No, they're moving. They've grown too big for their present office. I'll be working on top of the world! Sanders Brown is moving to the South Tower of the World Trade Center!"

Late that same night Jack called Veronica. He loved her, he missed her terribly. She felt the same. He told her he wanted to give the job a try. She did not resist too strongly. Of course, if he felt he had to, he should. They would be all right. Everything would be fine. They had all the time in the world.

# 14

September 8th and 9th, 2001

Jack had been at work almost two months now and Veronica was back in school. They only saw each other on weekends. Most weekends, he flew down to Durham. But this weekend, she flew up. He was still living at home but had decided on an area where he'd look for an apartment. He would begin looking seriously on Monday. This weekend, though, he just wanted to enjoy with Veronica. He was especially excited because someone in the office gave him tickets to the U.S. Open tennis tournament. He had great seats for the men's finals on Sunday, the ninth. He picked Veronica up at the airport late Friday afternoon.

They spent Friday evening at Jack's parents' house and that went okay. But Jack and Veronica wanted to be alone so Jack had booked a room at the Black Bass Hotel in Lumberville, Pennsylvania for the evening of the eighth. He loved the area where the hotel is located just above New Hope among a group of quaint villages banked along the Delaware River that are known for their historic and artistic charm. In mood, it reminded Jack a lot of Chimera on Taylor Island.

He had discovered the area on one of his frequent jaunts and thought Veronica would love it too. He had arranged to borrow one of his parents' cars for the weekend-the old Ford. So Saturday, they left Jack's parents' house mid-morning and drove about an hour away to Lumberville without stopping.

The day was glorious and warm so they decided to tube the Delaware. They drove up to Paradise, stopping once along the way in a small town that didn't seem to have a name but had a general store where they found bathing suits that neither liked but both bought. They got back in the car and drove until they found the sign for tubing they'd been told to look for. Veronica's tube was purple, Jack's bright red. With their colorful tubes and old-fashioned looking bathing suits, they looked like a throwback couple, one that could have used hula hoops and danced the twist but were here, out of time, waiting for their bus ride to the river. The line was not so long since things were just starting, so they got on the bus without having to show off their suits for long.

The bus drove five miles up the river and unloaded and the driver gathered all the tubers, some twenty of them, into a group.

"Now, we recommend you wear your life jackets because you never know about the rapids; they look small but they're powerful.

"Stay to the right of all islands and after about three and a half hours start looking for three big stone pillars in the water. That's where you come ashore."

Moments later Jack and Veronica were on the Delaware, drifting.

"The water's not that warm," Jack said.

"It feels refreshing," said Veronica.

The current was not too strong near shore but toward the center of the river got much stronger. Jack was ahead of Veronica and closer to the center of the river and the current took his tube swiftly downstream. He was sixty feet from her in a matter of seconds.

"Aren't you going to wait for me?!" Veronica yelled.

"What I want has nothing to do with it," he yelled back, "the river's a bit stronger than I am! Come out more and you'll see!" Veronica moved out and her tube got pushed downstream in the same swift rush as Jack's. She was next to him in a second, staring up with an expression of mock reproach.

"Drift away from me, will you?" She said.

"Not intentionally," said Jack, "I'm not that stupid."

"It would be foolish of you, wouldn't it," Veronica chided.

"No question!"

"Make sure it doesn't happen again."

"Never."

"And to make certain," Veronica said, "this should help."

She tied the ropes of the tubes together so that they floated tube to tube, resembling a floating figure eight. Together they worked their way out of the strong current.

"Now you're stuck with me." Veronica smiled through a whisper.

"I think I've already been stuck on you. But I like the idea of tying a knot. No slip knot either, one of those real good sailing knots that hold through everything." Jack spoke softly.

"I don't know about that," Veronica questioned, pretending confusion. "You're in New York now, in the big time. I'm afraid you might drift away from little old me."

"Not that easily, and you know it. That's why you have the confidence to joke about it."

"Are you sure?" Veronica asked demurely. Jack laughed, knowing Veronica was fishing for the assurance she already had. He played along.

"You know I am!" Jack said, saying what she wanted to hear.

More and more tubers floated the river now and they all seemed to be passing Jack and Veronica.

"Everybody's in such a hurry these days," Jack said.

"Perhaps they have some important business downstream," said Veronica.

"Silly them," Jack said.

"Don't you have important business downstream?" Veronica threw a coy look at Jack.

"Nothing that can't wait; my most important business is right here, right now," he said.

They faced each other, their feet interlocked at the ankles, and drifted languidly downstream. Veronica reclined her head back against the tube as if it were a pillow and looked up at the cloudless azure sky with contentment. Jack reclined as well but kept an eye on Veronica.

"How do you feel?" he asked.

"Dreamy, and you?"

"Divine!"

Other tubers passed them. And upstream, more and more came onto the river. Downstream, the river teemed with tubers, too, so that it looked like an armada of tubers, in all colors, covering the river. Everyone seemed in good humor and there was a lot of laughing and happy chattering going on all over the river. It was a like a great big floating party and they were smack dab in the middle of it.

From shore, even people in the yards of the riverfront homes seemed to join in the spirit of the party. One person on shore had set up a stereo with powerful amplifiers. As Jack and Veronica passed by, they heard the loud lyrical wafting of a perfectly chosen Beatles song:

*"Picture yourself on a boat on a river . . ."*

"I love it," Jack said, "but a tube will have to do!" he yelled out to whoever the genius disc-jockey of the shore was.

Soon after the music, they saw a large white sign made from a piece of plywood with blue letters painted across its face reading:

Hot Dog Man. Next to the writing was a large arrow pointing the way.

"Look, V," Jack said.

Veronica sat up and looked. "I hate hot-dogs," she said.

"Hot Dog Man," Jack said loudly. He began singing the name

"Hot Dog Man . . . Oh . . . Oh . . . . I am I and I am the Hot Dog Man," to the melody of some song he couldn't remember the title to but loved singing.

"Hot Dog Man," Jack said, "you've got it all together."

"Really," Veronica replied.

"Yeah, look where he works."

"It's not New York, is it?" Veronica smiled.

"God no," said Jack.

Veronica sounded more serious now. "But you told me it's okay?" she said.

"Oh, it's okay."

"What, Jack, what's the matter?"

"Nothing, it's okay."

"Is it the work? Don't you like the work?" Veronica worried.

"I'm not really sure. It's only been about a month and a half. But, I guess the work's okay."

"But you said that you could do it well?"

"I can."

"Then what is it?" Veronica pleaded a little now. She faced Jack with searching eyes. Jack had clammed up.

"Jack?"

"God, Veronica, don't you know?"

"No."

"I miss you!"

"Oh, Jack." She leaned toward Jack and they met in the middle of the combined tubes and kissed. Jack's hair was dry and reddish-golden and he took her face in his hands tenderly and kissed her. He looked her in the eyes.

"God, how I miss you," he said, looking as if it hurt.

"Can we find the strong current again?" she asked.

"Why?"

"I have some important business downstream."

In the Black Bass Hotel on the second floor the breeze from the river pushed the diaphanous curtains back. The white linen sheets of the four post bed were spread open to one side and the breeze came in and over their bare bodies. In the evening when they wanted food, they went downstairs and got a table in a room overlooking the river. The river breeze refreshed them. Nothing was on the river now but moonlight. They ate dinner and looked at the moonlight and after a while, went back to their room still hungry.

On Sunday they went to the U.S. Open. Veronica had a flight back to North Carolina at seven o'clock out of JFK. The match was not a good one and Jack couldn't stop thinking about Veronica having to go back to North Carolina. He didn't want her to go and he wanted to go with her. The match was not worth concentrating on, which was good, since Jack couldn't anyway nor could Veronica. Neither wanted the match to end, yet both couldn't really watch it.

Sampras looked like the old champ who could no longer keep up. The Australian, Hewitt, was ubiquitous! That is what Jack said about him. He knew that much about the match. When the announcer said that Paul McCartney was in the audience and the big screen showed him in his seat, Veronica squeezed Jack's hand, knowing what a fan Jack had always been.

"Wow," she said.

"Man," Jack said, "I wonder where he's sitting!"

"Yeah, let's go say hi," Veronica said.

"It would make coming here worthwhile," Jack said.

"I'll ask if he thinks Hewitt is ubiquitous," Veronica said. "I'll ask him what the key to happiness is," Jack said.

"He'll probably tell you it's the key of C," Veronica said. They started laughing giddy with the notion of saying hello to a Beatle and of the absurd response they imagined. Then, on the way out of the stadium they saw him: Paul McCartney. He was walking with his fiancée, Heather, ten feet from them. They were practically walking out together. Jack couldn't resist. He ran up to him:

"Paul, Paul McCartney!" Paul stopped for a moment. "Paul, what's the key to happiness?"

Paul looked at him askance but smiled. Veronica was off to the side about ready to burst. Jack looked to her for support.

"Love what you do," Paul said. He shook Jack's hand and walked on.

Jack turned to Veronica. "You didn't ask him about Hewitt?"

"I couldn't get the words out," Veronica said.

"His grip nearly killed me," Jack said.

"You are amazingly crazy." Veronica laughed. "My God, you went right up to him!" She was flush with excitement still.

"What a day, what a girl, what a world!" Jack said, "Paul McCartney and you and me. Maybe we can still ask him about Hewitt," Jack said zealously.

"He's long gone," Veronica said.

"He's ubiquitous . . . " Jack said.

Later at the airport the tone was subdued. They still smiled thinking about the match and seeing Paul McCartney but neither wanted to leave the other.

"I don't know, V, I don't think I can stay away from you much longer."

"But you have such a good job and, as you said, it won't be long. Two months have passed already. In a little over two more, I have a long break." Veronica felt the pain of the impending departure but wanted Jack to be strong about the separation.

"That's the same speech I gave you," Jack said, then stared at Veronica lovingly realizing what she was trying to do.

"I want you with me but also for you to be what you must be and do what you must. Yet, I love you so much and do miss you so too." Veronica's brave face began to change.

"V," Jack said, holding her close to him now, "you . . . are the only opportunity I need."

The plane was ready to board and they gave each other a long kiss.

"Goodbye, Love," Jack said.

"Friday." Veronica's eyes filled with tears.

"I can't wait," Jack said.

"Oh, Jack," she whispered.

# Book II

# 15

September 11th

He awoke before dawn. He felt restless, did not want to stay in bed. He wanted to run. He had time to so he got dressed and went outside. It was still cool, still dark. The world looked gray and misty. But by the time he started running, it was light and he could tell it would be a beautiful day.

He ran a different route. He normally ran a two and a half mile loop through town and back up the hill to his parents' home. Today, he chose to run farther. He ran the hills away from town up toward the old estates on back roads that still kept out the light because of densely packed woods.

The road looked canopied as he ran briskly on the old roads that divided the woods. He ran for twenty five minutes, three miles, before thinking of turning around. It was only just six in the morning when he came to the point at the top of a hill where an old, deserted estate was located. He ran onto the old cinder path to the estate. Where the path forked, Jack went left and there, with the sunlight bathing it; he stopped and looked at the remains of an old garden. He paused a moment. It was so serenely beautiful, even now. He wondered what the garden looked like years ago and what it could be again. He thought about staying home; it was such a beautiful day. The idea passed quickly. He was too new to miss days. He'd be responsible. But before leaving the old garden, he said a prayer.

He ran back the same way, quicker now that he was warmed up. He broke a good sweat. He ran down a hill, then up a long, slow, climb. He felt that in some way the best part of the day was done. He went back home and got dressed for work and was on the train by seven . .

When it came that day, it came with the suddenness of all true horror: mind boggling, devastating, and apocalyptic. And that day expectation didn't matter, played no part in it; nor did intention, except terrible intention. Good intention dissolved as if it were just some dreamy notion, some fantasy. When death and destruction came that day, the future did not matter; everything was pointless, nothing resolved.

Terror crippled perception, made what happened seem too unbeliev-able to be thought of as real. Fear and panic flourished, along with un-imaginable pain. Phrases attempting to capture the terror, such as "man's inhumanity to man" and "free will," failed utterly. "Free will" wrung falsely, sounding like God's small print disclaimer: I gave you this world, so now figure it out. Who can figure out terrible destruction, senseless brutality? Words didn't suffice. Action mattered: rescue squads, evacuation boats, and heroic safety measures. Action buried thought. Where in the Hell was God? It seemed an appropriate anthem.

For those immediately involved, no questions were asked. There was no time. While those directly involved but removed, were bombarded with questions, questions that shattered spirit and paralyzed reason. Pain would not stop and sense made no sense at all–no spiritual sense, no earthly rem-edy. Nothing reigned supreme! It made as much sense for a priest, during a baptism, to drown the infant as the facts of that day did. It made as much sense for a doctor, delivering life, to snuff it out in its first breath. It made as much sense for a father, knowing full well what it meant, to send his children into a war where everyone died. No sense on earth or in heaven. Jack's loved ones knew that.

That day Veronica was in class early. She was in microbiology lab look-ing into a microscope at blood cells, her right eye pressed against the ocular of the microscope. She sought to find the correct resolution for studying the difference between healthy and unhealthy cells. Her hands adjusted the setting of the lens as she looked intently into the microscope. When the setting was correct, she studied the cells, occasionally jotting down notes in her lab notebook. She wore a white lab coat. Her hair was pulled back tight-ly so that it was out of her eyes. She was alone in the lab for the moment.

Then the lab assistant came back into the room and came directly up to her. She didn't notice him at first. She focused on her work and did not see the young man standing there until he tapped her lightly on the shoul-der. She looked up, startled, looked at the wall clock, thinking he was telling her she should stop work now for her next class. But it was only 9:15. Her lab wasn't over until 10:00.

The lab assistant saw her confusion and looked solemnly at her. Ve-ronica straightened up in her chair and leaned toward the assistant with worried eyes. "What is it? What's wrong?" Her left hand gripped her pen as she spoke.

"Veronica, New York is under attack," the assistant said with a lowering look.

Veronica didn't understand. Her whole face contracted into a question: "What?" she asked perplexed. She had heard what the assistant said, but it made no sense to her. The suddenness and surreal nature of the message made it impossible to grasp. It was as if she was just waking up and someone came to her to tell her: it's the end of the world! Veronica, incredulous, sat silently. The lab assistant spoke loudly now, in an ominous tone. "It's on the radio, right now. New York City is under attack," he repeated.

"Where?" Veronica implored.

She ran out of the lab into the office where a radio was located, her heart pounding, mind racing. She crouched before the radio, every muscle in her body tense, her eyes wild and wide. The reporter spoke with utmost gravity as he described events taking place in real time: Both towers have been hit; two planes are involved, each hijacked and flown intentionally into the towers . . .

*"My God!"*

Veronica, horror stricken, appealed to the assistant, "Do they know about the people, I need a phone . . . my boyfriend's there, in the South Tower. . . . I need to know about Jack! Jack's there! Jack . . . "

She left the lab quivering. She tried calling Jack's cell phone. That failed. She tried calling his parents. That failed, too. The lines were overloaded and, when free, interminably busy. Her impulse was to go to Jack's Jeep and drive north. She went to her room, found the keys to the Jeep, and rushed out. She ran to the student parking lot where the Jeep was parked. She ran, frantically, tripping over one of the wooden steps descending to the lot. She braced her fall but the car keys fell onto the lot where they fanned out on the macadam surface, six feet away from her. A crowded lot made it hard to find Jack's Jeep. A gathering of students had formed in the parking lot. A mood of peril filled the air–a wartime mood-of imminent danger and pending disaster. The students spoke in tones of somber urgency. No reality ever felt as real as this horrible reality and Veronica literally shook with fear and torment. She moved ponderously towards where she remembered the Jeep to be. A short distance from the Jeep, she stopped.

A group of Jack's friends from the swim team surrounded the Jeep as if they were protecting it. They had heard the news and come to the Jeep. It was now after 10 a.m. These swimmers knew what Veronica didn't. Coach Ross had it on his computer: the South Tower had just collapsed. Many of the swimmers had tears in their eyes. All were grave. For Veronica, there was no mistaking what she observed. She saw the anguish of the swimmers. She looked beyond them. More students gathered. The word had spread. Veronica screamed in frightened disbelief, "My God, Jack, no!"

In Claremont Hills, at the same time, Catherine and Alexander were getting the news. Catherine was at home, organizing the final arrangements for a trip to the Loire Valley, France which she and Alexander were going to take at the end of the month. A glossy brochure for the Domaine des Hauts de Loire sat closed on the top of the granite center island in the kitchen. On a couch she had laid some clothes she had just bought, lovely clothes from Pulitzer and Talbot. She looked at the brochure and then at the clothes. The phone rang. It was Jack. While she spoke to Jack, the doorbell rang. The phone went dead, then a second call. The doorbell rang again. She listened. Then the second call ended. Catherine ran to the door. Several neighbors who had been watching the news were at the door. Catherine stared at them but said nothing. She ran back inside. She was trying to make sense out of what Jack had said on the phone. She could not think. Her whole body shuddered. She pressed trembling hands into the sides of her head, a contorted look of horror upon her face, and then screamed, "He's got to get out!"

She dialed star 69, nothing. She held the phone quivering and ran into her bedroom where she got the keys to the car. She continued calling Jack's number at work and his cell, still nothing. She had to get to Alexander at the Club.

"Where the hell is Alexander?" She ran outside yelling, "My God!" She tried calling the Club but couldn't get through. She ran to the car. Her next door neighbor, Allyson Simmons, intervened.

"We'll get Alexander," Simmons insisted.

"Get him now!" Catherine screamed.

Neighbors ushered Catherine back inside where she sat on a wooden chair at the center island, a few people beside her.

Catherine cried and those next to her attempted to console her. Other neighbors stood around the kitchen and living room in stunned disbelief. Words seemed useless; horrible silence. Catherine began shaking. Allyson Simmons returned after having called the club and gotten through.

Alexander was in the middle of putting on the third green when a golf cart drove onto the green as he putted. The caddie master told Alexander and brought him back to the clubhouse. Members gathered inside the club to watch the news on T.V. Alexander looked on in horror. He went to a phone and called Sanders Brown. The line was dead. He called his office and reached an associate. Tom McAllister confirmed the South Tower had fallen. Alexander couldn't stay calm. "Was it evacuated?" He struggled for words, pressed the phone tightly to his ear, his face froze in torment. "Did everyone get out? What do you mean? Somebody must know. No!"

On Taylor Island the weather was spotlessly beautiful. At Uncle Browne's neither Uncle Browne nor Aunt Millicent were outside. Nor did Aunt Millicent paint. Nor did Uncle Browne read. Today even Art seemed cruel. A desolation of spirit disabled them after hearing the news while on a CD the Beatle's song Yesterday played.

# 16

When they were coeds at Middlebury College, Alexander Conroy had doggedly pursued Catherine Browne. She was everything that attracted him- beautiful, elegant, and charm ing. Once they met, Alexander never looked back. He set his mind on being with Catherine and arranged his life to make that happen. When she transferred to Colby, he did to Bowdoin. Where she went, he followed.

Catherine had alluring light blue eyes that were so bright they sparkled. She had wonderfully full and golden hair that she wore in a ponytail and would sometimes let fall in cascades of gold over her shoulders and back. She had an athletic, trim, body with long shapely legs and arms with attractively defined muscles- the probable result of years swimming. Her face was square but not too wide and she had full, pert lips.

Catherine was a summer girl who seemed to carry sunshine and sea breeze around with her as part of her ebullient mood. She was a girl with laughter in her, and Alexander saw all of that. He saw her as not just physically beautiful, but as a beautiful companion for life.

She found in Alexander a winsome complement to herself. She admired his self-confidence, applauded his indefatigable effort toward accomplishment, and delighted in his apparently boundless zest for life. She was also instantly attracted to him.

After they married, they lived on Cape Cod. They had a lot of friends, played tennis, went sailing, and lived outdoors as much as possible. They wanted a child, but that did not come easy. Because of severe endometriosis, Jack was a long time coming and they felt commensurately blessed when at last he did. Their miracle, they'd called him.

But then, in a terrible instant, everything changed. Dreams died. Hopeless questioning began, tormented dissolution. Catherine looked gaunt and pale. Her youthful spirit shaken from her, she appeared alarmingly sedate. Her smart-alecky attitude gave way to a moribund reticence. In the months following the tragedy, she became a flower in decline.

Physically, she looked worn, wracked. Her hair had grayed completely and looked dull and not brushed. She pulled it back in a youthful tail but that only revealed the pallid tone to her skin. Her face, at times in the light, looked powdered-whiter than white, and where once an intelligent clarity had filled her eyes they now looked out at the world with stolid detachment.

These physical changes had their equivalent in Catherine's blunted spirit. She became a shadow in the shadow of her own life. By stages of terrible immediacy with the horror and then exceptional distancing from it, Catherine entered into one world and removed herself from another. She would stand for hours at a window in the house and hardly move. At other times she'd simply stay in bed.

First, it was the incomprehensible terror that immobilized her—the heart wrenching agony of loss that nothing could undo, nothing could abate. Then the shock of the tragedy filled her so that she was dumb, insensible. After that, there was an apparent absorption of the facts of the terror and details of its tragic proportions. These facts she recounted one by one with exact specificity. But even with the deliberation her mind insisted upon, to take in the scope of the horror, she could neither fathom nor accept the irrevocable conclusion that applied: Jack was dead.

Then a second wave of terror took hold-an insidious, quiet and consistent terror. This terror came after all the initial days of waiting for some word. It was a terror of silence, of unanswered hope. This terror bore on the surface some morbid pretense of normalcy but was in reality an utter desolation of spirit. Sustained mourning, irreconcilable anger, and the eventual abandonment of hope cast long shadows over Catherine so that her presence took on the pall of death.

Lost in his own torment, stung by guilt, Alexander wandered about the house, cognizant of Catherine's dissolution but unable to do anything to stop it. The surcease of joy had left them both with a living death.

At some point in the winter, Catherine's ostensible understanding of the tragedy gave way to a tacit then complete denial. She rejected immediately the suggestion of a memorial service. "It's premature. . ." she said.

By March, six months after Jack's death, all Catherine could think of was the first nine months she'd spent carrying him. Once pregnant with his life, she now carried him in death. At least in their townhouse, part of Jack was with them still. All of his things were there-everything he had on earth. At first these things were painful reminders of his absence. But then they became the connection between her and Jack that sustained Catherine. The pain of birth and the pain of death she made into the same thing. They were the last vestige of Jack. And gradually, as her mind fought against the truth, these things fostered in her the pitiful notion that Jack was still alive.

Such is the place Catherine lived in. She could not go. Nor could she stay. And time was the void between the two places she could not be. Break the last tie and Jack would be gone. Jack is gone. She felt these things; she did not think them. A fragile cord connected her to Jack. A fragile cord connected her to life. She threw off despair to cling to the illusion her mind fell into. On her birthday, Catherine spent the entire day waiting in Jack's room.

"It's my birthday today. I know he'll be home. He always comes home for my birthday," Catherine spoke mildly with detached calm.

She didn't address Alexander; she was speaking abstractly thoughts said out loud-undirected, ungrounded.

Alexander looked at her without saying anything. Tears formed in his eyes, but he did not cry. He chose to listen. There was nothing he could say. He wasn't being addressed nor, in his quiet attention to her, acknowledged. She had slipped from him and was somewhere else, but always in Jack's room.

She rose from her seat on the bed and then strode with a sleep-walker's quality around the room, appearing to survey all the room disclosed.

Blue ribbons he had won swimming hung tacked to the circular wood frame of the wall mirror. Next to the ribbons around the top of the mirror, photos were snugly pushed up into the space between glass and wood, photos of Jack, and one of Jack and Veronica.

At his desk, under the chair, a pair of swimmer's slippers lay as if he had just kicked them off, exhibiting that carefree attitude that defines the impulse and ease of life in the lived in room of a young man. In one corner of the room goggles spilled out of an open swim bag that sat propped up against a wall, its zippered mouth wide open as if it were being cleaned out. In another corner a small wooden cabinet fitted with slots for CDs had a few CDs pulled out, one of which now played at low volume McCartney's voice in plaintiff resonance, jumping waterfalls over and over again, as tribute to a song Jack had listened to on a trip with his father and loved.

Loose change spread across the top of a blonde bureau and next to it, among the coins, car keys fanned out. Pressed shirts covered with drycleaner wrap hung on a hook behind the door. Books piled on a night table had markers slid in place-an open Outdoor Magazine lay on the bed like the reading was still in process, like the reader would at any minute return. The whole room felt in process, suggestive of activity-incomplete, still going on. It was a still life of a young man's room interrupted. After circling the room sufficiently, Catherine sat down on the bed again and began speaking. "It's my birthday and all I can think of is the day you were born. I've told you about that so many times. I always tell you about yourself on your birthday. But I want to tell you again today. You love it so. I've told you since you were so young, from as far back as you could listen and understand: You were born on July 3rd, 1979. You weighed nine pounds and four ounces. You were not full term. I developed diabetes when pregnant with you and you came a full month early. We still lived on the Cape then. You were the special event of that July 4th weekend. We had tried so long and hard to have a baby, and you were our blessing. All our friends showed up when you were born. You were the celebration.

"The doctor who delivered you worried your father and me. He was too nonchalant. But, of course, it worked out. He induced the delivery with an injection of Pitocin and I was in labor from three in the morning to five the next afternoon. When they gave you to me to hold, I felt such joy and happiness. I adored you from the moment of your birth. When they took you from me, I objected. 'Wait a minute, this was not easy and he is so perfect,' I said.

"You had a healthy pink tone to your skin. Your cheeks were rosy and full in your infant face. Your hair was golden blond and they put a skull cap on you-a little blue and white skull cap. You had a long body and sprawled out in the plastic bassinet they placed you in. You stretched out with all your newborn might-as if happy to be free and wishing to use all of the space you could. Your eyes were closed and you wore that tiny blue and white sailor's cap and looked as robust as a little captain. From the very start you seemed comfortable-comfortable and at home in your space.

Your dad smiled delightedly when he first looked at you, commenting on your forearms. You had big forearms for a baby.

'He's going to be a major league hitter,' he said. You were a happy baby. You hardly cried. You slept through the night right away. I think you were born considerate. You've always been considerate, considerate and perfect.

"When you were a toddler I brought you with me to the beach. The sand dunes at Marconi Beach and the hills of golden green grass around Truro-the sea air and surf and the gulls with their high-pitched cries-the sunlight and the sound of the tide moving in its rhythm, all of this fed you with sensory wonder. You loved being outside. When I would start packing up to go home, you'd try to get away. I can see you now streaking into the high grass of the dune. I couldn't get you to leave.

"We had a garden at the house in Truro. It always seemed loaded with sunlight. You were my helper in the garden, always trying to arrange things. I was so haphazard about it and you always made it neat. . .Didn't we love the garden then? Oh, didn't we. . .I sometimes wish we never moved. Sometimes I wish we were all back there again. The house was small. We were just starting out. We had enough, though, didn't we? Didn't we have everything then?"

Catherine's voice trailed off. She seemed to be lost in a reverie, at a place where no one on earth could reach her. Perhaps it was the feel of something like the sea breeze she knew once-she tossed her head slightly back. A breeze had come through the open window with the sounds of the world outside-birds calling-somewhere off in the distance.

She got up off the bed and went to the mirror. From the top of the mirror she removed two photos. She brought them back to the bed with her where she sat down and stared at the photos with unflinching intensity, as if searching for something-some dimension not apparent but absolute.

# 17

She looked at two photos that had been taken at the ranch in Montana the week Jack had learned about his new job. They were tubing on the Gallatin that day. Jack loved it. He also loved the fact it still meant a lot to his parents. Their times together were not so frequent after he'd gone to college, and his parents seemed more alive in Montana. In Claremont Hills his parents' life had become stilted, even bloated with excess. Not so Montana. Being with them in Montana was special.

In the first photo, Jack stands tall against a background of sky. He is tanned and his golden hair shines, luminously, suffused by sunlight. Catherine had sat down taking the photo, which made Jack look monumental up against the sky. All you can see is Jack and sky. He was six feet-two but in the photo, against the hazy clouds and at that angle, looks giant. What reins the photo in and makes it real is Jack's expression.

He is a boy and a man at the same time. Jubilance shows in his eyes and mouth. His eyebrows slant downward from inside to out in ecstatic play. An impulsive wrinkle of the forehead, just above the eyebrows, catches Jack's delight like a fossil of emotion. So immediate is the feeling in his expression, that it defies the temporal constraints of the snapshot. Joy is there still, in the eyes, his beautiful blue eyes.

A radiant twinkle flashes from the eyes-ignited by an irrepressible spirit, a spirit that cannot but glow and will at any second burst out of the frame and into his mother's eye, and then, infinitely, outside of time.

He wears the gold-cross Veronica gave him and it glows brilliantly. And the sun catches a swatch of his green shorts as they twist with his body's turning. And in the foreground of the photo, framing the scene, two green shoots of river lily project out from the bank of the river toward Jack. One of these, prominent in the foreground and at the center of the photo, seems to reach up and softly brush Jack's shorts just below the hand of his arm hanging down. The second lily, almost out of view, points to the river.

As she looks up from the tip of the lily reaching toward Jack, Catherine sees Jack's right hand closed in a fist with the thumb up and a large blue-stoned ring on his ring finger. It's his Duke ring and with it his hand is that of an accomplished man.

There are two parallel lines in the photo; the line of the lilies in the foreground, and in the background the line of the rolling river. In front, the line of the lilies crosses Jack standing in the river; and the line of the river crosses behind him. The river is all that moves in the photo. In swirls and rolls, the river splashes over rocks from left to right, upstream to down, crossing over and rolling on.

Catherine Conroy stood still in the center of Jack's room; intently viewing the photo. She seemed, with her unblinking stare, to have moved out of the room she was in and into the photo with Jack. "I know when you are home, I hear you singing up the drive," Catherine spoke joyfully, looking all the while at Jack. "You bring happiness with you wherever you go, that's what one of your earliest teachers said. And it's true. You come in from outside and you bring me flowers, my thoughtful boy, my considerate angel.

"There were times when I was ill and you would not leave me. Your friends wanted you outside and you would not go. You sat with me, unable to leave despite my complaints for you to go. In sports, that niceness sometimes hurt you. . . feeling badly for opponents when they lost. Someone's got to win and someone's got to lose. But you never cared much for that philosophy. I used to say to you, Jack, you are too unselfish. You must take some time for yourself . . . think of yourself just once. And then you'd clear the table, looking at me as if what I had just said was a symptom of my illness. You would clear the table and make room for something you thought I might need. What about you, my son? There is no need to deny yourself; I want you to care a little less sometimes."

Branches of trees stirred in the wind that blew outside. And the shadows of those branches jumped about the room when the same wind that stirred the trees stirred the blinds. Catherine's mind stirred, too, and she said what she was thinking in a way that suggested she was more aware than she seemed to be.

"Dance with it. Take care to dance in your own time and to be light-hearted."

Again she looked intently at the photo in her hand. With a puzzled look she spoke to Jack in the photo.

"I cannot see you beyond the frame. Can you see me inside the frame? I am inside, just out of view. But you must see me. Do you see me? I can't be outside. I'm with you . . . inside. All of it is inside. . . . We were going to take the wagon out to the field and fill it with everything we could. But the wagon is so empty now. It was the wagon of our dreams. And it is so empty now. Will it always be so empty? Only you can tell me. I cannot see now."

She had colors in mind. They were colors of the beach with its sun-gold grass and high-pitched, billowing white clouds. She had those colors in mind along with the azure sky and the faded red of the wagon. As she recollected those colors now all of them were bathed in a golden light. But in her thoughts, the wagon remained empty and then the gold began to thin. And then all of it, the gold and the perfect blue and white, and the red of the wagon-diffused into an empty, lifeless, off-white and Catherine felt blind.

One arm reaching out blindly crossed over her other arm. Her left hand still held onto the photo she was lost in. With blind fingers she gripped the photo, feeling for something that wasn't there and only feeling the thinness of the photograph. Catherine dropped to her knees and with her left hand held the photo up. And then she fell deflated to the floor. She had fallen into the scene in the photo. She fell with the falling moment and with the fading colors of the empty wagon. She fell with her failing perception, believing that she could reach out with the river lily and touch Jack's hand. . . touch the hand of her son again. But then she rose up and looked at the second photograph.

Alexander had taken the second photo, Catherine remembered that. The photograph spoke for itself. It said it all:

"*Come on, Dad, let's go in head first,*" *Jack said to his father.*

"*You go; I am getting too old for this.*"

"*Dad, come on, we always do this. It's the best part of the river. Just don't bang up your back like you do sometimes.*"

Then Jack went in. Into the river, he was underwater, piercing the rapids. He couldn't be seen. Not to see him. . . a second maybe. It felt too long.

Alexander had not gone into the rapids but raced ahead—pushing the uncooperative tube like a beleaguered sea turtle. He turned the tube around in time and had the camera pointed at the rapids.

When the photo came back from the shop, it was all white water, the mad face of a surging rapid-a turbulent whiteness shooting up and up, crashing and exploding-white rage. Then, Alexander found what he was looking for in the photograph: In the lower right hand comer of the photo, protruding from a crashing wave-Jack emerging, but not just emerging-laughing. Part of all that whiteness was Jack laughing loudly coming out of the tumult of the rapids-his mouth wide open in laughter-his white teeth showing. The wave sprayed out its surging foam and Jack, coming up from within the foam, sprayed out his laughter. Alexander had heard the laugh and by instinct shot the rapid with Jack coming out.

Catherine recalled what Alexander had said:

*"That's my boy," he yelled, snapping the photo, "that's Jack!"*

She remembered more about that day and that later on in the evening of that day on the shore of the river how Jack had thanked her and his father. He was always thanking us, she thought. She remembered that.

*"I love it here-thanks. This is so special to me."*

*"You do love it, don't you," Alexander said.*

*"Yes, Dad, I really do."*

*"It makes me wonder," Alexander said.*

*"Wonder? I did well getting that offer, didn't I, Dad?"*

*"And you will do very well there. Better than I did."*

*"Dad, come on-you were an excellent money manager. I know that."*

*"I was good. But you have more heart. You're great with people, Jack. You'll do better than I did. Just watch."*

*"If I do half as well as you, I'll consider myself a fortunate man."*

Catherine looked again at the second photograph. She could not see Jack. She was angry at Alexander for taking a photograph that didn't show their son. She was angry with Alexander in ways she could not fully understand. She remembered what Alexander had said on the evening that second photograph was taken:

*"Jack is a special young man. To see him now and listen to him speak as a young man with true modesty, I am amazed. I know I should not be. He's always been great. I'll miss this all too soon."*

Catherine held both photos tightly in her hands now. It was his birthday, she thought. She looked at the photograph without Jack in it. She walked to the center of his room. She looked at it again. Then she looked out the window and saw nothing. She went back to the center of Jack's room and collapsed.

When Alexander found her, she was prone on the floor of Jack's room still clutching the photos. She wouldn't get up. Alexander called for an ambulance. He looked at the photographs in her hands and was bulled over. He looked at Catherine lying on the floor not moving. He felt utterly incapable of helping and was relieved by the sound of the ambulance coming into their drive.

A paramedic came into the room and took her vitals.

"She's unconscious, I'm not sure if it's the heart," the paramedic said. Alexander nodded blankly. "I'm going to give her an injection," the paramedic said, "okay?"

"Yes," Alexander said quietly.

Momentarily, Catherine was on a stretcher being transported out of the house to the ambulance. Once inside, the ambulance went out the drive and down the road with is siren whirling and piercing emergency signal sounding. Neighbors gathered in curiosity and concern and one older man who lived alone approached Alexander.

"Can I bring you to the hospital?"

Alexander had stayed behind and said he'd be at the hospital as soon as he could change.

"Thank you," he said to the neighbor.

"We all know how difficult it's been for both of you," the man said.

They were at the hospital in ten minutes and Alexander left the neighbor and went to ICU. A doctor came up to him there. "There's nothing physically wrong with your wife," the doctor said. "Can you give me her history?"

Alexander gave the history and the doctor's face changed expression from perplexed inquisitiveness to empathetic awareness.

"We'll take care of her now. But I think you should contact your family physician and have him suggest a psychiatrist. I think your wife is under a tremendous emotional strain and has collapsed because she's unable to handle it."

"Yes, Doctor, I will," Alexander said numbly.

# 18

On the evening of her admission, which was the evening of her fifty-seventh birthday, Catherine slept under the influence of a sedative. It was late; Alexander had gone home and would be back early the next morning. Catherine's roommate had been discharged earlier that evening and, thus far, no one had replaced her. She fell into a deep sleep and dreamed.

In the dream the sun shone brightly in a limpid blue sky. Catherine was in Battery Park in lower Manhattan walking slowly and alone. With no humidity in the air the slight breeze from the water felt cool as it touched her face. She walked down a long promenade between two beds of roses. She looked a long while at the sign naming the garden: Hope Garden.

The rose bushes were full and in the light looked golden green. They seemed crowded in the space of the beds. The roses were brightly lit by the sun. Their wide heads loomed up in magnificent red filling her vision. Their fragrance stayed with her as she continued walking.

She followed a path out of the park toward the water. She turned into a terrace that was arranged in a series of graduated and self-contained squares with several small gardens of summer flowers decorating each square—lavender, black-eyed Susan and golden-red ornamental grasses mixed together like miniature Eden's. And beyond the squares of flowers borders of glossy green ivy spread splendidly over a wall of stone.

Now she was in the Robert Wagner Park-walking the Esplanade, a red brick pavilion with a series of arches on her right. There were outdoor tables on a patio in front of the pavilion and in front of the patio an enclosed green lawn, lush and brilliant in the morning sunlight. Sunlight touched everything she saw now-highlighting it and making it all radiant. Arches of sunlight bent luminously above the sun splashed pavilion whose bricks burned tawny red in the light. She turned and everywhere she looked she saw light everywhere she moved, she was in light.

She walked on the lambent Esplanade along the river to her left. The water glimmered in scallops of light. Waves rolled suffused with radiance.

Catherine walked on through this shower of illumination. Light streamed down and splashed the walls of the buildings she passed-the walls of the Jewish Heritage Museum looked vivid white. Light reflected from the windows of the residential high rises that bordered the Esplanade. The flowers she passed glowed. Light fell over railings-illuminating their tops and making them shine. It touched the leaves of the trees. It filled all the empty spaces below the trees and on the earth and ground. Light washed the hulls of boats that rocked on the brilliant water; it rested on the benches along the walkway. The sea walls sat in light. Light cleaned the earth and made it fresh and clear. Then as she came to a point in the Esplanade where she could see the plaza of the World Financial Center, she stopped: Above everything above the bright and wonderful world-like two gods rising against the sky, the Twin Towers stood crystal clear in the full light of morning. Their enormity staggered her. She stood in awe-time froze. Ascending brilliantly, climbing in spectacular effulgence, the towers rose above the world like monuments of light. Gloriously they stood; radiantly they appeared.

She walked on across the wide and shimmering plaza and turned toward the water. At the landing near the Mercantile Exchange she could see the canopy that covered the dock where the ferry boats came in. She stopped and waited, out of the way. Rush after rush of commuters came up the landing passing her without seeing her urgently on their way. They came off the boat as if walking the gang plank. She looked across the water and got the time from a colossal clock. It was 8:30. Another swell of people came off the boat.

In a wave they came off and up, passing her. Their first burst out as a group resembled a stampede or soldiers taking a beach. Then there was a gap with no one. Sun filled the gap. Then she saw Jack.

Among a group of commuters he stood out. He moved more calmly then the rest but with definite purpose. He marched, looking straight ahead. His golden hair glowed. His blue eyes as limpid as the day looked out with their own warm light. Catherine waved at her son. She called out his name. She ran toward but could not reach him. So she ran harder and finally reached him and looked at him and called loudly to him-all to no avail. She was close enough to, but could not touch him. He walked on. She saw his golden hair move steadily away, and then vanish. The gold was gone.

The next morning, Catherine awoke disoriented but with the certainty she had seen Jack. She asked the nurse on duty if her son had been there.

"Not a soul has been here," the nurse whispered.

But Catherine believed that was wrong. She rose from bed and opened the blinds of the hospital room window. Nothing about the day outside hinted at the truth of the world's golden fragility. Nowhere could she ascertain the depth of darkness just beyond the light. Everywhere the vacant world shined.

# 19

The weather changed on Taylor Island sometime around November. Sea winds blew cold and brought with them icy rain. Cloaked in gray, the island wasn't the same. Summer grasses lay stiff, frozen by the chilling wind, flaked with ice. Crystals of ice covered everything, like winter jewelry worn by a dead earth.

Where the water ran in the summer on the side of their house, Aunt Millicent could only glimpse stubbles of the ice-flaked grass. From the window of her studio, a view of the outside world rebuffed her determination to feel better. Nothing outside caught her eye. Nothing out and nothing in, she thought. She didn't want to stop the clock as she usually did when inspired so as to have her imagination zoom in. Her imagination had deadened, it wasn't so much dormant as gone. She turned on her round swivel stool, away from the gloom outside to the gloom at hand.

Next to her, looking as stiff as the ice-flaked grasses, her brushes sat atop a wooden table. Their bristles, devoid of color, were all dried up. Aunt Millicent made a movement with her left arm toward the brushes but then, gazing at the easel mounted canvas, aborted her reach and let her arm fall limply down.

The pattern on the canvas fit the pattern of a bunch of sunflowers, tall stalks with large circular heads close together. But the stalks on the canvass were twisted and the round heads of their flowers black, as if their dark centers had spread outwardly and subsumed the whole. Aunt Millicent whispered, perhaps to the canvas, since no one was with her in the room, "flowers dead do not wither, but won't have a spring, no, not anymore." Then, she got off the stool and left the room.

In the kitchen she turned on a lamp and it was like lighting a match in a pitch black room the way the light concentrated at the center of the room, accentuating a gray periphery. Aunt Millicent moved quickly apparently agitated, putting things in order. She put away dishes, moistened a rag and cleaned the counter tops, picked up and stacked a pile of correspondence as if it were a deck of cards, opened and shut closet doors and drawers to cabinets all hastily, as if by her burst of energy, active life might resume around her for good. She caught her movements in a wall mirror and paused, considering herself futilely. But she started again after that. She rushed into the living room with a look of anticipation. "Where is he?" she asked out loud.

Uncle Browne wasn't in the room. The books sitting on a table by his favorite reading chair were closed and the reading lamp turned off. Aunt Millicent gave another quick look around the room, then went and opened the door leading out to the deck. She walked out onto the deck and saw Uncle Browne. He was in the yard, seated in an Adirondack chair, looking numbly toward Smith Point. A layer of icy droplets shone on his blue parka. His hair was soaked and looked liquid silver. He hardly moved, just gazed out, and didn't hear his wife call to him. He didn't turn to look at her until she was right beside him. Then he stared up at her with the tired eyes of a lost man.

"Browne, you must come in. We have to do something to beat this," Aunt Millicent urged.

Uncle Browne studied his wife blankly. Then he dropped his look and peered out at the frozen grass. He felt the wet coldness of the chair's arm. He adjusted his sitting position, keeping his eyes on Smith Point as he did so and then turned back to Aunt Millicent with a look of forlorn recognition.

"It's too damned cold out here," he said, touching her hand with his.

Inside, Aunt Millicent and Uncle Browne sat in the living room. Uncle Browne had laid a fire and soon heat filled the small room. They sat on a love seat facing the fire.

"I can't get him out of my mind," Uncle Browne said, stretching and straightening his lips in sad contemplation. His look was averted from his wife so she took her hand and softly raised his face under his chin. She studied his eyes for the truth of his broken heart. Her own eyes were clear blue behind hanging tears.

"Me too," she said. Her glistening gray hair was pulled back and secured by a velvet band. "We need to make contact with the others and see what we can do, your poor sister and Alexander, and Veronica, that poor girl." She got up from the love seat angrily shaking her hands in front of the fire. "Damn this world. Damn this foolish, terrible world."

# 20

The first two weeks of her treatment did little to alter Catherine's mood. She sat in her room with the blinds drawn and looked tired and gaunt. Her hair was pulled back, showing her face, which was inexpressive, without make-up and pale. Her high forehead, clearly visible, looked sallow, accented by a few gray hairs around her widow's peak. Occasionally, she took her right hand and with the flat palm stroked her hair just above her forehead in a repeated rhythm. Her eyes did not move in her head. They seemed not to see. They seemed not to blink or react and they seemed lifeless-like those of an old toy doll. Dr. Simon recognized her fragility and treated her with remarkable care.

Nothing about Dr. Simon stood out but the almost tender way he handled his patients. He dressed informally in plain khaki pants and a white button down shirt. He did not wear a watch. He had dark brown, wavy hair that he brushed off his forehead but was in no way styled. When he moved, the bangs of his hair fell forward and he regularly pushed them aside.

He seemed in no way extraordinary until he spoke and then, instantly, one felt the care in his voice. His voice worked like a salve that he seemed to pour gently into the ears of the injured soul he cared for. His presence itself provided solace. For one knew, in some ineffable way, that Dr. Simon's first concern was to help.

He held sessions with Catherine daily. Often he saw her twice a day and while she sat, he spoke. He spoke calmly and with certainty. His voice, even while making a statement, seemed to incorporate his listening. He listened. Always, he listened. He listened to her silence and spoke to it as if he somehow knew what the silence meant and where, deep inside her mind, Catherine resided. He addressed her unspoken thoughts, her inarticulate pain.

"There is reason to go on. You must realize that. Certainly, based on my understanding of him -your son would want that. He would want you to stop suffering. He would want you to go on with your life, even if in its diminished state that seems to you impossible and pointless. He would tell you, it's not."

Dr. Simon looked at Catherine while he spoke to her. He tried to meet her eyes with his. He spoke softly and with great care to be clear and to be certain that what he said, at some level, Catherine heard. Catherine's burden could only be raised with the utmost care and that is how Dr. Simon approached her. He spoke, trying to get her to acknowledge him. He spoke deliberately for a tacit acknowledgment. Yet for two weeks, Catherine did not say a word and did not even look at him.

It was late in the afternoon on a Friday of her third week at the hospital when for the second time that day Dr. Simon came to see Catherine. Light shone through the window in refracted beams that left Catherine partially shadowed. She sat still in the shadows, in some tormented confusion. A palpable pain showed on her face. Dr. Simon sensed some greater torment this afternoon. Her expression at first was of impassive calm, then agitation—her forehead wrinkled in distress.

Dr. Simon sat in a chair away from Catherine but, to be sure she knew he was there, he pulled his chair closer to her. Gently, he placed his hand on her shoulder in an effort to comfort her. When there was no reaction, he folded his hands and addressed Catherine softly. He did not coax or ply but gradually solicited a reaction. A twitch of the eyebrow, a slight wrinkle in the forehead or a pursing of the lips-a quivering-something to suggest a penetration of what he had said into her mind and heart. He spoke affectionately of Jack, the way he might have if Jack were his own boy. And his voice carried a weight of sadness.

"I know that you loved your son deeply and cherished him beyond the capacity of words to describe. . .I know that your boy, your beautiful boy, was most precious to you. I know how beautiful he was and how immeasurably you suffer now with him gone. There is no way on earth, as glorious and wonderful as it can sometimes be, to remove that pain or not feel in every breath of the empty air and fiber of your fractured being-his absence. But I am compelled to aid you now in learning to live with a pain that at some level will never go away. I am here to help you with this burden of death that is so inextricably linked to the burden of love. For it is love's burdening that you now bear. And through love that has not died, you must learn to live again. You have not died. Your son has. Your love for him is not dead either. . . that love you shared with your boy is alive still. That is what you must learn to carry, in time."

Catherine remained still and impassive as stone and Dr. Simon left her with a second gentle touch on her shoulder. In his touch there was an awareness of Catherine's body that seemed at that instant so fragile-so diminished. It was an awareness that knew those thin arms-limp in spiritless fact-had once cradled a boy.

In the dusk of the late afternoon alone in her room, Catherine moved about restlessly. She went to the window and with weak and groping fingers spread open slats of the Venetian blinds. A muted light filtered into the room, touched her face and covered her eyes so that their watery-blue looked gray. She raised the blinds.

Outside it was raining. And with the light drizzle that fell, coating the afternoon world-a cloudy mist extended throughout the grounds of the hospital and into the street and buildings along the street, and to the horizon beyond so that the world seemed draped in a diaphanous gray veil.

Within the mist, gloom spread to the edge of her world. Rain fell harder. In sheets it poured down. Rivulets of water washed over the street into the storm drains and cars passed along the street in a steady flow that to Catherine looked like the water the whole world looked liquid-the whole world seemed to be draining away from her. And suddenly, welling up from deep within her, from the quiet, hidden recesses of her being that Dr. Simon's words must have found-a pouring forth began. Another draining started. Catherine sobbed a mother's hardest tears. She cried continually for the rest of the afternoon and into the evening. When Dr. Simon returned for the last time that day, Catherine lie on the bed, spent. He ordered a sedative for her and as he exited the room for the first time since she'd come in to the hospital, she spoke.

"It's premature, premature." She spoke these words as if she were speaking a mantra-without inflection, repeatedly. Then there was a rising in her voice and Dr. Simon stopped as if ready for something he knew was coming. She rose up in bed: "It's premature," Catherine spoke loudly now, not in the same way she had previously. Now, it was an assertion.

"What is premature?" Dr. Simon asked.

Catherine turned to Dr. Simon now, her body trembling, her voice quivering with the movement of her chin. She looked up at Dr. Simon who stood waiting as if to receive her back from a long, arduous, journey.

"Jack's death," she said.

Dr. Simon moved to her and guided her as she collapsed back down. Now his help could make a difference.

# 21

Gradually, Catherine spoke more and more and Dr. Simon listened. He listened and tried to elicit the range of feelings she had about her son and his death. It was Dr. Simon's intention at this point to have Catherine articulate her loss, to have all that she held inside spoken about. Dr. Simon wanted it out in the open, out of her mind, into the room.

That was the way to relieve her. That was the way to lift the burden of suffering from off her shoulder and see her, eventually, walk out of the hospital as unencumbered as she could now be.

"What is it that you feel the most?" he asked softly.

"I feel everything . . . too much. I feel sorrow. . . waste. . . anger. . . hopelessness. I'm confused. Over and over I ask myself, why? Why he had to be there? I don't know why he had to be there. I don't know why the buildings had to be so tall? Why we put people in buildings like that? What's it all about? I don't understand the hate it took to murder so many people who were just going to work-just doing their jobs. And how this country could have let it happen. I'm very angry about that. We were too fat, happy and arrogant. I think it is arrogance. And I am angry that my Jack was there. He shouldn't have been. It wasn't him. . .he didn't belong there."

"What do you mean?" Dr. Simon asked.

"All of his life before college he wanted to be outside. He loved being outside and for the longest time talked about working outside. He designed gardens and arranged trees even at home. He'd been offered a job doing that. He had even sketched his ideas. I found some of his sketches at home before all this happened. I felt a kind of sadness then. I feel much worse about it now.

"In Montana, he used to talk about bringing nature into our lives through landscape design. He used to say he wanted nature close to home. Jack did not belong in an office. I see that now."

Catherine's face flushed red with the certainty of her conviction and then in an instant the color faded to a bleached out pallor. She turned to look at Dr. Simon.

"The idea of working at a brokerage house wasn't his," she said.

"But that's what he did," Dr. Simon said.

"Yes, he did."

Catherine turned away again and looked out the open window at a sweep of elm trees that lined the front entrance to the hospital.

"So much promise gone," she whispered. "He was exceptional, so much promise."

"Tell me about Jack," Dr. Simon said.

"Jack was wonderful, people loved being around him. From the time he was a very young boy he was a joy to be around All of his teachers said so. That was the first thing they said. I remember when he was in fourth grade; he had an excellent teacher-a real caring person, Mrs. Dawson. She told me at a school conference 'I'd rather go to lunch with Jack than anyone else I know- he is such a pleasant person to be with.'

"He was so personable. And he was kind and mild mannered. He was an excellent swimmer, too, just so good. Once at a State meet there was a false start. The official didn't blow the whistle quickly enough to stop the heat so Jack swam. Someone on another team had yelled 'Go' trying to confuse him.

"He swam the entire race while all the other swimmers waited. Because of his concentration he didn't hear anyone yelling to stop. It wasn't until he finished and saw no one else in the water that he knew something was wrong. And when he was told there was a false start, instead of getting angry at the person for yelling or the official for not stopping the event immediately, he just shrugged it off and laughed at himself.

"There was another very good swimmer in the heat whom Jack should have beaten. But Jack swam the race twice and was tired. The other swimmer won-just barely-but he won and Jack never complained or said a word. He was gracious. He was such a nice young man, such a class act. And he was too considerate."

Catherine lied down on the bed, rested her head on the pillow and rolled away from Dr. Simon.

The next day Dr. Simon met Catherine again. He began their session by reminding her of what she had said the day before. "You said yesterday that Jack was too considerate. What did you mean by that?"

"He shouldn't have been in the building. When he was a toddler I used to walk him in the stroller along with my husband down to the train station. Alexander got his promotion and we moved down here from Cape Cod. Alexander's job was in lower Manhattan. Many mornings then, we walked him to the station."

"Your husband worked on Wall Street?" Dr. Simon asked.

"Yes, he was made for Wall Street, excellent there."

"Is that where Jack got the idea?"

"Yes. . . from my husband. My husband belonged there. Jack didn't."

There was a break in the session while Catherine got up from her chair to use the bathroom. She looked at the clock. It was almost ten in the morning. Alexander usually got there every day at ten o'clock to say good morning, since Catherine's morning session was usually over by ten. When Catherine came out of the bathroom, she looked at the clock again. Then she sat back down in her chair across from Dr. Simon.

Alexander had arrived by this time and was on his way down the corridor to her room. He paused at the door when he heard Dr. Simon's voice realizing their session was still going on. Alexander waited at the entrance to the room and heard Dr. Simon resume the conversation by referring to him.

"You said your husband loved Wall Street. What about your son? Did Jack love it?"

Catherine looked at Dr. Simon impatiently. "Alexander loved Wall Street," she said again.

"Did Jack?" Dr. Simon asked again.

"No!" Catherine said. "Jack went to Wall Street to please his father."

It was as if Alexander had been kicked in the stomach violently; he couldn't breathe. He fell backward away from the room and crashed into a chair out in the hallway. The sound of his body crashing rang through the hall and silenced Catherine. Dr. Simon got up and, as soon as he saw Alexander, realized what had happen. He called for a nurse. The nurse applied a cold compress to Alexander's forehead and put smelling salts to his nostrils. Revived, Alexander stood shakily at the entrance to the room where he had just overheard Catherine. He shuddered and stepped back, not wanting to enter.

He gave Dr. Simon a wounded look. His lips drawn, his shoulders slouched, his whole body drooping. Then, bracing himself against the chair he had struck moments before, he stood up straight and announced he had to go. He said he'd be back later, but he said that so perfunctorily it didn't mean a thing.

He fled the room and tried to race away from the feeling that had made him fall. He rushed down the corridor and did not look back at all. Dr. Simon watched him go and then came back into Catherine's room where the two looked at each other without a word.

# 22

Alexander did not handle Catherine's hospitalization well. All that he had held dear suddenly seemed so fragile and questionable, like a bubble that had flown high in the bright sunlight just to burst and vanish.

At home he felt a profound sadness and aloneness. The world he'd had was gone. Financial security seemed moot without that it was meant to secure. Everything had the quality of illusion—of ghost-like insubstantiality. Everything seemed immaterial. A blast of fate had destroyed happiness and left inconsolable emptiness. He lived now in a purgatory of gloom without hope, with immeasurable solitude.

How quickly, indiscriminately, and completely his whole world fell with the death of his son—and along with it, the death of dreams for his son and himself. The only thing left that mattered was Catherine-her love-their love. But after the incident at the hospital even the roots of that union seemed too delicate and insecure. In his present state of mind, their love seemed improbable. It felt to him as if all love had ceased flowing and all life perched upon death.

He did not like being alone in the house-alone with his thoughts. None of which were good. Guilt added to guilt, now plagued him. Had he been selfish in suggesting Wall Street to Jack? He had never been introspective before. He had always acted with a pragmatic confidence, as if there were no question about his choices and why they were good ones. But recently and now, intensely, he felt riddled with self-examination and doubt. He looked back over his life, questioning it, wondering whether he'd become too consumed with the wrong things wondering about his values-was he too interested in money? Did he want his son to somehow reflect him, his success, shine as an extension of him? Was it all a facade that after all did not mean a thing? Then he turned to thinking about Jack.

*Did I really know Jack? What about Jack?*

In this weary state everything was abstruse-a diabolical puzzle that sent his mind into a whirl, revolving around the same question-ending in the same blunt horror-his son was dead.

"Jack was my boy!" he cried out.

He went into the kitchen, pulled a bottle of bourbon from a cabinet. He took down a tall glass from another cabinet and poured the glass full with such haste the bourbon spilled over the rim of the glass in a golden-brown stream and across the brown granite counter top to the floor. Alexander thrust the glass to his mouth and drank the full glass down without stopping. Then he walked rapidly across the kitchen and stopped suddenly when he entered the family room. Hung on a wall in the family room that faced Alexander as he entered was a gift to him from Jack. In a beautiful, rustic wooden frame enclosed by glass, a homemade trout-fly, its yellow and red feathers spun in a filigree style over a hook, sat against a background of brilliantly blue water. It was a memento of a trip made for him by Jack. They had gone out west to Montana and fished the Gallatin where it cuts into Yellowstone Park. Alexander recollected the trip in all its details: seven days of fly fishing in a velvety green meadow surrounded by awesome mountains. Eagles flew over them, elk appeared at the edge of the woods and he and Jack were as happy as best friends sharing something they both loved in a place they both loved. The memory of the trip and Jack's memento shook Alexander and tears welled in his eyes.

"For Christ sakes!"

He went back into the kitchen, opened a drawer, and took a section of the Claremont Hills News and read:

> He was a hometown boy. You probably saw him around town if you've lived here any length of time. He was an attractive young man who people wanted to be around. He loved to walk the sidewalks of this town growing up, and you never had to smile first when you saw him. He was Jack Conroy: good student, great athlete, one of our own. And he perished too soon in the madness of September 11th.
>
> Jack Conroy was the pure heart of America—the offshoot of our best roots and the flower of our American Dream  When he perished in the sudden madness that killed the Towers and all the dreams and lives the Towers stood for and contained, he left a void larger than the Towers were in the lives of those who loved him and whom he most definitely loved.

Reading his son's obituary in his emotional state was like a blind man playing with a loaded gun. He went into the den and found an album of photographs mostly of Jack, Jack at different ages. He went into the living room with the album and to the fire place and took out some twenty or more photos and set them side by side and just gazed at them. "No success," he said. He took out a book of matches from a wooden box on the fireplace mantle and started to light the photos. Then he looked at one of Jack looking out at him from a stage at school. He remembered the event. He stared at Jack's loving gaze. He dropped the matches, doused the flame, threw all the photos into a heap and left the room. He took a set of car keys, got into a car and rushed off under the influence of heartbreak.

It was now late in the afternoon. Shadows fell across the narrow roads Alexander drove on in the Claremont Hills. All that he passed now had a distorted quality-as if it were the reflection from one of those carnival mirrors that makes everything oversized and exaggerated. Trees came out obtrusively toward him-wide and squat. Flowers looked overly big and not so much pretty as gaudy. Bushes buckled and bulged, bent and burst into the path of the road, like obstacles in a maze. The land and all the growing things along the road seemed impediments.

All that he passed went by in a whorl, in a whirlwind of emotions. Too many reminders jutted out at him-roads where they had taken bike rides-schools that Jack had attended streams they had fished together and all the accompanying conversations shared between them came up to him like snippets of love torn from his heart and thrown down like road kill. Everything, under the cloak of Jack's death, seemed offensive-grossly enlarged beyond reason.

Alexander sped up and drove with reckless frenzy around blind corners, over the limit, on roads barely big enough to fit the car. He drove in a cloistered labyrinth of roads that served the denizens of those exclusive hills. And as he passed by properties, he felt accosted by excess. Every yard was an estate-all of the homes were exceedingly big marvelously appointed and exuded abundance and such a surfeit of wealth that Alexander imagined he could taste the money involved. Higher up in the hills he drove. And the higher up he went the larger the houses got, until at the summit of the hill the land seemed gorged with estates set down like castles in a glutinous heap. Alexander felt sick to his stomach. It was all too much and it was nothing at all. Alexander's thoughts became a jumbled mess:

*Nothing the stone castle without love, love required so much less, gave so much more. People living with their heads in the clouds their*

*heads in the clouds-blind to what's around them. More truth can be*
*found in one fallen leaf than of all these castles in the air.*

He drove on, out of the glutted wealth. He started down the moun-
tain-down the road called Jacob's ladder, out of the paradise of wealth into
the fallen leaves. He wanted to go into town. He wanted to get away from
what seemed to him at that moment the preposterous wealth of the hills
surrounding the village. There was a local pub he thought of that was in
town—a place he would occasionally stop at after work when he worked in
New York. The Station was in town directly across from the railway station.
He wanted to go there. It is a regular place with ordinary people. That is
what he thought. That is what he wanted. He wanted ordinary life.

He parked his car in a lot up above The Station and took the stone stairs
down to the bar entrance. Inside, it was dark the way a bar can be dark even
in daylight. Some of the regulars were at the bar making small talk with the
bartender whom Alexander remembered from when he used to stop there.
The place looked the same. It had that barroom smell of spilled beer and
alcohol and the smell of cooking hamburgers came out from the kitchen of
the bar. A couple guys were shooting darts. Two others in softball uniforms
sat at the bar, expiating their team's recent losing streak and generally airing
their opinions on every subject that occurred to them with the brazen and
authoritative conclusiveness of practiced barroom philosophers.

Alexander entered and brought with him the morose atmosphere that
all afternoon had been his domain. He sat a few bar stools down from the
ball players and loudly called to the bartender. The bartender whose name
was Scotty knew Alexander by sight and recalled that Alexander's boy was
lost in the Twin Towers. He glanced at Alexander, continued to mix the
drink he was making and said he'd be right over.

Alexander called at the bartender again, again loudly. His attitude and
loud voice attracted the attention of those sitting at the bar. One of the men
dressed in a softball uniform looked at Alexander with reproach, as if to say
you are being rude. Alexander ignored the reaction and testily called again.

"May I have a drink?" he said, with exasperated emphasis.

Scotty turned toward him and rather than objecting to Alexander's
surly behavior, apologized for being slow.

Alexander ordered bourbon. When the drink came, he took a large
gulp and looked around the bar room. A talkative couple chided each other
about some recent exploit. Alexander immediately turned them off. He
looked to his left at the two men in softball uniforms who continued their

discussion of the world's troubles, occasionally eliciting Scotty's opinion as if it were the final word on all matters. One of the men addressed Scotty now: "Hey Scotty, what do you make of the beating the market's taking?"

"Christ, don't remind me," Scotty said.

The other ballplayer spoke next. He addressed his teammate and Scotty at the same time. "That's why I never put any money in the market. You could lose it all in a day."

"That ain't why you're not in the market," his friend said.

"Yes it is. I don't plan on losing everything I worked for," the other one said.

"No, that's not it at all. You ain't in the market because you don't have any money. That's why."

"Well, that too," the one not in the market said, laughing. "But if I did, I'd stay out of the market. To me it's just gambling."

"Tell me you don't like gambling a little," the first one replied.

"Not with my nest egg."

"Your nest egg?" the first ball player laughed again. Then turning to Scotty he asked, "How are your investments doing."

Both ball players looked to Scotty. Instead of speaking, Scotty held out his right hand pointing the thumb to the floor.

"I have an IRA," Scotty said, "and I've lost a hell of a lot of it."

Alexander listened with a disdainful impatience and then interrupted.

"While you Wall Street wizards discuss your losses, may I get another?" he said with a sardonic grin on his face.

Scotty fixed Alexander another drink. The two ball players eyed Alexander and whispered something to each other. Alexander finished the new drink almost as soon as Scotty set it in front of him and then, in a contemptuous tone, addressed the ball players.

"So you boys are a couple of financiers, huh? Well, let me tell you something," he went on, "you, my friend, are absolutely correct." Alexander pointed to the ballplayer who had objected to getting involved in the market."

"On Wall Street," he said, "you can lose it all."

The ball player he'd addressed now tried to bring Alexander into the conversation.

"So, do you work on Wall Street?"

"Not any longer. But you're still correct. You can lose everything."

"Did you get hit hard?" the ball player asked.

Sensitive to the tone of the conversation, Scotty waved a hand at the ball player, as if to say-leave it alone. But it was too late. Alexander looked around the barroom with wild, angry eyes that finally fixed upon the un-suspecting ball player.

"I lost it all!"

"God!" the ball player responded, withdrawing a little as if this might be why Alexander was so bitter. Alexander couldn't stop now. He wanted to get it out.

"I lost everything there is to lose on earth, last September!"

The ball player straightened up on the stool. His friend suggested they get going. Everyone began to understand. Alexander pressed the ball player. He stood up at his barstool and turned toward the ballplayer he'd spoken to, "You want to know how much?"

The ballplayer took on a sudden seriousness. "Take it easy, buddy," he said.

Alexander, pointing to the ballplayers and then to himself, command-ed Scotty, "Set us up with another round of losses," he said, "losses for us three, losses for everybody. But make mine a double because I lost it all."

Scotty walked out from behind the bar and in a soft voice asked Alex-ander to sit down and take it easy.

"Yeah, sure, I'll sit down but first I want to show these gentlemen how much you can lose on Wall Street. Alexander fumbled for his wallet, opened it on the bar, and looking at the ballplayers took a photo out of his wallet.

"Here," he said, "here's what I lost." He held up a photo of Jack. "Every-thing, every damn thing."

"Please, sit down," Scotty urged.

"To hell with you," Alexander answered, "To hell with you, and you and you, and Wall Street."

He got up, chugged his drink down and walked out the front door.

In the street outside he felt the fresh air hit his face and smelled his own alcohol-heavy breath come back at him in a warm wave. The remain-ing daylight hurt his eyes. And as he walked away he felt loaded and empty at the same time.

He walked around the corner behind The Station to get to the stone stairs that led up to the lot where his car was parked. He was halfway up the stairway when his left foot struck a stone jutting out from the side of the stair casing. He lost his balance and fell backward all the way down the stairs. When he hit, the right side of his face struck a metal drain at the center of the landing.

He awoke in an ambulance. He knew because he heard the scream of the siren. But his right eye was swollen and his right cheek very tender and he couldn't see and didn't care to try and see. And he couldn't speak without more pain so he just laid there.

"You'll be all right now," someone said to him in a kind voice. "You've had a hard time. But you'll be all right now."

Alexander knew the voice even if he couldn't see the person. But almost immediately after hearing it, he became faint and blacked out.

At the hospital, in the operating room, things happened quickly. He found himself looking up into blinding white lights. A doctor stood over him with suture scissors mending a gash over his right eye. A fractured right elbow had been stabilized with pins.

In all the commotion, Alexander never saw the person who'd been with him in the ambulance and whom he was certain he knew. But he felt more at ease now in the hospital than he had in a long while. His physical pain diminished. There was an exultation of spirit. He felt as if lifted up, as if weightless, above the turbulence and attention of his own turmoil. It was as if in an instant a great weight had been raised from off his shoulders, carried away for the moment, suffering and strife. He felt absolved, anointed. The weight of loneliness, the weight of sorrow, the weight of guilt, gone, replaced by a soaring peace. He went to sleep. In sleep, he was in heaven's soaring calm.

There was a torch light. There was a candle light. There was green and gold. He felt honor. It was as if he was in a skyway. He was wise at heart. He felt boundless and free.

All that he remembered from this post-operative dream was that still, soft voice-saying he'd be all right.

# 23

In the morning Catherine met again with Dr. Simon. With Alexander now in St. James Hospital too their discussion turned to him.

"Your husband is doing okay," Dr. Simon said.

"How badly was he hurt?" Catherine picked at the nail on her right thumb and didn't look at Dr. Simon.

"He fractured his right arm around the elbow and has a fairly deep laceration over the right eye." Dr. Simon spoke with concern about Alexander but also watched what Catherine was doing to her thumbnail.

"What else?"

"He's distraught."

"He's blamed himself all along." Catherine stopped picking at the nail and looked up almost ashamedly.

"That will do him no good. It's exactly what he doesn't need," said Dr. Simon.

"I know." Catherine's voice sounded compassionate.

"Do you think what he heard yesterday has anything to do with this?" Dr. Simon asked. It was a rhetorical question and Catherine quickly grasped the implication.

"We both know it did," she said, "and it wasn't fair."

"How do you feel about what happened to him yesterday?" the doctor asked.

"Are you asking if I feel responsible?" Catherine looked away.

"How do you feel about it?" Dr. Simon repeated.

"So much has happened, hasn't it? But. . .it's not Alexander's fault. It's not his fault at all."

"Go on," said Dr. Simon.

"Alexander has always been caring, always, from the beginning of our marriage and before that. It's what I loved about him and still do." She looked at the doctor intently now. "I had a difficult pregnancy with Jack.

For the last trimester I was confined to bed. The doctor said I could lose the baby if I didn't stay in bed. It was a long, delicate situation, an ordeal really."

"How did Alexander handle that?" asked Dr. Simon.

"Nothing. . .I mean, nothing was more important to him than how me and our unborn baby were taken care of. He did it pretty much all by himself. He stayed home and took care of us. For the last three months, and at a time when it was important to his career to be at work, he was home every day taking care of us. He made my meals, served them, fed me. He washed me. He sat with me, never complaining-always willing, always there. He's always been there for us, for me. He used to read to me then-and to Jack."

"What did he do about work at that time?" Doctor Simon wondered.

"Nothing, that's just it. His star was on the rise at that brokerage house and he walked away from it without hesitation. Nothing meant more to him than we did."

"What about the idea that he put Jack in danger?" Dr. Simon crossed the fingers of his hands and held the clasped hands under his chin.

"Alexander is pragmatic. He came from a relatively poor family. He's worked hard because he knows how much money it takes to have a rich life, to have opportunity. He suggested Wall Street because he truly believed Jack could have a nice life if he did well on Wall Street. Money is important."

"How important is it to Alexander?" Dr. Simon asked.

"He knows you need money in our society if you want the best things- a nice house, good community, nice schools and all the other opportunities. Without money, there's a lot you will do without."

"But, how important is money to Alexander?" Dr. Simon asked again.

"If you're asking if money meant everything to Alexander, I just explained it to you. . ."

"I mean how important is money to him?"

"What do you mean?"

"How important is money to Alexander? Is it more important to him than you are? Was money more important to him than Jack was?"

Catherine became noticeably uncomfortable. She walked across the room and turned around abruptly.

"Jack meant more to Alexander than anything else in the world."

"And what about you, how important are you to Alexander?" Dr. Simon's tone was pointed but not threatening.

"It's not about me," Catherine raised her voice.

"Isn't it?" Dr. Simon asked quietly.

Catherine paced the room again. She sat on her hospital bed. She looked away from Dr. Simon, out the window at the wide blue sky.

"I came from a well to do background. My father was a successful businessman. My grandfather was an executive for Alcoa. Alexander would never have met me unless he had a promising career. He's made his money for me. But it was never more to him than I am. He's the most considerate man I've ever known. And what he has done, he has done with me-with us in mind. And Jack was his father's son, if anything, too considerate."

"You've said that more than once that Jack was too considerate," Dr. Simon said. "What aren't you telling me?"

Catherine looked pallid and frail. She stumbled a little getting off the bed. Then she sat down in a chair next to Dr. Simon -just feet away. Color rose in her cheeks and she seemed flushed with anger.

"I can be selfish. I can be that way. Perhaps that is what drove Alexander. It's possible. But he's too intelligent to be misguided by what he thinks I want and only that. Still, with us, he gave me what he felt I wanted and what I'm certain I made him think I wanted and did want. . ."

"You didn't answer my question. What do you mean exactly when you say Jack was too considerate?"

"I don't mean anything else but that he was like his father, a good man."

Dr. Simon did not press Catherine though he felt she was still holding something back. He changed the subject back to Alexander.

"Do you think it would be useful to have Alexander hear what you think?"

"I'm sure he needs to hear it."

"I will get him then." Dr. Simon turned and walked away. The previous day the Conroy's family doctor had asked that Dr. Simon check on Alexander. It was not a surprise to Alexander to see him there. When Dr. Simon arrived, Alexander looked at him desperately. He looked small in bed, enfeebled his face flushed-his right eye swollen. The right eye was black and blue and sutures closed the laceration. With an unsteady left hand he clutched the side of the bed. He wore a cast on the right arm. He looked completely vulnerable.

"How are you this morning?" Dr. Simon asked.

"I've been better."

"How did you handle the night?"

"It started out okay at first but after a while, it wasn't easy," Alexander said.

"Tell me about it?"

"When I first came in, I felt unusually peaceful but then in the middle of the night I couldn't get certain thoughts out of my head. Those thoughts took over," Alexander said.

"What thoughts?" Dr. Simon asked.

"Thoughts that came in phrases that played over and over in my mind, like a broken record."

"What phrases?"

"Oh, there were several phrases that kept repeating and running into each other."

"Tell me what they were," said Dr. Simon.

"I couldn't stop thinking World Trade Center. Then it was Ground Zero and then the two together. Then, just some crazy equation played in my mind like a formula," Alexander said.

"What formula?" Dr. Simon asked.

"A crazy formula. . . Center = Zero," Alexander said. "It just kept repeating in my mind so I could hear it in my mind's ear.

*Center= Zero. 11.*

"Was that it?" Dr. Simon asked.

"No," said Alexander. "After that, the phrase changed."

"What did it change to?"

"To something crazier, more upsetting, and it repeated continuously."

"What was it?" Dr. Simon pressed.

"It involved Jack."

"What was it? What was the phrase?" Doctor Simon repeated.

"Center = Zero; Center = Jack; Jack = Zero. Jack = Ground Zero. . . Zero. . . Zero." Alexander looked tormented.

"Jack will never equal zero," Dr. Simon said.

"I know that," Alexander said. "It's crazy."

"It's not crazy," Dr. Simon said. "It's a horrible fact that Jack died."

After a moment, Dr. Simon continued. "Let me give you another phrase or two," he said.

Alexander looked at him blankly. Dr. Simon went on. "Jack and Alexander," Dr. Simon said.

"Yes," Alexander said, "he was my pride and joy."

"What about Alexander and Catherine?" Dr. Simon asked next.

"That was always first. But I feel less certain about it now, much less certain."

"Do you feel less certain of yourself?"

"Yes." Alexander's head was down.

"Your wife doesn't. I just met with her. She wants to see you."

# 24

Veronica's ordeal began on September 8th and became terrible on September 11th when she saw a crowd of people gathered around Jack's Jeep. At that time, she had hyperventilated and was rushed to the emergency room of the Duke University Hospital. At the hospital she was given oxygen and calmed down. She did not remain calm long, however, before she began asking questions about New York. But no one had any answers.

The details of the disaster were still unclear. Confusion dominated. Nobody knew who had lived and who had died. People thought to be dead were later found alive. An Emergency Hot Line was set up in New York but it was impossible to get through. Veronica found a kind of refuge in the confusion. Still, she was desperate to know about Jack. She called the Conroy's in New Jersey but their line was constantly busy. Uncle Browne's number was unlisted. After a while, not knowing how Jack was, she grew increasingly agitated.

The attending doctor suggested she remain in the hospital overnight. He prescribed a sedative. Veronica was reluctant to stay and didn't want the sedative but was worn out worrying. When she called home, her father convinced her to follow the doctor's advice. They would come down as soon as possible. They understood her anguish. They shared it. Speaking to her father allayed Veronica's anxiety enough to take the sedative.

In the morning when she awoke, her parents were by her side. It was a comfort to see them. They had flown down from Maryland the night before after having arranged for a family friend to take care of Veronica's younger brother. The doctor had apprised them of their daughter's condition. Except for the breathing incident, nothing else had occurred. Her vital signs were good. But she was still at risk. Uncertainty plagued her. Any bad news could be devastating. The doctor recommended they stay with her for the next few days, at least. They arranged that and, under their care, Veronica was discharged around noon on the 13th.

After her discharge, Veronica and her parents walked across the East Campus of Duke on a path that took them by the parking lot where Jack's Jeep was parked. They were on their way to Veronica's dormitory. She had not intended to check the Jeep but when they reached the parking lot her attention was drawn to a bright yellow spot at the far end of the lot. That's where Jack's Jeep was parked. Instinctively, she moved toward the yellow spot. Her parents tried to stop her but to no avail. They followed, anxiously, sensing something amiss as their daughter hurried toward the yellow area. When Veronica got within ten feet of the yellow spot and saw what it was she trembled, her eyes widened hysterically. Her father tried to hold her back, but Veronica ran to the Jeep. No one was near it now, but it had been covered with yellow roses. Swim caps, too, had been laid across the hood. A photograph of Jack had been slid under a windshield wiper to rest on the windshield. Veronica screamed: "What the hell, have they killed my Jack!" She ran frantically around the Jeep wiping off the roses like she would have gotten rid of snow, her outstretched arm acting like a broom. She pushed off the swim caps with the roses and everything fell in a heap onto the parking lot next to the car. She took Jack's photo in her hands. "How can people be so cruel? They don't know. Nobody knows what I do."

She looked at Jack's face in the photo. She looked into his blue eyes. For a moment, she believed she could smell his hair. A few nights before, they had made love. There was no way he was dead. Her memory of last Saturday night was so immediate, so vivid, and so fresh. It absolutely defied the meaning of what she now observed, of what she looked at in her hands. The yellow roses, the swim caps, the photo, all lied. Nobody knows what I know.

"Get these things the hell away from me!" she yelled violently at her parents. She screamed and screamed, "Nobody knows!"

Her parents moved to their daughter's side and enveloped her in their four arms. Veronica cradled the photo. She stood next to the driver's door of the Jeep. "I have to keep all of this off the Jeep. I won't let anyone near it, anything touch it." Then she said, "Call New York, find out where Jack is."

Her parents felt their daughter's torture and knew they had to take her home.

The next day Veronica returned home with them. So much of her recent life was defined by her relationship with Jack that the home she'd grown up in felt foreign. She felt without an identity there. There seemed to be an impassable gap between what she had come to know with Jack, and what she had with her parents. And the prospect of never being able to return to her life with Jack horrified and immobilized her.

Her first couple of weeks at home was some kind of living hell. Emotionally, she had declined to the point that a breakdown seemed imminent. There were instances when she acted catatonic. And when she didn't appear dead, she appeared sorrow laden. She spoke little in those first two weeks, did not eat and barely slept.

She began losing weight. She had always been thin, so the weight loss was immediately noticeable. It left her looking frail. Added to that, she had dark circles under her eyes. She presented a stark figure, ghostlike and lost. And she seemed always to be preoccupied. Her parents wanted so much to see her smile. It was unreasonable to expect that under the circumstances. Nevertheless, they wanted to see it. But the light that had been her smile went out. They did not know if it would ever return, so morbidly altered did she appear.

When people came to visit her, they were disturbed by her appearance. It was as if she wore an invisible mask of death. Well-meaning people reacted oddly toward her now, too earnestly sorrowful, too readily conclusive in their opinions of her permanent change. And these reactions only increased her isolation.

Though she'd had no choice but to come home, she did not like being home. She let her parents know that. She did not like anything. And her parents suffered deeply with their daughters sorrow. Their only hope was that time might do what place and people could not. What would time hold for her? What would she be able to hold onto? Her parents wondered. The psychiatrist who treated her kept saying to them, "Time will tell."

Veronica Cashmiris came from Damascus, Maryland, a small town forty miles outside of Washington, DC. She lived there growing up, in a middle class neighborhood, in a small house. Her father, Nadid, worked for the Federal Government as a computer programmer. Her mother, Maria, stayed at home, taking care of Veronica's younger brother, Cabal. Her father was of Lebanese and her mother Italian descent. It was easy to see where Veronica got her dark coloring. Both of her parents looked exotic.

The Cashmiris loved their daughter unconditionally and felt helpless in the face of her present pain. All they could do was love her and that didn't seem to help. Veronica seemed afflicted. She told them one morning about a month after coming home, that she knew Jack was dead and that she wished she were too. She said she'd never felt so alone, so lifeless. She said all of this impassively, and with such remove that it seemed to come from a disembodied voice. Her parents worried about suicide. They contacted her psychiatrist.

They advised her doctor exactly what Veronica said and how she'd said it. To their surprise, the doctor said this was important and could, possibly, portend her gradual recovery. The Cashmiris felt somewhat relieved to hear that until, two weeks later—six weeks after the disaster, Veronica became very sick.

She awoke very early one morning and started vomiting. So loudly and wrenchingly did her vomiting sound that it woke up everyone in the house. Her mother went into the bathroom to take care of her and was frightened by her daughter's deathly appearance. Veronica looked so drawn and feeble. She vomited continuously while her mother attended her. This time the Cashmiris called their family doctor.

Dr. Hatcher saw Veronica right away. He reviewed her symptoms and did several tests. He called the following day. He wanted to see Veronica again that morning. She was not dying. That was not it. There was no question about her condition.

Six weeks after September 11th, time became something else again for Veronica. Six weeks before, going back to that Saturday night so vivid in her memory, she and Jack had made love. There was no question at all about her condition. Veronica was pregnant.

# 25

The news of her pregnancy struck Veronica like a cruel joke. It was supposed to be a miraculous event. But that's not how it felt. It felt like a consolation prize. In the insanity of her pain she failed to understand its significance. She yearned for Jack and desperately wanted him. Of all the events in her life in which she wanted him to be with her, and needed him most, this one was first. And he was dead. She wanted a miracle but not this one.

"I'm going to refer you to a high risk obstetrician," Dr.

Hatcher told her. Veronica said nothing.

"Your mother's with you, isn't she?" Veronica still didn't speak. The doctor thought her parents' involvement was crucial now because of Veronica's emotional fragility. He looked at Veronica and said firmly, "I'm going to invite your mother in to discuss this. If you object, tell me now."

Dr. Hatcher had been the Cashmiris's family doctor for years. He knew the family, could guess how they'd react, felt confident their first concern was their daughter and that they would want to help her as much as possible now. So he invited Veronica's mother in and Veronica did not object.

Maria Cashmiris entered the office with trepidation. When Dr. Hatcher closed the door and asked her to sit down, she feared the worst. She believed her daughter might actually be dying of a broken heart. Maria Cashmiris looked plaintively at Dr. Hatcher. "What is it, Doctor?" She sat like stone in a chair near the doctor.

Dr. Hatcher put his elbows on his desk and hands up to his glasses, and with both hands held the arms of his glasses near their lenses, and then he looked down at his file and across at Mrs. Cashmiris. "Your daughter is pregnant."

Mrs. Cashmiris looked incredulously at the doctor. She placed her hands together as if to pray and said softly, "Are you sure?"

"Yes," Dr. Hatcher spoke authoritatively.

Mrs. Cashmiris looked at her daughter lovingly. She was a devout Catholic and practiced her beliefs. One of her strongest beliefs was that life begins at conception. She also knew her daughter and had known for some time how much Veronica loved Jack. She believed the love was mutual. With respect to this specific development, she believed that, had Jack lived, he and Veronica would have been married. They would have had the baby together. She knew that in her heart. She was in no way angry with her daughter. But she was worried about her and worried about the baby.

"What can I do to help my daughter?" She spoke stoically but tenderness in her voice disclosed her love.

"I've suggested to Veronica that she see Dr. Hollins. He specializes in high risk pregnancies," said Dr. Hatcher.

"Is this a high risk pregnancy?" Maria Cashmiris appeared worried again.

"It is because of Veronica's emotional state as well as the fact she's anemic. But Dr. Hollins is excellent. Your daughter will be in good hands," Dr. Hatcher assured her.

Veronica apparently ignored this discussion. She looked at neither the doctor nor her mother. She hardly moved but then got up from her seat, walked to the door and, without turning around, said, "You're wasting your time."

Mrs. Cashmiris glanced toward her daughter and then at Dr. Hatcher. "Doctor," she said, "please let me have Dr. Hollins's number."

Veronica, about to exit, abruptly turned back to stare angrily at her mother. "Do you have any idea how I feel?"

"I am trying to understand, Veronica." Maria Cashmiris's voice filled with compassion.

"You have no idea, Mother. No idea. . ." Veronica's assertion seemed to obviate any effort made on her behalf. Her pain approached the unutterable; her spirit remained aloof. "I know the pain of my daughter. I know how badly you hurt and I want to help you."

"You cannot, Mother. He can't either," she said, pointing to the doctor. "No one can." Veronica's words rang with finality. Dr. Hatcher closed his mouth tightly and pursed his lips in a grave expression. He wrote Dr. Hollins's number onto a prescription sheet and handed it to Mrs. Cashmiris.

"It's a very difficult situation, Veronica. But I must tell you that it is critical to the life inside you that you see this doctor and that you begin taking better care of yourself immediately," said Dr. Hatcher.

Veronica looked angrily at the doctor with unflinching intensity.

"I do not want the life inside me, Doctor. I want Jack."

"You don't mean that about the life inside you," her mother said, rubbing her hands together.

"I absolutely do." Veronica's frail body clenched with the force of her response.

"That's a problem, Veronica," Dr. Hatcher said, "and it's a terribly difficult one on almost all levels but one, the life inside you. That life inside you is struggling to live. He or she cannot do so without your help."

"I cannot live without Jack," Veronica said and walked out.

In the office, Dr. Hatcher laid it out for Mrs. Cashmiris. "Veronica's overall health is surprisingly good. It's better than it appears. But she must start eating well and sleeping appropriately. She has to have additional iron. She needs care for herself and for the developing baby. It's all tied into her feelings now. She needs a psychiatrist?"

"Yes," Maria Cashmiris said.

"Make an appointment with Hollins first. See if the doctor will come to her if she refuses to go to him. This should be done today."

In the car, Veronica sat in the front seat holding her head with her hands. She couldn't get Jack's voice out of her mind. She imagined Jack's reaction to her pregnancy. She imagined his absolute joy. Is it possible he's still alive? I know we get married right away then. We'd return to Durham.

When her mother got in the car Veronica looked at her with wildly ecstatic eyes.

"Mom, is Jack still alive?"

"Oh my daughter," Mrs. Cashmiris said, "Oh my blessed girl."

# 26

Veronica began daily sessions with her psychiatrist. Dr. Kate Nomis, a relatively young doctor at thirty-five. Dr. Nomis took a modern approach to her clients, using medication wherever she felt it could make a quick impact. But the fact that Veronica was pregnant caused the doctor to proceed cautiously and adhere to more traditional psychotherapy.

Dr. Nomis office adjoined her house that was built of light wood, not too big, with large windows that let in a lot of light. It was a cheerful place, as tidy in appearance as the doctor's mind seemed to be when asking questions.

In session, Dr. Nomis sat opposite Veronica in a large brown, well-worn leather chair. Behind her on a bookshelf was a photograph of her and her husband with their two children. She intentionally sat so that Veronica, whenever she looked up, would notice the family photo.

The photograph looked like an advertisement for the happy family. The children shone spotlessly, as if they'd just been washed and polished. They looked out with gleaming, jubilant smiles and eyes that seemed to summon all good things into their welcoming innocence. Doctor Nomis's husband looked handsome and proud; he had an unmistakable look of contentment within his warm brown eyes. And Dr. Nomis it seems had left the role of her profession sitting in the studio waiting room when the shot was taken. For in the picture, her hands rested lovingly on the shoulders of her two cherubic children while her left cheek pressed against that of her husband's on the right. The photo could have been named Family Love.

The Cashmiris had an instant rapport with Dr. Nomis. They liked that she was female and a mother. They hoped because of that an additional empathy might develop that would foster a speedier recovery for their daughter. They were pleased that Dr. Nomis had gotten Veronica to start talking but the problem remained the extent of Veronica's depression. She still did not eat properly and slept only sporadically, usually due to sheer exhaustion.

Dr. Nomis tried to get to the root of the depression. She felt sure that below the surface, tremendous anger was involved, anger that surfaced occasionally in the form of incensed expressions, and terse, caustic statements. Kate Nomis believed bringing the anger fully to the surface was essential if recovery was to occur. She was keenly aware of the urgency involved because of the pregnancy. The Cashmiris kept her informed of Veronica's behavior at home, particularly her eating and sleeping habits, and Dr. Nomis wasted no time in addressing the pregnancy.

"Veronica, I understand you're pregnant," she said. "Will you tell me how you feel about that?"

Veronica sat slumped in the chair, head down looking away from the doctor. Without raising her head she answered,

"It doesn't."

"Doesn't what?"

"Make me feel." Veronica sat in the chair like a shadow, her voice distant, vacant.

"Not a thing?" Dr. Nomis reached out to Veronica with her question.

"Nothing."

"What will you do about the pregnancy?" the doctor asked.

"I don't know. What is there to do, anyway? I will either have it or I won't." Veronica hardly moved answering.

"There is a lot to do if you want the baby, less to do if you don't. Do you want the baby?" The doctor's voice did not challenge, just inquired.

"No."

"You don't, why?"

"I didn't want the baby before. I especially don't now."

"Will you have an abortion?" Dr. Nomis hung the question up in the air by the gradual rising of her voice, as if Veronica might consider it by sight.

"I might." Veronica's eyes looked nowhere and her voice followed.

"Why?"

"Because, I don't want the baby."

"But right now a life is beginning inside of you; does that make a difference to you when you think about it?"

"Why should it? I mean especially now, why should it? Should I want to deliver a baby into this Hell of a world? Should I be happy about having a baby whose father's dead, about going through this alone? And what about the way he died, why the hell would I want to bring a life into this damn world?"

Veronica lifted her head defiantly looking at Dr. Nomis as if Dr. Nomis was the world she'd just condemned.

Nonplused, Dr. Nomis continued. "You recognize that there is a life inside you then?"

"I don't feel life." Veronica shrank into the back of her chair.

"But there is nascent life. That's the fact. You may not want the baby, but in its nascent form, you have it. Does that make a difference?" Dr. Nomis got up from her chair and walked across the room to a water cooler. Veronica looked up. Without the doctor there, she saw the family photograph.

"What kind of life would it be? It wouldn't be like that cute life you have there," Veronica said, pointing to the family photo. "It'd be a hell of life. That's all." A sudden flush of color surfaced in Veronica's face. In her anger, she looked revitalized.

"But with a new life, such as there is inside you, isn't there new hope?" Dr. Nomis stood solidly before Veronica, her voice measured and direct.

"What hope, for what? There's no hope, no hope ever."

"Maybe you're talking about the world, Veronica. Maybe, you're correct. After all, we all die. But are you thinking about the life inside you when you say that? Because, there is hope for the life inside you."

"What hope? Do you think whatever it is inside me would one day sit in a pretty type photo like yours over there? There's a father there?"

"No, I don't. That's not possible. But it is possible that whatever is inside you could sit with you. As a matter of fact, you're the only hope for that life inside you now."

"Well, that's not what I want."

"What do you want?"

"I want Jack."

"But Jack is dead, you know that."

"Yes, he's good and dead." Veronica's mouth slanted downward, framed by lines of bitterness.

"He was a good man? Is that what you were trying to tell me?"

"I'm not trying to tell you anything, you're trying to ask me!"

"Okay. Was Jack a good man?"

"Are you stupid?" Veronica appeared angry.

"Sometimes, but was Jack a good man?"

"You are stupid. I loved Jack. Don't you think I'd say he was good?"

"Yes. But I wanted to hear you say it. He was good. How do you think Jack, as good as he was, would have reacted to your pregnancy?"

Veronica twisted in her chair and began curling strands of hair around her right index finger. "I don't know. He's not here to tell me. He's dead." Veronica began to cry.

"But would he have wanted your child?"

Veronica was silent. She pushed away tears with fisted hands. Bereavement sat in the room with them, unseen but plainly there at the center of their session and heart of Veronica's affliction. Dr. Nomis saw Veronica's spirit sink in her body. She saw in Veronica's sunken shape and saddened eyes all the sorrow and pain of the last two months. She chose to discontinue the session now but felt it incumbent upon herself to say one more thing.

"Veronica, you have had an inconceivably horrible time in the last eight weeks. And now you find yourself hopeless and pregnant. It's a terrible combination. I believe, however, that some part of you wants Jack's baby. That baby will not live unless you want it to. That means you must forget your own pain now and think only of keeping the life inside you."

Veronica, who had turned her head as Dr. Nomis spoke, feebly raised it up again.

"I can't do that. I can't stop thinking about Jack. I don't want to go on. I don't want that constant reminder."

# 27

Based upon Veronica's severe depression, Dr. Nomis consulted Dr. Hollins as well as her parents. Both doctors felt she needed to be hospitalized. Her own physical and emotional well-being depended upon it, as did the viability of the fetus. Since they saw no change in her willingness to take care of herself and were now convinced she might die, her parents agreed.

Mrs. Cashmiris was in Veronica's room on the morning of November 20th, preparing a bag for her daughter to take to the hospital. Veronica came out of her bathroom hunched over, holding her stomach with one hand and bracing herself by grabbing the bed post with the other, moaning in pain.

Mrs. Cashmiris shuddered in alarm. The white nightgown her daughter wore was stained with blood near the vagina. Veronica moved toward her mother. "Please help me."

Mrs. Cashmiris dialed 911. Paramedics arrived in minutes and rushed Veronica to the hospital. They contacted Dr. Hollins who met the parents at the hospital.

"How is she?" Mr. Cashmiris asked.

"She's stable now." Dr. Hollins held a chart in his hands and looked at it as he answered them.

"Was it a miscarriage?" Mrs. Cashmiris asked beseechingly. "Don't know yet. She lost a lot of blood, so I ordered a transfusion. Then we'll do the ultrasound. I should know within the hour exactly what happened. I'll let you know what's what as soon as I do." Dr. Hollins walked away from them down the corridor, the sounds of his heels thudding away.

The Cashmiris went to the Hospital Chapel to pray for their daughter and the unborn child. They returned about thirty minutes later to find Dr. Hollins at the nurses' station holding a chart in his hands.

"Good news. She didn't have a miscarriage."

"What was it?" Mrs. Cashmiris asked.

"Severe cramping with a vaginal discharge, but the baby's alright. Your daughter's anemia may have contributed. I'm treating her for that. You can see her now."

Dr. Hollins led the parents to an ultrasound room. Veronica was sitting up in bed. There was an ultrasound machine with a screen alongside her bed and several lines attached to her stomach connected her to the machine. Mr. and Mrs. Cashmiris paused at the entrance.

Veronica looked at the ultrasound screen. She had more color in her face at least partially due to the transfusion. She appeared more alert than she had been recently but her attention stayed entirely on the screen. She looked with fascination at the pulsing heartbeat of the baby. A little over two months and the baby's heart beat clearly showed. Veronica sat, transfixed by the steady movement. At the same time, she listened to the regular beep of another machine that measured her blood oxygen. She was tired but didn't want to sleep. The machine was hardly loud enough to keep her up but she concentrated on its sound as she stared at the heart beat. She imagined that one was related to the other, that the regular beep. . . beep. . . beep of the machine that gauged her oxygen and the steady opening up on the spot of the ultrasound screen that signaled her baby's heartbeat worked together. She chose not to sleep, believing in some way, that if she went to sleep, the heart beat would stop. So she made herself listen and let herself see-her baby. Only with a great effort could Veronica maintain her concentration. And while she was fairly sure from an intellectual standpoint that her sleep and the baby's heartbeat were not connected, at that moment, looking at the heart beat, she could not relinquish her fear.

To keep herself from sleeping, she thought of everything that had happened in the past two months. For the first time since September 11th, she was able to recollect the events with greater objectivity, as if she had suddenly emerged from the cloud of her own emotions.

She recalled her startled confusion after being tapped on the shoulder by the lab assistant in microbiology lab that morning, and all that had transpired. The chain of events in its surreal magnitude replayed in her thoughts, scene by scene, but with greater sharpness and order. She recalled the position of the lab clock hands at the moment the lab assistant said: New York is under attack. She thought that perhaps time itself died then, at that precise moment.

She recalled the heavy weight of her body as she left the room and the way the air outside the building felt thick with tension, the invisible but oppressive burden of calamity, and the pitch of contagion among students just at its breaking point. She thought she had died, that her time had died. She thought that life was a series of deaths. And she thought of Jack.

She thought of Jack in all their time together, the beginning, the middle and the end of their time, his constant caring for her, his true attentiveness, his good humor, his laugh, and his eyes. She saw him in all his moods, recalled his soft voice, his kind words, his loving manner and his vitality, his active nature, his spiritual zeal.

She thought of their life together, what they had planned for it to be and the diminished present, all of that unrealized promise, the seeming impossibility of his death. It made no sense to her. It never would. She was still under the power of his life. His spirit was with her. She felt anger and remorse, and his spirit. Watching the screen before her, she felt a dizzying juxtaposition of death and life. In her thoughts, her burden remained. But in the room then, her breath in unison with the heartbeat on the screen. What I have left of Jack is that life inside me. My heart beat, his heart.

When her parents entered the room, Veronica addressed them. "I can see the heart beat."

In the weeks that followed, a remarkable change occurred in Veronica. She did all that she could to take care of herself. The baby became her reason to be, the positive direction to which she could channel her own purpose. She continued seeing Dr. Nomis. In her sessions now they dealt with the emotional residuals of loss. They dealt openly with Veronica's anger: anger about Jack's death, anger with Jack's parents, with the country's leadership, her need to know how such terrorism was possible in the United States. And they dealt with Veronica's guilt.

"You said you hate Jack's parents," Dr. Nomis said.

"Yes."

"Why?"

"I think he's dead because of them."

"How, they did not kill him?"

"Not directly."

"Not in any way."

"Oh yes, they did."

"Tell me how."

"He was set up from the time he was born."

"Set up?" Dr. Nomis made an expression of doubt.

"You know, to be a chip off the old block."

"Was his father a bad man?"

"No, but he wasn't Jack."

"Who was Jack?"

"Jack? He was Nature's boy. He never should have gone to New York."

"He didn't want to go?"

"He was afraid to. I was afraid, also."

"Afraid, why was Jack afraid?"

"He didn't want to fail, didn't want to disappoint his parents."

"So he didn't want to fail. But did he want to go to New York?"

Veronica didn't answer. Dr. Nomis left the question out there and asked another.

"Why were you afraid?"

"Excuse me?" Veronica asked.

"You said that you were afraid, too. Why?"

"I thought Jack would be unhappy in New York."

"That concerns Jack. Why were you afraid?"

Again Veronica was silent. Dr. Nomis looked at her. She got the feeling Veronica wanted to say something.

"Veronica?"

Veronica looked on the verge of tears. "I didn't want to lose Jack."

"Lose him, how?"

"To a career, to another girl, to his parents' way of life, I was afraid he would forget me in New York."

"Did you tell him that?"

"Kind of," Veronica spoke softly.

"What did you tell him?"

"I told him I thought Durham would be good for him but didn't want to stand in his way."

"Why didn't he take the nursery job?" Dr. Nomis asked.

"I don't know. I think he wanted to please his parents."

"Is that it?"

"No."

"What else?"

"He wanted to prove to himself that he could do the Wall Street work. And he wanted to make money."

"He wanted that?"

"Yes."

"How did that make you feel?"

"Hurt, angry." Veronica pressed her hands into closed fists.

"Did you ever tell Jack exactly how you felt about him going to New York?"

"Not exactly."

"Well, what did you say?"

"I told him whatever he wanted to do, I'd be behind him."

"But you didn't want him to work in New York, did you?"

Dr. Nomis looked directly into Veronica's eyes. "No," Veronica said, her eyes watering.

"If you had told him the truth, would he still have gone to New York?"

"I would never have stopped him from doing what he thought he had to."

"Are you mad at yourself because you didn't try?"

"Yes."

"Are you mad at Jack?"

"Yes."

"And you are mad at his parents?"

"Yes, I'm mad at them."

"I see."

"What do you see?"

"I see a lot of anger. I see a lot of blame. I think there's some guilt going on."

"Guilt, what do you mean?" Veronica implored

"Yes, guilt." Dr. Nomis spoke calmly.

"You think I'm guilty of something?" Veronica zeroed in on the doctor.

"Absolutely not, I don't think that at all, but you may feel guilty."

"I don't understand."

"I think you feel guilty you didn't insist he stay in Durham, that you feel in some way like you didn't do enough to keep him out of New York. I also think it's possible some of your anger at his parents is redirected anger at yourself. And I think you're mad at Jack for doing what he wanted to, at least to some extent, when it's not what you wanted him to do. I'm certain you're mad at him for leaving you. There's so much going on. It's normal under the circumstances. Anger and guilt are the typical offspring of sudden and premature death. Anger's understandable. But guilt in this case is completely irrational."

"You don't think I'm guilty of anything, then?"

"You're guilty of loving Jack, in other words, not guilty at all. And I don't think you are really angry with his parents. You've erroneously transferred your guilt to them. Really, you should feel no guilt at all. Also, you blamed them for what Jack wanted, working in New York. In the intricate interweaving of your troubled mind working in New York is the equivalent of Jack not wanting you. His parents wanted him to work in New York. You didn't. Therefore, as your injured psyche sees it, they wanted him to not want you. All they really wanted, I imagine, is the same thing you did, to be near Jack."

Veronica erupted in tears now. She seemed inconsolable. Dr. Nomis let her cry. She sat next to her and let her cry and said nothing else for a long ten minutes. Finally, Veronica's tears abated. She looked at Dr. Nomis.

"We should have had what you have there," Veronica said, pointing to the family photo that had haunted her all these sessions. "His parents at least had that."

"We suffer in different ways with tragedies such as this one.
Do not mistake their blessing with their suffering."

"Sufferings and blessings seem so much the same to me."

"They're two sides of the same life, same love."

"Why me, though? Why do I have to suffer now? Why couldn't I have been blessed like them?"

"You have been, Veronica, twice. And they suffer now; they do not have the family snapshot any longer."

Veronica got up from her chair. She walked to the family photo on the shelf.

"I can still imagine this scene with us, me and Jack and children."

"That's not possible. Nor is a family photo for the Conroy's possible. You might want to consider what is, "Dr. Nomis said.

"What is?" Veronica spoke with a beleaguered voice.

"Yes, Veronica. What is, and what soon will be."

# 28

About the same time Veronica's ordeal peaked and her real healing began, the Conroy's reached an apparent dead end in their recovery. Outwardly, they seemed okay. But that was just the face of it, a stolid reticence. Their pain remained so potent that even the most benign incidents wreaked emotional havoc on them when perceived wrongly. They were living in a kind of denuded state, their hearts and souls exposed. Stripped, laid bare, they could not avoid pain but were continuously at the mercy of it. Their only protection was to try and remain aloof. And so they lived somewhere between life and death, here but not here, ostensibly better but actually still hurt. They suffered time, trying to elude it.

Dr. Simon addressed their emotional state with Alexander and Catherine in his latest session with them. He told them it was crucial they make some changes in their life. He did not want to see them live like shells of themselves. But he knew that in every aspect of their lives their son's death tormented them. To some extent, their son's death was killing them. So Dr. Simon urged them to get involved in something new. "You don't ever really break with your past. It's with you and will always be. But something new, now, may help you take part more fully in the life still available to you."

The Conroys considered what they could do to follow Dr. Simon's advice. They had had a full life before and were now looking for satisfaction in the ruins of it. Whatever they did, they agreed it must honor their son. Jack was still so much in their thoughts, so much a part of them. How could they lay to rest Jack without somehow going to the grave with him?

It would be easier to just continue living numbly. Catherine especially had become resigned to the relative emptiness of their life. To her, it would forever be lacking that which they held most dear. She felt it would be impossible to ever feel the same.

Alexander worried about her. He wanted desperately to salvage what life he could for himself and his wife. He worried Catherine might one day spiral all the way down into the abyss of loss she rested on the brink of since

9/11. So his wife's tenuous condition distracted him from his own pain and he thought all the time about what they could do to begin again. He came up with the idea of finding a new place to live in Claremont Hills.

He thought about this for months and urged Catherine to agree. Finally she acquiesced and they got rid of some of the things that had characterized their life in the townhouse: a pool table, a large screen television, a bar with stools. They no longer wanted these things. What they wanted was some sort of peace. How they would find it, they did not know. But they felt, together now, that things only got in their way.

All of Jack's clothes they gave to charity, saving just a few as reminders and those they boxed and stored. A good many paintings they sold at auction, giving the proceeds to charity. Some ornate furniture was also auctioned off. They gave to a reputable relief fund. They gave to the fire and police departments of New York and to their local departments as well. Then Alexander saw a property of interest in the Claremont Hills News. He and Catherine drove out to view the property by taking a quick drive around the grounds.

It was an old estate located at the foot of the Claremont Hills, not too far away from their townhouse but more remote because of its secluded setting. It had been in the same family since it had been built more than a hundred years ago and had come on the market, due to the death of its elderly owner. They called a local real estate agent, Mary Kelly, about it. She was glad to show it to them. She told them thus far there'd been little interest. The property had fallen into disrepair so its condition turned people off. Someone with vision might find it appealing though.

Alexander liked the property for its land and proximity to an historic preserve. Catherine, too, admired the natural aspects of the property-it had a stream running through it and remnants of an old apple orchard. It also had a large garden, albeit much unattended. They both liked the stone architecture of the house, garden walls, and field walls that enclosed the entire estate.

On the south side of the property across the road some development had taken place. They did not care for that. But the development was limited to a few new homes on spacious, five acre lots. And while these monstrosities extended the dominion of the hills, they could only go so far because of the historic preserve and the old estate's property.

The property consisted of thirty acres of woods, meadows and fields, with a picturesque stream cutting through its northern limit that served as a natural boundary. A long time ago it had belonged to a New York financier named Upton Millfen who built it as a summer retreat. It was once part of a colony of summer retreats, existing at a time when wealthy New Yorkers came out to Claremont Hills to relax in country elegance. Most recently, however, it belonged to Millfen's great granddaughter. But she did not have the money her great grandfather did and now, a hundred years after its heyday, the estate was a rundown ghost of what it had been. Nevertheless, the Conroy's were interested in getting a complete look.

They drove out with Mary Kelly on a Wednesday in late May. Despite predictions, the weather was lovely. The sun shone through the trees as the Conroy's drove their Lexus up Jockey Hollow Road which was heavily shaded and uphill, gradually inclining for about a mile before leveling out. If they hadn't known the estate was there, it would have been easy for them to pass by. But just after the road flattened they knew to look for the sign to turn.

It was an unassuming sign, orange-brown in color except for the name in white letters "MILLFEN GRACE." It was mounted to a thick-trunked tree, distinctive because, relatively low in the trunk, the tree split in a Y before ascending some seventy feet. The estate house itself was well hidden within a system of natural barriers that separated it from the rapacious pace and business of the outside world. The first of these barriers was a traverse of meadows apparent upon first entering the grounds. The driveway transected these meadows, dividing them into two pools of golden grass. They were wide and gleaming under the late spring sun and when the Conroy's saw them, they were covered with light and shadow in a crisscross fashion. There was stillness to the fields that suggested something primeval. These peaceful meadows had the effect of providing a quiet interlude between two acts of history occurring, so it seemed, simultaneously: the frenzied world of new construction cutting into the adjacent woods on one side of the property, and the sublime tranquility of the historic preserve on the other side.

The Conroy's were also impressed by the symmetrical arrangement of trees lining the driveway on both sides. The trees here acted like guards standing face to face and completely still. Coming down the road, Alexander and Catherine felt like they were in a processional being escorted by these sentinel trees. They drove slowly, taking in what they saw, feeling welcomed.

At a point where the driveway forked, the two columns of trees ended. There, to the left of the forked road, a bulwark of woods stretched deeply back to where it merged into the woods of the historic preserve. One path of the forked road now led to the mansion and the other toward an empty lot where a stable had stood. The Conroy's took the road that led to the mansion. They followed the contour of the road now made of gravel as it bent slightly to the right. Ahead of them a tunnel of vegetation covered the road, thick foliage on both sides and overhanging limbs of giant fir trees. At the end of this tunnel, the only part of it not dark with shade, they saw the door of the mansion. It looked tiny at a distance, not so much like a door as a portal. And the door shone, lit by the sunlight that fell before it at the end of the tunnel just before the house.

The Conroy's proceeded into the canopied passage, still with the sense of being ushered in. All that they saw thus far, the meadows, the trees; the verdant corridor approaching the mansion beckoned them. They felt more like returning occupants than first time visitors. Mary Kelly waited for them near the mansion's front door and suggested showing them the outside first.

A massive structure built of huge blocks of poured concrete, the mansion was two stories high. It had a pitched, red-tile roof and green shuttered windows. The windows ran along its wide face on both floors. Extending from the main body of the mansion was an L-shaped fieldstone addition. This addition projected out at a right angle from the original structure another forty feet. Alexander noticed that the foundation of this addition had a large crack running almost as long as the addition itself. A raised terrace at the east end of the home and pillared sun porch at the west end, served as opposite limits of the enormous structure.

All around the mansion a wide, green yard sat enclosed by a stone wall, three-feet high. This stone wall curved in a serpentine pattern following the edge of the lawn, separating it from the gardens, woods, and fields on the other side. Within the walls, several grand, old trees stood like symbols of ancient permanence, echoing nature that beyond the stone walls thrived. One such tree at the center of the back yard, twelve-feet in circumference, radiated massive branches like the ribs of a giant green umbrella. That tree seemed to be the center around which the estate had been built. For at all angles, from all places in the yard, it dominated the view. After they toured the outside, Mary Kelly commented, "You can see for yourself how the land alone makes this property appealing. There's so much potential."

"Potential," Catherine said dubiously.

"Of course, look around, this home could be the showcase of the hills," Kelly said.

"May we see inside?" Alexander asked.

"Absolutely." Kelly got a key out of her bag and unlocked a lock box and then the front door. "Follow me," she said.

Inside the mansion was dark with many small, compartmentalized rooms. Thick walls separated the rooms that little light found its way to. There was an amazing den with recessed bookshelves all in a deep brown, dark and dusty, walnut wood. There was a wine cellar as big as an average liquor store in the dank basement. All the shelves in the wine cellar were empty but for a coating of dust and stale air, which was damp and smelled of mildew.

"Needs a good cleaning," Kelly said.

"Didn't the woman that owned it live here?" Catherine wondered.

"Not much, not for the last ten years. She stayed in Florida most of the time." Kelly was ahead of them answering the question as she scoped out another room.

"Did anyone take care of it?" Catherine followed up.

"Doesn't look like it," the agent said.

They continued looking around.

Fireplaces occurred throughout the mansion-a small, arched fireplace in the master bedroom; a walk-in fireplace in the kitchen; and a formal, elegant, wide-mantled fireplace in the ballroom.

The ballroom itself, with its enormously high ceiling, parquet floor, and chandelier as big as a car, created a feeling of disbelief. It was opulently impressive even now in its dusty disuse. In its day, it must have been stunning. For it seemed theatrical in its grand elegance and filled one with the kind of amazement experienced at a play or musical-so dramatic was its setting. Standing in the room, facing the sculptured garland above the mantle, and catching the occasional glimmer of light off the many faceted chandelier-one could almost hear the music of a waltz played long ago and the perfect, light, steps of a bedazzling couple as they danced across the floor that for so long now had felt not a soul.

"Don't you agree with me now," said Kelly, "the place is a diamond in the rough that a quick polishing would splendidly reveal? Imagine the parties you could have here." Kelly seemed lost in her own reverie. But immediately after saying what she did, she appeared apologetic. She'd let herself get carried away with her own musings, forgetting the recent history of Alexander and Catherine. But a look at Catherine set her straight.

"I'd like to go back outside if you don't mind, Mary," Catherine said softly.

"Of course." Kelly appeared embarrassed. She hung back when the three walked outside.

Outside again, Alexander walked the property close to the house and then through the backyard, past the giant oak and into the old garden. Catherine walked with him and they hardly spoke. Mary Kelly told them to take their time and waited for them out front near her car.

Alexander stood near the garden as he looked back at the house. It was easier to look at the whole house from that distance. He pointed to the crack in the foundation of the addition first.

"They didn't plan that right. The whole addition looks like it tilts upward. That crack is just the tip of the iceberg. I don't think any part of the addition is worth a damn."

"Seems a shame," Catherine said. "It was a good idea."

"Ill conceived, I'm afraid," said Alexander. "Somebody was in a terrible rush."

He pointed out a series of other things in the addition he felt were no good: soiled eaves, water stained window sills, dilapidated stone walkways around that part of the house, a roof that sagged in a section.

"A cracked foundation and a roof that's ready to collapse. Up and down, it's no good. What do you think, Catherine?" Alexander turned to Catherine.

"I don't know," she said sadly. Suddenly, Catherine looked deflated, like some more dreams had vanished. She began to cry.

"Honey," Alexander said, holding her, "what's wrong?"

"Please forgive me, Alexander. Please forgive me," she said, trying to rub away her tears.

"What is it, darling?" Alexander looked at his wife with eyes desperate to console.

"When Mary said that in there, about the party, I felt so badly."

"She wasn't thinking."

"But I was. I'm sorry, dear. I was thinking about Jack getting married and a reception in that room. My God, I know I shouldn't. But I thought that. Oh where the hell did our heaven go? I'm sorry, dear. I'm so sorry."

Alexander felt a lump in his throat. He did not let himself think such things. It pained him terribly that his wife had. He wanted her to be joyful again. He wondered if she ever could be, if they ever could be. His spirit sank in his body which looked suddenly defeated. Catherine kept her eyes on him.

"I didn't even ask you what you thought of some of the beautiful parts of the house, like the ballroom." She was trying to be considerate upon reflection.

"I think it was excessive, and now it's obsolete."

"It's so much, isn't it," Catherine said, "and it's so empty."

They walked on, into the garden. They passed a huge silver maple tree. Its crown was so great it completely shaded them. A pleasant breeze blew toward them from the area of the historic preserve. They felt refreshed by the shade and the breeze. Under the giant maple they saw a small chair positioned so that the back of the chair was in front of the trunk of the maple. The chair was made out of carved stone, granite, smooth in the seat- a child's chair, empty now. That did not bother them though. They looked into the garden. It was May and flowers bloomed. Birds flew around the garden, butterflies too. There was a humming of insects.

Standing in the garden, they felt an overwhelming sense of peaceful-ness. It was a feeling similar to the one they had coming onto the estate. In the mansion, the feeling was gone. But out here, it was with them again, a welcome feeling, like an accompaniment, like a blessing.

"What do you think?" Alexander asked.

"I don't feel badly out here. I like it out here. It looks a ruin, but I like it." Catherine spoke with rising animation.

"Me too. Shall we try, then?" Alexander asked.

"To make something of it," Catherine returned.

"Yes," said Alexander.

"We should try," Catherine answered.

They arranged to buy the property. Mary Kelly was very surprised, though, when they hired someone after they bought it to raze the addition. All the Conroy's said to her about it was that they felt the addition was superfluous.

# 29

Closing on MILLFENN GRACE happened quickly since no one was living there. Within the month, the Conroy's owned it. They made changes immediately, bringing in a contractor and crew to raze the addition. Large piles of debris formed from the wreckage and dust covered everything. The more time consuming clean-up was now underway.

The Conroy's slept at the townhouse but spent their days at MILLFENN GRACE. They planned to put the townhouse on the market once the clean-up was complete. Without the addition, their new home would be much smaller. It had been a ten thousand square foot home with the addition, but after the work, it was about three thousand. Even then, it would be too big for them, they thought. But they would keep it modest as far as amenities, keep it simple.

They spent their time at MILLFENN GRACE checking on the demolition work and planning a restoration of the gardens. These gardens became their focus, for they had decided to honor their son by rejuvenating the gardens at MILLFENN GRACE.

Alexander still wore a cast on his right arm as he and Catherine looked at the gardens, planning the restoration. They stood near a long stone wall that wrapped around the property and separated the gardens from the backyard. The gardens appeared hopeless. They had been so long neglected. It exhausted them to think about the work required to restore them. They sat down together on the stone wall and pondered the project.

They watched as a front end loader filled two dump trucks and listened to the thunderous sound of stone and cement crashing into the steel basins of the trucks. When the trucks were fully loaded, Alexander and Catherine watched them leave. The trucks sounded like angry dinosaurs as they shifted gears, then like trumpeting elephants as they applied their brakes before pulling on to Jockey Hollow Road. These hauling operations punctuated their day which went from terribly noisy during them to serenely quiet after the trucks had gone. This day when the clean-up halted, they got up and went to the garden gate.

They tried to discern a pattern in the green chaos. But confusion flourished: a tangle of weeds and bushes. Here and there, hidden within this jumbled mess, they spied remnants of the old garden-surviving flowers. But these were scattered and barely visible, having to be searched for to be detected. Alexander and Catherine looked at each other with beleaguered resignation. Everywhere they turned, their challenge con fronted them. Here, overgrown ivy; there, tangled up vines; and weeds, weeds, weeds.

Along one path Alexander bent down and pushed a cluster of weeds off a tiny Reseda, its diminutive spikes concealed by the cloak of weeds. "I don't know how this thing survived, choked by weeds," he said, handling the dull white spike. He pushed his hand around in the weeds, trying to free the Reseda and withdrew it instantly. A tiny spot of blood dotted his left index finger. He'd been pricked by a thorn he couldn't see.

"Christ, who knows what's in here," he said, pressing his bleeding finger with his left thumb.

After a pause to attend to his finger, Alexander and Catherine resumed their walk in the garden. They walked for only a few moments before they heard the sound of a car coming up the gravel drive, its tires rolling over and crunching the gravel. They moved toward the driveway, each relieved in a way at an excuse to postpone the daunting work before them.

"Are you expecting someone?" Alexander asked.

"No," Catherine answered, surprised.

Presently, an old white Valiant worked its way toward the mansion. It drove slowly, coming up to the circular part of the driveway just before the front door. Alexander and Catherine saw a woman behind the wheel of the Valiant who appeared to be wrestling the steering wheel and didn't bother completing her turn around the circle to parallel park. She stopped the car with a jerk and parked it, diagonally, a few feet in front of the door. She wouldn't have far to go to knock.

A woman about five-foot four exited the car and came to the front door. She pressed the bell that didn't work and then, with animated insistence, knocked on the door. As she knocked she turned around and looked at her parking job.

"Oh Christ!" she said loudly enough so that Catherine and Alexander heard her.

The woman seemed as exasperated with her parking job as Alexander and Catherine had been surveying the garden. She waved a hand at the car as if to dismiss it, then turned back to the door and continued knocking.

She wore a wide-brimmed straw hat, the brim of which flopped like a fish in a boat whenever she moved. This ample brim shaded and hid the lady's face. Once revealed, the face looked youthful and somewhat made up like a stage actress, rosy cheeks and eyes dark blue with mascara. Her clothes fit loosely so that she seemed to float inside them. She gave the impression of a child playing dress up, the clothes were so haphazard. In one way, they didn't fit her. In another, they fit her perfectly and made her appear playful and flamboyant. She was probably sixty-five or so Alexander and Catherine guessed when they spied her in full sunlight as she looked impatiently at the mansion. But the woman had an energy about her that defied age, an aura of ebullience that acted like an accompanying corona.

Now, she turned away from the front door, apparently frustrated that no one was home. She started toward the stone wall and gate at the side of the house, evidently intent on accomplishing her mission. For clearly this woman was on a mission. She had that tenacity of spirit so detectable in a woman set upon something.

Alexander and Catherine saw her more clearly now. Catherine thought she recognized her, something vaguely familiar in the woman's quick movements and "nothing's insurmountable" attitude. They had met this woman before, had known her, but had not seen her in years. She was Mrs. Donogan, Jack's kindergarten teacher. Before Jack was ever categorized, after that doctor's assessment, Mrs. Donogan had rendered her own less formal opinion. "Fooey," she had said. Then Mrs. Donogan had taught Jack how to have fun.

For forty years Regina Donogan was the only kindergarten teacher at the local parochial school. She was a one-of-kind teacher who kept a pet kinkajou in her classroom that she treated like a house cat. At various times in each school year, she'd don boxing gloves, tap shoes, a Napoleon-like hat, stilts, and a Buffalo Bill jacket. Her classroom was a parade of novelty; it was fun in motion.

She played the classroom piano like a cigar-smoking, razz ma-tazz showman in a vaudeville hall and approached life and teaching with a gusto that bowled parents over while it filled their kids with joy. Her school kids were everything to Mrs. Donogan and she remembered every one of them.

She had recently retired. But in the time spent teaching, she seemed to have absorbed all the joy of every child she had ever known and made happy. It was as if one thousand singing hearts sang in her, and somewhere among those was Jack's.

As Mrs. Donogan approached Alexander and Catherine, Alexander recognized her. Without a word, she went up to them, held out her hands and took theirs and squeezed them tightly.

"I'm so sorry about Jack," she said.

"It's good of you to stop by," Alexander said.

"Nice cast," she said, "want me to sign it?"

"You'll be the first," Alexander said politely.

"I thought you were in North Carolina now," Catherine said.

Catherine appeared somewhat unsettled.

Mrs. Donogan noticed that and lowered her energy level as she responded. "Most of the time I am. But I'm up visiting my daughter so I thought I'd try and see you. I heard you bought this old place."

She looked around at the debris and the dust covered yard and at the garden. She couldn't resist herself now. "You've done wonders with it," she said.

Alexander gave a quick grin. Then he saw that Mrs. Donogan was looking at the site of the demolition.

"We didn't think we needed it so big," he said.

"Who would?"

They walked together and Alexander told Mrs. Donogan about their plan to bring back the gardens.

"A long time ago, they were magnificent gardens," he said, as they entered the main garden. "We want to dedicate them to Jack."

"Jack was a wonderful boy," said Mrs. Donogan, "I remember his first day at school. He was the only boy who, without ever being told to, held the door open for me going into school. He did that his first day. What a little gentleman. What a fine young man he became."

"You really remember that?" Catherine asked. She seemed to doubt Mrs. Donogan.

"Oh yes, I've got a memory like an elephant. I remember it all." Mrs. Donogan was looking around trying to make something out of the patterned confusion.

They walked farther into the garden. Vestiges of garden paths showed up in places, but were covered by a knotty mix of growth. Weeds predominated. An old rose bush, practically strangled by weeds, still survived and Regina Donogan looked at it encouragingly.

"It's amazing that's still growing," she said. Then they walked on amid the overgrowth. Hostas tangled by clusters of wildly spreading ivy looked like heads of green hair, half in curls and half straight and flowing-all uncombed. Regina Donogan looked around.

"This reminds me of the first draft of a kindergartner's letter to his parents," she said. "All the words are big, but nothing much is said. Oh, but the possibilities are enormous."

"It will be a challenge," Catherine said. Catherine sounded fatigued. She had not warmed to Regina Donogan. She seemed to be performing, in a wholly obligatory manner, the function of a hostess receiving a guest. But Regina Donogan was not put off by that. "There's some poetic license at work here, but I think we can make it tidy," Mrs. Donogan said.

"We," said Catherine.

"Of course. . . it's all about We. . ."

"We," Catherine said, "are less these days."

"Let me help you be more again," Mrs. Donogan said, and then continued, "In my classes at school I used to have the kids plant a garden. We'd start it from seed and they'd observe the garden throughout the year. I'd assign responsibilities for watering and sometimes even weeding-I hate that part-and by May we'd have a full enough bed of flowers so that we could pick some for the May crowning. Maybe you remember that.

"Well, anyway, we'd pick some flowers and there would be an empty space for a time. But the garden is a funny thing and to some extent, it attends itself. By the end of the year, where the empty space had been, the other plants had filled in and another sprout appeared. The garden healed itself. And the kids loved that. Jack loved it. He was a little gardener, you know?"

"Yes," Catherine said, upset now. Alexander squeezed his wife's hand. He knew what she was feeling. At the same time, he knew Regina Donogan was trying to share something with them. She was attempting to fill in the hole just like the garden story she told.

"Jack was always trying to take care of things. I remember that very well. And he loved colors? I'm sure you know that."

"Colors," Alexander said, weakly.

"Yes. Jack loved bright colors. He delighted in drawing in class. And his drawings were always very bright. I didn't use to place much emphasis on what my little ones drew, but with Jack I recall splashes of brightness all over the page. Colors loomed up at you when you looked at his drawings. Color always meant more to him than whatever it was he was drawing." She paused for a moment, and then continued.

"I remember, too, how he loved to sing. In my class we sang a lot. I played the piano and they gathered around it and we had a hullabaloo for a while, usually until I got exhausted. They never did. First, I'd sing the song. (I'm a frustrated singer from way back-born for Broadway and bound there still.) Anyway, we sang! Oh God, we sang up a storm! And Jack was a loud and happy singer. He loved Yellow Submarine. I'd played it on the piano and when the refrain came Jack's voice rang out above all the others: We all live in a YELLOW Submarine. He liked the color of the song, I think."

Catherine walked away now. Farther on in the garden, she sat alone on a bench under an arbor. She sat so quietly. Alexander tried to express appreciation to Mrs. Donogan but it was the shadow of appreciation, really. Regina Donogan's recollections of her son had hurt Catherine. Alexander, too, found them hard to take.

"I'm sorry," Mrs. Donogan said.

She hadn't realized the Conroy's were still in the place where pain was the currency of their life and where even kindness paid to them wrung up as sorrow.

"I should have known how badly you still hurt," she said. The floppy brim of her hat fell down over one eye. She looked at Catherine Conroy. "She's hurt so terribly. We won't let the roots die."

Alexander looked at Regina Donogan. He did not know what to say. Regina Donogan spoke again.

"To me it's the same as one of those withering flowers over there. What are needed are time and a lot of care. We'll figure it out. There's a group of women that can help you with this garden. Let us do that, The Women of Claremont Hills. We can help; we can come out here and get you started with this garden. My, it is a mess. But we will do it together."

"Thank you," Alexander said. But it was a dead thank you.

Really, it was so hard to feel grateful about anything.

# 30

That evening Alexander and Catherine sat together on the terrace of their townhouse. The sun had just gone down and Catherine wanted to tell Alexander something that had bothered her for months.

It was dark so Alexander lit the candle at the center of the table. He could make out enough to see that Catherine was anxious.

"Alexander," she said sorrowfully. "I must tell you about what still haunts me. I must tell you something I know that you do not."

"What?" he asked.

"Jack was always such a good boy," Catherine said.

"I know."

"He was the same as you-always so considerate of others."

"He got that from both of us," Alexander replied.

"I don't know about that," she said.

Alexander gazed at Catherine. He didn't listen to what she said as much as notice her agitation. She was struggling with something.

"He called, you know. . ." she said suddenly.

"What do you mean?" Alexander looked at Catherine intently with an expression of alarmed surprise.

"Jack called in those last minutes," Catherine said.

Alexander didn't say anything but appeared baffled. He was unsure of Catherine at this point. He was worried about her again.

"He called on his cell phone," Catherine said, "after the first plane hit. He was okay. Then he called again fifteen minutes later. Everything was different."

"Why didn't you tell me?"

"I couldn't," she said.

"What did he say?"

"When he called the second time I could hear that things were bad. He said he loved me. He said he loved you. He loved us so much. I told him to get out, to leave immediately, and to get to the stairs as quickly as he could. To get out. . ."

"What did he say to you?"

Now the candle on the table flickered with a passing breeze. The breeze pushed the leaves of a nearby oak tree sideways toward the house and the candle flame bent like the tree's leaves in an arc but toward the bowl that held the wax, and then the flame blew out. Alex lit the candle again. A less vigorous breeze blew but it was still difficult to light the candle. When he finally got the candle lit, its light reached up to Catherine and showed she was crying.

"What is it, Catherine? Please tell me," Alexander stroked her back.

"He was too considerate for all of this," she said.

"Catherine, what did he say when you told him to get out?"

"He said some people were trapped in an office. That a door had jarred shut. He was going to get them out. . ."

Alexander took it in. He sat quietly. After a long silence, he spoke.

"Jack was the very best a man can be," he said.

"That's not all," Catherine said. "I told him to get out again. Again he told me about the people that were trapped." Catherine looked Alexander in the eyes.

"I said to him, to hell with them. Get out! Save yourself, Jack!"

Catherine turned away. She stared down at nothing, vacantly, before she spoke again.

"He said, 'I can't do that, Mom. . .I love you!' Then nothing.

Alexander," she cried, "do you think me terrible?"

Alexander rose and came to Catherine. He sat beside her. He put his arms around her and hugged her.

"You loved your boy," he said, "what else could you have said?"

They left the terrace and went upstairs to bed. When he finally got to sleep, Alexander dreamt of September 11th and of Jack.

At first, he dreamt of the NEWS coverage of the event as he'd seen it so many times. Then, still dreaming, he dreamt he was in the NEWS and was in Downtown Manhattan as the events unfolded. He saw himself, as if on Television, on his way to work on the day of the attack:

> *Riding up the escalator he looked at his watch. It was 8:50 and he worried about being late. At the top of the escalator, those worries changed. Police had cordoned off the area to the right of the escalator so that he could only move to his left or straight ahead but not toward the Towers. Alexander looked at the officers. They were in a line and they all looked very young, like kids, he thought. Behind them a long, empty, corridor stretched, receding toward the Towers.*

*All the way down the corridor at the far end, where it met the lobby of the South Tower, another line of officers stood. In the shadows of the far end, their uniforms looked like a wide, black, band and behind them, nothing. Alexander started walking toward the street. He passed a row of stores with no one in them-some were closed, others open but deserted. In the dream their emptiness loomed. Then from behind, a wave of commotion swept across the concourse toward him. A rushing of people came at him and passed him, a faceless crowd defined only by their agitation. A palpable fear accompanied these people, as if something invisible but absolutely terrible chased them. Fear ignited the growing group as it dispersed, exiting in a sweeping rush into the street outside.*

*A solitary man dressed in black passed the group going outside in the opposite direction. As he passed them, walking away from them he seemed to grow in size and his muffled voice in cautionary tones said, "Stay away from Liberty Street." Another man came immediately toward Alexander and as he did Alexander saw blood dripping from a gash in the man's forehead, blood obscured the eyes of the man. Alexander reached out toward the man to help him and the man disappeared. Alexander ran now and dreaming, felt his heart pounding in his chest.*

*Once outside, he looked up. Office memorandums on company stationary glided down eerily from someplace far above him. Some were singed and all floated down with a terrifying incongruity. Now Alexander looked up past the hellish confetti. High above the earth the North Tower stood wounded-a gaping black hole in its side, smoke and fire bleeding out. On the street everyone ran. In all directions they ran. In his dream Alexander ran too. He ran up to Trinity Church and then down Wall Street to William Street where he turned right and ran for another block. At the corner of William and Beaver streets, standing to the left of a huge empty lot and in front of Delmonico's Restaurant, he heard a resounding BOOM! In the sky above him the gray air had turned black. Now, all he could think of was Jack.*

*He ran hopelessly toward the Towers. Sirens blasted the air all through Lower Manhattan. He ran toward the sirens. And more horrible than what he heard, was what he imagined he heard, high above the sirens . . . voices crying out. He ran back up William Street but at Wall was stopped by a police barricade. He ran down Wall Street to Water Street. Wherever he ran he met barricades. And at every barricade and every turn he thought of Jack. He could not go West on Water Street. So he ran down Water Street toward Battery Park to try and circle around. It was the hopeless running of a* dream. He tried to run to Jack but only got so far. Finally, everything in the dream stopped-the sirens died and all motion ceased in time for a tumultuous din. In the sky fire balls fell like Hell's own tears. Then shards of steel and glass rained down. The ground trembled and shook. Then, a surging, sweeping, darkness eclipsed all light.

After the longest stillness, his dream resumed. Skyscrapers projected up through the dust in Jersey City across the river. Traffic froze on Broadway, on Water Street, and South Street from Lower Manhattan as far as one could see uptown. And uptown seemed to him like the Promised Land, away from everything going on, presumably safe, impossibly distant. He wanted Jack to be uptown. Alexander couldn't get there except by walking and he'd have to walk through Hell first. He looked ahead up the deadened street.

A huge Coca-Cola truck, solitary and abandoned, diagonally cut across Water Street blocking both lanes where nothing came or went. On both sides of the street on the sidewalk, people marched out of Lower Manhattan. Many coughed. All held clothes or paper towels up to their faces covering their noses and mouths. A rain of soot and ash fell over everyone and everything. Some people were coated in ash. One young African American woman walking alone on the sidewalk was entirely gray.

The Brooklyn Bridge had lines of people moving across it, out of Manhattan. From Water Street they looked like ants marching. Giant plumes of smoke spread across the sky like sinister hands pushing everyone out. When the wind blew, the hands broke apart and flew in giant shadows the other way, thinning then collecting again until monstrous black clouds loomed over the Hudson River where they stood like Death's sentinels.

In the dream, he was watching the NEWS on a TV in a store window. On the ground below everything was ashen. Soot and ash covered trees, churches, cars. Faces of stores along the streets, smeared with gray dust made the stores look as if they had on masks of ash. The air tasted pasty, like air inside a fireplace when the wind blowing down the flue throws it back in your face. It had an acrid smell and taste that choked him as he tried to breath. Men, women, girls, and boys cried. Everyone was scared.

At the Seaport all kinds of boats crowded the East River-fishing trawlers, tug boats, Police and Fire boats-all the Waterway ferries. There wasn't enough room for them all and there were too many people to evacuate at once. Convoys of boats carrying people plied the turbid waters. And people crowded the piers, anxiously waiting to get out. Everyone went to the water or walked uptown or out across the Bridge, and Alexander started back the other way toward *the Towers. The last thing he saw at the pier was a seagull, its white wings dusty gray, scavenging for food.*

*Now in the dream he walked up an empty Wall Street through an ominous silence and stillness. He got to Broadway and it was empty. Distantly it seemed, very distantly, sirens screamed. But the sirens were muted-dulled. In what seemed a lifeless void, he could barely hear them. He made it to the Park at Liberty and Broadway. The bronze statue of a businessman sitting with an open briefcase was black and gray-the briefcase loaded with cinder and ash. Alex stopped and looked up at nothing. He could not get closer. He could no longer move. At this point he saw it. The Twin Gods of thirty years lay dead on the ground-a million tons of dust and in front of them, dozens of shoes. Now there was a sudden change in the dream. The sky around Alexander began to disappear. Whatever light there was had gone. And with that strange, surreal, thinking that char-acterizes dreams, Alexander thought that darkness had come too early- too early for anyone to know just how to find their way. How could anyone get home?*

*So suddenly, night had taken away light. The whole world had descended into grades of darkness. And Alexander felt himself breathing in the dream the way a lost child might, heavily, panic stricken. There was nowhere to go. There was nothing to see and nothing to shed light upon what was happening. Almost blindly, he walked on.*

*A gold standpipe on Wall Street loomed, nicked and marred, then turned ashen, then black. The entire street was like that, as if sucked into a black hole. And the buildings darkened.*

*The buildings around him became gray and then, in one blurred instant, black. Next, it was as if the black buildings extended over the streets and sidewalks and the people and all movement stopped. In the dream Alexander looked at a small scrap of paper in front of him on the ground, a lottery ticket, strewn on the gray street that he saw gradually darken, then become black, like a fadeout in a movie.*

*The Sun had died and with it the light of the world. Alex walked on in his dream. He walked sorrowfully now, feeling that the world mourned its own disappearance. He walked purblind to all but the certainty that in the unyielding darkness he was at death's door. He would never again see his son and he sobbed: "Jack . . . Jack . . . Jack!"*

Catherine woke Alexander up. They lay together awake until morning. In the morning they almost felt normal.

# 31

The next day Alexander had some business in town. Catherine was tired from a restless night's sleep but wanted to get out of the house. In her fatigue she imagined going back in time to a place that existed before pain. Less fancifully, she wanted to find a quiet place in the gardens of MILLFENN GRACE where she might hide from the world for a while. She'd been thinking too much, painfully, since meeting Mrs. Donogan and wanted not to think at all. So her intention was to go to the gardens and immerse herself in work.

She drove the old army road. About a mile up stood the giant red maple that marked the estate where Tommy Dorsey once lived. She imagined being back in time when Dorsey lived there and would bring Frank Sinatra out to practice their songs. She wanted so much to get out of the present that she fancied Sinatra in the house now, practicing. She slowed her car and slid a CD into the CD player. A Sinatra CD of songs he sang in the forties, songs he might have practiced in the Dorsey Mansion. She stopped her car in the road and looked at the mansion, hoping in some way to transcend time. Sinatra sang Time after Time and at the point where the song rose to a crescendo, Catherine pictured Frank Sinatra singing it inside the mansion. She put down the window so the sound of the song in the car could go out and connect to the sound of the song she imagined being sung in the mansion, so the present could meet the past, and some lingering moment from yesterday become alive again, awakened by its recorded life. She got goose bumps because her fantasy became so real that history took life. If there were a way for her to disappear into the thin life of that song, and linger eternally with it, she would have. After the song was over, she felt let down. She drove on, slowly now, heading toward MILLFENN GRACE. Farther up the old army road she turned left onto a hard gravel road and took that road through woods and around turns for another mile until she turned right onto Jockey Hollow Road. It was only seven-thirty in the morning.

The clean-up crew was somewhere else so Catherine was alone on the property. She drove in slowly, watching the light filter through a wall of trees like golden needles coming through a dark green blanket.

At the gardens she opened the outer garden gate with the peg handle of the door. She slid the lock out of its slot and opened the gate, then closed it, watching the pulleys connected to the swinging gate door go up and down, and hearing the knock of the sliding lock as it fit back into its slot. Beyond the gate she looked at a green channel of lawn, fifteen-feet wide, that came between rows of mountain laurel above it, closer to the house, and a natural border of hosta and rhododendron below it, next to the interior garden. The grass had been freshly cut and looked neat and lush. It was bright green and glistening as the sunlight hit the dew. Catherine walked across the channel of lawn and came to the natural border.

The rhododendrons stood fifteen-feet high and were thickly packed together, extending the length of the interior garden and adjacent to a garden wall. The hosta below was so gigantic they looked prehistoric, like plants where you might find a dinosaur egg. Their luxurious green leafs were as big as elephant ears and looked attentive, while the rhododendron looked impressively erect. Catherine felt as though she were at a checkpoint and must pass by the plants according to some prescribed procedure suggested in the appearance of the plants. She walked on past the plants and up to the interior gate and pushed it open.

Once through the interior gate she was in the shade of a wisteria covered pergola. The pergola ran one hundred and fifteen feet and was covered by wisteria vines its whole length. It created a shady path below. This path made of cinders was cool and quiet, pleasant to walk along. Colonnades supported rafters and cross beams that were the bed of the wisteria vines. These vines sat upon the pergola in a twisted and tangled cross, looking like snakes covered in flowers. Catherine walked under them but, in the shade under the vines, her thoughts darkened, so she stepped out and walked into the light of the upper interior garden. She walked on a ways and then down three red brick stairs to the lower interior garden. She found a bench in the northeast corner and sat down.

Here she was in the most sheltered area, in a garden within a garden, sunk below the rest of gardens. The upper and lower interior gardens were square with the same dimensions, forty feet by forty-feet, with smaller squares within each of them. Huge terra-cotta cisterns sat in two places in each garden. One blocked the view to the gate from where Catherine sat.

She started taking things out of the canvas bag she'd brought: a straw hat, gardening gloves, a trowel, some string and a big gray thermos of coffee. She reached for the thermos and poured herself a cup. The steam of the hot coffee looked like a small smoke signal. She watched the steam and felt its heat touch her face. The morning sun had not yet heated up the world and Catherine felt fine drinking her coffee. She was glad not to think, to be out of the way, in the most remote part of the estate and hidden even there by the cistern and the overgrowth of plants. She sat quietly, sipped her coffee, and looked around, listening. An owl repeated its melancholy hoot at regular intervals, sounding forlorn and enervated. Song birds sang. Some sang short bright songs, others whistled a long time in strands that seemed to slice open the silent air.

She heard bees buzzing around the plants and the rustling leaves of trees, stirred by a slight breeze, and fluttering wings from a dove flying away from its perch in a tree. Nothing was harsh. It was all pleasing. She was out of herself, enjoying the privacy of her seclusion, and the steady rhythm of garden life: sounds and silences. A bee whizzed by in its evanescent hurry. Catherine heard it fly. Then she watched as sunlight coming into the garden alighted on the face of a half hidden flower, making the flower look deep purple. Catherine sighed. Momentarily, she began weeding.

She chose a section of brick walkway covered by overgrowth right next to her bench. She used her foot to search for bricks in the walkway that she couldn't see because of the overgrowth. She took some string and lined what she determined to be the perimeter of the walkway and then weeded along that line. She looked up when she thought she heard the thud of the sliding lock to the interior garden. But she saw nothing. She resumed her work, weeding in no hurry. Then, she definitely heard a thud. This time there was no mistaking. She looked up and the interior garden gate had blown open. She was surprised since there was hardly enough wind to push it open so forcefully. The garden gate swung on its hinges and knocked into itself without closing. Catherine looked around and still saw no one. Then at the far end of the pergola, away from where she'd come in, she saw what looked like a figure of light. It was so brilliant she had difficulty looking at it. Catherine didn't know what she saw. She assumed someone had entered the garden but she couldn't see anyone, but she could hardly see because of the angle of the sunlight. She said hello and no one answered. She walked back to the bench she had her stuff on and sat down. It was just a gust of wind, she thought, nothing else, no one's here. After that, for a long while she weeded in peace.

Just before lunch time, she went back to her bench and sat down. She drank from her bottle of water and looked down at her work and noticed her progress. She could see the full red brick walkway for a good twenty feet. She got up and walked down the cleared walkway and tripped over a raised brick, spilling some water from her bottle. The water fell onto the bricks, bright in the midday sun. Catherine was struck by the pattern the water made on the bricks. It was a straight line with two circles of water on each side of the line and above it. It looked like a face. Catherine experienced a rush of feeling, a sudden heightening of emotion, an immediacy of sensation. Then she thought of Jack. She tried not to but did. My God, I can imagine my baby's breath. Catherine steadied herself and walked back to the bench and sat, slumped over, her head hanging down almost to her lap. Why did you die? Why did you die? Did you die because we did not love you enough? Agony sat with Catherine on the bench. Solitude suddenly seemed a curse. And life felt like solitude and life seemed a curse. Catherine wanted Alexander with her now. She heard a different, louder, more intrusive noise at the gate.

She glanced anxiously toward the gate and this time saw a line of women coming into the garden. They all wore dark blue smocks. They huddled in the shade of the pergola like a black cloud, and then dispersed and Catherine watched them, dumb struck. Who are they? What do they want here? Where's Alexander? Catherine could not differentiate, in her state of mind, between genuine kindness and patent remorse. The Women of Claremont Hills had come to help but Catherine wanted no part of them. She went at them now. "What are you doing here?"

Some of the women had seen her and were approaching her when she said that. They stopped short. And all Catherine saw was a blotch of dark blue, her hand rose trying to block the sun.

"Get away from here. You're like vultures to me. All you mean to me is death. Get out! Get away from me!"

Regina Donogan came up to Catherine. She just stood with her. She directed the other women to leave. She waited with Catherine. When Alexander arrived, Regina Donogan explained what had happened. Catherine didn't say anything at first. Then, she turned to Alexander. She looked at him with tortured disappointment.

"Who let death in?"

Alexander called Dr. Simon and later brought Catherine to the hospital as the doctor had advised.

"She's emotionally exhausted," Dr. Simon told Alexander at the hospital. "She knows Jack is gone but she can't accept it. She needs some rest. She will be all right. But she needs rest."

"Of course," Alexander said, and as he thought about his wife's love for her son, his heart broke again.

# 32

After Catherine was released from the hospital and had been home a week, the Conroy's received a phone call from a New York City Recovery official. Something had been found at the site, the official said. An investigation determined it could be their son's. He would have a personal courier deliver the property the next day so that they could see if it belonged to Jack. The Conroy's gave the official directions to MILLFENN GRACE and said they would meet the courier there. Ten months had passed since the terror occurred and this was the first news that something of Jack's might have been found.

It was with mixed feelings that Alexander and Catherine accepted the news. Of course they wanted anything that might be Jack's. But if it were Jack's, the final shreds of lingering doubt would be removed. And some secret doubt along with an accompanying, infinitesimal, measure of hope still existed—had not gone, but it seemed entirely futile and, as Dr. Simon said, delusional, to hold onto such a remote possibility. It was necessary to look for closure. The wound, open too long, would only continue to fester without closure. Closure of a kind, that is. Since in a larger way, there never could be closure-the wound could never really completely heal. The doctor said that as well.

The next day brought a lovely, mild and sunny morning—a blessed day at their country retreat. Alexander and Catherine sat outside on the terrace of the original house drinking coffee and enjoying the quiet beauty of the morning. They looked out over the stone wall in the back yard toward a meadow—green and golden in the fullness of summer. Beyond the wall in a small grove of apple trees, a doe and her white-spotted fawn fed on apples in harmony with the unhurried pace of the world around them. The doe stood on her hind legs from time to time and gingerly, it seemed, plucked an apple from a bough and then dropped it on the ground in front of her fawn. Then the attentive fawn moved to sample every dropped apple.

"It's amazing," Catherine commented, "how she handles her job as a mother."

Alexander looked away to the woods to the left of the meadow on the opposite side of the apple tree grove. The wall of trees framing the meadow was dense and rigid looking against the supple grass of the meadow that seemed to flow in as much lazy ease as the deer ate. A morning breeze, somewhat chill for summertime, came up and rustled the grass. Some goldfinch darted across the meadow so low to the ground they risked getting lost in the grass. It was the kind of day that made you feel happy to be alive and Alexander looked back toward Catherine now. He reached across the table and took Catherine's hands in his.

"You were a wonderful mother," he said.

"I think I was," said Catherine.

"You did everything right. You always did," Alexander said, holding Catherine's hands tenderly in his own.

"It was so easy with Jack-so easy to love him," she whispered. "He made being a mother like having a treasure that every day became more precious without ever being more than it was: Our beautiful boy."

For a moment they shared a heartfelt silence in which all things in life are considered and what matters most is known. Then they heard, faintly, the sound of a car coming up the drive. Assuming it was the courier from New York they walked to the front of the house. They were surprised to see that the courier was a Police Officer in dress blues. He was a young man-polished and polite. His red hair was cut short and neatly combed off his forehead to one side. It shone under the gloss of a gel he must have used. He was a fair skinned, green-eyed, Irishman with the comportment of a knight.

In one hand he carried his dress hat that he had tucked into his chest and arm. In the other he held an iron box about the size of a music box but deeper than that. The box was partially covered in a small American flag as if it were something of a soldier's now carried by a soldier home. There was dignity and solemnity in the moment and an anxious, sobering, fear on the part of the Conroy's that the young officer must have seen before.

"My name is Officer Joseph Brady with the New York City Police Department and I am here to present to you property that may have belonged to your son."

The officer spoke in a professional tone but with kind and respectful eyes.

"Sir and madam, after you have had an opportunity to examine the contents, if you agree they belonged to your son, I will need you to sign these papers so that I can release them to you," the officer explained.

With that, he handed the draped iron box to Alexander. Alexander suggested they go around to the back of the house and sit at the table on the terrace to open the box. They walked around the house to a wrought iron table they had brought out to MILLFENN GRACE. There, the three sat down. Alexander and Catherine sat together on one side of the table and the young officer sat down opposite them.

The sunlight that had shone so brightly earlier that morning now dimmed behind a passing cloud. The young officer took out a small key from his jacket pocket and handed it across the table to Alexander. The iron box sat in the middle of the table, heavy and dark in the muted light. Alexander stared into the officer's eyes as he accepted the small key. Just for a moment he held his hand out with the key in it, the palm facing toward the sky. Slowly he withdrew it, folding the key in his closing fist. He glanced toward Catherine, and saw she reflected the same reluctance he had about opening the box. The officer's attention remained on them. He seemed to expect their look of apprehension. In his manner and expression, the officer made it clear there was no need to hurry.

"If you prefer," he said, "I can leave the box and return later this afternoon."

"That's not necessary, officer," Alexander said, "but we appreciate your courtesy and the fact you made the trip out here to deliver this face to face. But we don't want to hold you up."

"Sir," the young officer said, "this is the only appointment I made today. I am in no rush."

"Thank you," Alexander said.

"I suppose you'd better open it," Catherine said to Alexander.

"I suppose so."

Alexander turned the key in his hand and pressed the head of the small key between his left index finger and thumb. He felt the smooth rounded surface of the head of the key. With great deliberation and an unsteady hand, he placed the key into the key hole and turned it but nothing happened. He had turned it the wrong way and now turned the key clockwise and with a quick twist of his wrist the lock clicked open. He and Catherine watched as the lid of the iron box rose slightly. Then, Alexander opened the box.

Now the clouds passed away and the sun shone again, its rays falling down in golden streams through the branches of the grand, old, oak sitting at the center of the back yard. The massive oak stood by solidly like an aged and dignified witness to a tragic and defining truth. And in full light the box looked brilliant silver and the items inside, burnished gold, gold and crystalline blue. And when Alexander and Catherine gazed upon the contents of the box, it was as if their hearts both died inside them. Alexander requested the officer give them some time to be alone.

When the officer left, Alexander took the contents out of the box and placed them in Catherine's hand. Then he held her hand in his and they both looked intently at what they held.

In their hands were Jack's Duke College ring and his gold cross necklace, the one Veronica had given him before his last birthday. The two items were bound together. The necklace was looped through the finger opening of the ring and tied there. It was looped and tied in such a way that the cross of the necklace fell down over the blue face of the ring. Nothing could have said more sadly what the ring and cross necklace did.

They sat quietly for a long while and passed the jewelry back and forth. First one held it and stared at it, then the other. They held it as if the combined object was heavy and very fragile. They each felt it-every part of it, like blind people feeling an object for the sense it makes to them. They each held the object as if they were in some way holding their son. It signified so much and yet in actuality was so precious little of their son. Each had questions. They shakily groped for some reassurance that was impossible. Neither wanted this relic and neither could let it go.

They were in the garden when the young officer returned. They waited until he got to the garden fence and then went to meet him. Alexander approached the officer and asked him, "Officer, do you know how the cross got tied to the ring?"

"Sir, it was found that way."

"How did it survive the fire?" Alexander asked.

"It was found beneath two beams and under some insulation, I believe," the officer said.

"No one at the site tied the cross to the ring?" Catherine asked.

"No, ma'am, that's how it was found."

"How did you know it belonged to our son?" she asked.

"We identified the ring by his initials and the school and year. In our database, your son's name came up. He was the only match."

"Thank you, Officer," Catherine said softly.

Then Alexander turned to the officer. He placed his right hand on the officer's right forearm, causing both to stop and look at each other.

"Was my son's. . .his. . .anything else recovered?" Alexander struggled.

"I'm sorry sir, but nothing else was found," the officer said. "I'm very sorry."

The officer went to his car. Before getting in, he shook hands again with the Conroy's. Then he got in and drove down the drive. The Conroy's watched the car move slowly away from the house. They watched it turn toward the main road. They watched as it moved out of sight, beyond the woods that sheltered that part of the driveway from the rest of it leading to the road.

# 33

At first it was her anger at them that kept Veronica from contacting the Conroys. Then it was her fear. Early in her pregnancy, she feared the baby would not survive. Then, when she knew it would, she feared the Conroys might use their wealth to take the baby from her. There was no rational basis for that fear. But since she had already lost Jack, she was not thinking rationally. But in early July, several things combined to make Veronica change her mind about contacting the Conroys. First, Veronica opened a box that had been sent to her from Duke about a month after she'd come home and beneath her incomplete application to medical school found her folder of mail from Jack. In that folder she had kept all of Jack's emails and letters to her. After all these months, Veronica finally read these. She read them in her room alone and then she shared most of them with her mother. The emails were so typical of Jack in their concern for her and in the way they illustrated Jack's fundamental optimism that the mother was moved to tears. Mrs. Cashmiris felt right away that Veronica owed this picture of Jack created by the emails to Jack's parents since some were specifically about them.

Veronica weighed sending them to the Conroy's. She believed it was possible the emails might be more of a distress than solace.

"No, Veronica, they would not be," her mother said. "If he were my son, I would want to see these emails. I would cherish them because they are of him."

"If he were your son, Mother, he would not have gone to Wall Street."

"Veronica, you don't know that. Here," her mother said, citing a specific email, "he says he wanted to go to Wall Street. Do you not think his parents need to read that? My daughter, they suffer too."

Veronica knew her mother was right. And when she thought about Jack and how much he would not want his parents to suffer, Veronica felt she had to send a copy of these emails to the Conroy's.

She had called the Browne's immediately after the incident but couldn't get through to them. Once the tragedy came home in its full force she couldn't make further attempts, but Uncle Browne and Aunt Millicent had tried to contact her. She had received numerous letters from Uncle Browne over the past seven months. She had put them aside and did not read them until now. Uncle Browne's caring voice permeated the letters and his recollections of Jack, and her and Jack, were so vivid and affectionate they returned Jack to her. His letters also passed along, with poignant clarity, the sad ordeal that had become the Conroy's life. Not without effect were these insights that read like verbal echoes of her own torment. "Too much pain, all around," Uncle Browne had said near the end of one letter before asking, "What can I do about it but care?" The question resonated for Veronica. Veronica finally returned a letter to Uncle Browne and Aunt Millicent and after that sat down and wrote one to the Conroys.

She had all her emails from Jack copied. She chose one to send to the Conroy's with a letter, the one her mother thought they'd appreciate. Then, should the Conroys want the rest, she'd send them. She told the Conroys something else she thought they'd want to know about too.

> Dear Mr. and Mrs. Conroy,
>
> I hope you are okay. I am sorry for not having written or called sooner. I'm sure, though, that you understand the last ten months for me, as for you, have not been easy. It is only recently that I have felt like reaching out to others. I do now in the hope that I may bring to you some joy after all the sorrow.
>
> I include here for you an email from Jack that I thought you would like to read. I hope you find it something of a comfort. My mother thinks that it will be. I also have something else to tell you.
>
> Forgive me for not letting you know sooner. I have no excuse but my own blind pain. But now I am telling you, and I am happy to tell you, I gave birth to a healthy baby boy on June 8th. He is Jack's son. When he is old enough to travel, I will bring him up to Claremont Hills for you to see. In the meantime, know that your grandson is healthy, that he has brought me great joy and that I hope he brings the same to you.
>
> Sincerely,
>
> Veronica Cashmiris

The Conroys received this letter in July, not long after Jack's cross and ring had been returned. They had been at MILLFENN GRACE all day. They returned to the townhouse around eight at night and Alexander went to their mailbox to retrieve the mail. Walking the mail in, he noticed the return address of Veronica's letter. He brought the mail in and pointed the letter out to Catherine. They sat together at the kitchen counter while Alexander read the letter out loud. When he came to the part about the baby, Alexander paused. He read silently now. Catherine saw the change in his face. For a moment, she imagined the letter said that Jack was still alive.

"What is it, Alexander?"

"My God," Alexander said.

"Alexander, what, what does the letter say?"

Alexander looked confused in disbelief. Catherine took the letter from him. She read it quickly, up to where Alexander had paused. She read out loud now, falteringly:

"Forgive me for not letting you know sooner. I have no excuse but my own blind pain. But now, I am telling you that I gave birth. . . to a healthy . . . baby boy. . . on June 8th. He is Jack's son. . . "

Catherine turned to Alexander, astonished, and agitated. "Is this possible? Alexander, is she telling the truth?" Catherine sounded as if she suspected she was being teased. She couldn't believe what she read. Why hadn't they been told sooner? Alexander got the phone. He had taken the envelope with him. He called information for Damascus, Maryland. He got the Cashmiris number and wrote it down. In the background Catherine stared at the letter, would not let it go, read it again and again.

"Call her now," she said, her voice quavering. "I want to know what this is all about."

Alexander dialed the number and listened as the phone rang. He listened to four rings and was afraid an answering machine would come on, but on the fifth ring, Mrs. Cashmiris picked up the phone.

"Hello."

"Hello, this is Alexander Conroy, Jack's father."

"Did you receive Veronica's letter?" Mrs. Cashmiris asked.

"Yes, we did. We just read it."

Maria Cashmiris heard in Alexander Conroy's voice someone whose spirit had been jostled. In his voice was a plea for assurance that Veronica's message was true.

"I will call Veronica," Mrs. Cashmiris said, and then she said something that made Alexander have to put down the phone.

"She's with the baby," Alexander echoed.

"My dear God," Catherine said.

Alexander arranged for the Conroys to visit Veronica and the baby. They would go down the next day. Veronica and the baby had a doctor's appointment but they could come down. There is no way to fully describe the effect of the news upon the Conroys except to say they were still somewhat doubtful but also cautiously starting to believe. At the same time Catherine was angry.

"If it's true what she's said, don't you think she should have told us?" Catherine interrogated Alexander. Alexander could say nothing. He was not so much angry as in some way desperate for a certainty that had seemed for him to have disappeared from the world.

Then, after almost an hour, he read the email Veronica had sent with her letter. Again, he read out loud to his wife:

> *Dear V,*
>
> *About my parents whom you will meet this weekend, of course I'm biased, but soon you'll know why. When you are an only child like me, I guess you get spoiled. But my parents never really spoiled me. My dad, he's always worked very hard and been a great example that way. And my mom-she's just terrific. She's got a great sense of humor and has always been a great friend (my dad too)! They are, I think, with you, my best friends. I know what they want for me and why. It's not the typical get good grades, get the good job, make a lot of money cause that's what counts scenario, they have wanted for me. It's not really that. And while sometimes we disagree about certain things, I know deep down they are trying to take care of me. I know life is not just money to them. I also know money is important. But we know, they and I, it's not everything.*
>
> *When my dad encouraged me to go to Wall Street it was because he knew I'd be good at it. I think he also knew I wanted to try it, to prove myself and he always gave me a vote of confidence. He knew if I did well, my options would be open. But that's just the surface, the tip of the iceberg. What they both really want is that I am happy with my choices. I will go to Wall Street and I will do well and sometime when I am around thirty five, I will leave and open my own nursery and all those designs I have shown you will come to life in gardens and landscapes and life will be fine and full. I will write about it, too. I think you know I like to write. And one day, our garden will be the garden of the world. (That's the only Eden possible.) That's my plan. They will think you are GREAT!*
>
> *JC*

# 34

Veronica did not recognize the Conroys. It was as if she were meeting two different people. Alexander was no longer the robust, confident, presence she'd met at the Claremont Hills Club. He appeared weak and defeated, like he'd aged ten years. He was thin and his hair had whitened at the temples. Catherine, too, had physically dwindled and walked as if she needed Alexander's continuing attention. Their imposing aura was gone.

Veronica had gone through changes as well. But the decline of her appearance and fragility after 9/11 had given way to a more vibrant air brought on by her role as mother. Color had returned to her cheeks and her hair was once again full, rich in texture, and chestnut.

At first their meeting felt like a confrontation. Veronica, upon seeing the Conroy's in her home instinctively went to the baby as if to shield him and then removed him to his crib to sleep. Catherine had impulsively reached out both arms toward the baby almost as if she considered it hers. But Alexander took her hands and held them.

"Why didn't you let us know sooner?" Catherine asked, staring at Veronica with injured eyes, searching somehow for the answer to her whole diminished existence. Alexander shook his head from side to side. He stroked his wife's hands and said, "No, dear, it's the wrong question." He focused intently on Veronica, said nothing for a moment, but took in the girl before him with gratitude. "How are you, Veronica?" He hesitated then continued, speaking softly but distinctly, "How are you and our grandson doing?"

Whatever trepidation Veronica had felt before, seeing Alexander and Catherine somewhat shattered by the misfortune shared among them, she could not fear them. She even saw in Alexander an expression she knew with Jack, a flash of vulnerability in the eyes and slight upturn of the lips.

"I did not tell you earlier because I was afraid to," she said to Catherine.

"Afraid?" Catherine uttered.

"Afraid that you might take him away from me," Veronica confessed. Catherine's shoulders relaxed from their tense erectness. She slid into Alexander's arms.

"No, no," she said to Veronica, "never."

Veronica came up to the Conroys now. Her mother who stood to her side nodded her support to Veronica. Veronica stretched her hand down to Catherine where she sat on the couch in the Cashmiris's living room. Catherine looked up with faint appreciation. She let her hand be taken. Veronica led her into the room where the baby slept. Alexander followed and so did Maria Cashrmiris.

The child was in a room that was fairly empty of furniture and had been turned into a kind of nursery. Catherine and Alexander did not notice how relatively poor Veronica's family was compared to them. They did not notice the lack of furnishings, the barren walls, the rather old sofa, nor did they care. Everything that was in the room had been reconfigured for the baby. The small oak coffee table was pushed off to one side of the room and a large, thick, sky blue quilt lay on the floor.

As they entered, the baby awoke and Veronica took him out of his crib and laid him gently on the quilt. He rolled and cooed and sucked his fingers and then stopped suddenly and looked up at his grandparents who adored him. His baby eyes were intelligent and rather than cry from not knowing these two, he seemed to be studying them as they fawned over him.

"What's his name?" Alexander asked.

"He's Jack Jr., but I call him Duke," Veronica said.

The Conroys had to momentarily look away. When they looked back, Catherine made an observation: "He has a long back," she said. Alexander nodded. "And big forearms," he added.

Alexander and Catherine moved closer to each other and embraced, then focused on the baby. Their expression was full of both affection and sad longing. They took turns doting over the baby, rubbing his tiny feet, feeling his long fingers that automatically squeezed theirs. Catherine picked him up in her arms and felt his complete body in her hold and against her chest, listened to his breathing, felt his warm, pure breath on her neck. The baby gurgled and twisted, jerked his legs frenetically this way and that and shot out jabs with his infant hands that made Alexander laugh.

"He's a tough little guy," Alexander commented.

"He's a little gentleman, aren't you?" Catherine whispered, kissing his cheek. Then the baby did something that stupefied Catherine. He squirmed upward in her arms, turning his body around so that he faced her and stopped. He looked for a long unblinking moment into his grandmother's eyes, perfectly content, utterly enthralled.

"Oh Alexander, Alexander." Catherine handed the child to her husband, put her head in her hands and cried. Alexander took the baby while rubbing his wife's back, held him like a football so that the baby's feet were tucked into the corner of his grandfather's elbow and his face pointed upward so he could see who held him, "You're your daddy's son, aren't you?"

At the entrance to the room, in the doorway between that nursery room and the living room, Veronica watched these last events without intruding. She had witnessed Catherine's recollection and reaction and empathized immediately. Twisting, the baby caught sight of his mother and squirmed in Alexander's arm so much that Alexander put him down again on the soft quilt, and Veronica came and took him up in her arms. Then she sat Indian style on the blue quilt and rocked her boy in her arms until he went to sleep. Catherine watched quietly and Veronica gazed at her. Veronica could see before her in the presence of Catherine, a woman broken, diminished in spirit so much that she appeared smaller. And she could see that Catherine was still fragile, irrevocably altered, and incomplete. Veronica rose with the baby, went across the room to where Catherine sat on the sofa, sat down next to her and placed the sleeping baby in Catherine's arms. "He will need you, too."

"Oh my blessed child," Catherine said, almost voicelessly.

After she had held the baby a good while Catherine returned him to his crib, sound asleep. She and Alexander and Veronica then went back out to the living room. The Conroy's asked if they could read more of Jack's emails. Veronica hesitated. She'd read through the emails again and thought twice about having the Conroy's read them. Most of them had to do with Jack's feelings for her.

"A lot of the emails are personal," Veronica said. Catherine and Alexander appeared disappointed.

"I don't mind if you read them, I just wanted you to know that," Veronica reconsidered.

"May we?" Catherine asked considerately. She had to ask no further. Veronica went and got her Duke box. She brought out the album with all the emails and handed it to Catherine then left the room. The Conroy's read and in his emails it was like getting a picture of their son and his love of Veronica.

Above the first email Veronica had written a comment:

*This letter came very early the day after Jack took me to the Lake, my freshmen year, just before midterms. He calmed me down by taking me for that ride. Then he sent me this the next morning.*

*Dear Veronica,*

*Yesterday, everything I saw when I was with you and everything we did together was touched by a different and remarkable light. I know it must seem rash of me to say so, but yesterday, with you, Duke and Carolina and the roads and fields and trees and plains of grass, the whole, sleeping, world of possibility lit up for me-with you. I'm not really here right now, Veronica. But I am in all those places we went to. . . with you. God, I am so with you.*

*Jack*

He wrote other emails and in all of them Veronica felt she could see Jack.

*Dear V,*

*As I sit here looking out the window of the Library toward the field and the garden across the field above it, dreaming when I should be reading, I think about what I need to be happy. I don't need all that much. A small house would do. But, I'd like it filled with books. And I would like it set down at the right place too-near a river. If it had a picture window facing the river and I had a book, my guitar, a small piano and you-I can't imagine ever needing more. I could look at the river always. I could take a book I like from a shelf and read, read all around the world and never leave home- read one and then another book-and you by my side-reading too or, perhaps singing, singing while I read. I could listen to you sing always. We could have lunch on the lawn that borders the river; bring our music and our books and our love. We could picnic under the soft sun as it filters through the leaves of the trees, listening to the music of the water and our own. We could dream together while we live the very dream we dreamt. We, we are a dream! Aren't we? We could dream always.*

*Then we could go inside and with the moon up in the night sky, we could lie side by side-watching the moon watch us, bathing us in its light while we, like eternal lovers, make love. We could make love always. Oh V, there's very little that I need.*

*JC*

One email must have been written after an argument.

*Dear V,*

*I should not have ruled out working in Boston. I know you talk about going to medical school there. I say Boston is not New York, but it really doesn't matter if you're there. If I were in New York without you, I wouldn't like it. I had a dream about a future without you.*

*In my dream it was Christmas at a corner of the city where there were beautiful red-brick clothing shops that had great glass windows with dark wooden frames. And the rain that drizzled down around us brought tints of gray to the green and red of the season. And the air was cold. It made your cheeks lovelier and more red. You were dressed in Scottish plaid and your hair hung long and shiny brown. And you smiled as we walked somewhere together then; it must have been in Boston.*

*Then you looked at me as if in question of the time-but not at all sadly. You loved so very much the season and your eyes were happy eyes. . . and then you were gone and I walked again and again those timeless streets of Scottish plaid that were so lovely in our Christmas youth and saw them no less lovely but sadly, alone this time, and loved in them your happy eyes.*

*JC*

Later on in the album other aspects of Jack surfaced:

*Dear V,*

*Academics draw their superiority out of a different account, from the think-tank bank. It's the same elitist snobbery that goes into a label on your shirt or logo on your hat: The Snooty White Club or the Brilliant Mind Club, it's all the same snobbery, a craving for distinction, and a way to be superior.*

*Give me a plain shirt and a club where every color shines. Then I'll give you something useful-a better world. I would like to be able to say someday that I hold an advanced degree from the School of Life. My major was in kindness to my fellow man and I graduated with honors. Everyone on Earth was in my class and our Alma Mater: Mankind.*

*JC*

*Dear V,*

*You asked me whether I believe in Heaven. I'm not sure I believe in Heaven as it's conventionally described. If there is such a place, such a state, it seems to me that it would be the place where love exists without desire and wants and needs are gone. But then, I think, I cannot conceive of knowing you without wanting you-without needing you. Desire is a part of paradise with you!*

*JC*

*Dear V,*

*Some days, in this business, at this place and time, it seems like it's only about money. But it's not. It's about Liberty. I look out my window and I can see her standing in the harbor. I can look right into the eyes of Liberty and I thank my lucky stars that I am here-here and now. I am in the heart of the heart of freedom. I doubt I will be here long, it's just not me. But I'm glad I came, know I can do well here, and anywhere. And I know I want to be near you.*

*JC*

The last email had been written September 11th:

*Dear V,*

*Good morning! I miss you! But when I think of the future, I feel great. I think of you and me together. We will be together doing all we can, being the best we can be. You will go to Medical School. I will start my own Landscape Design Co. Bellini will help. So will my dad. We will live wherever. All the possibilities! I love you!*

*JC*

Alexander and Catherine stopped reading. They felt so many things. But mostly what they felt was Jack's deep love for Veronica. And they were not saddened by that, except sad for Veronica. She, too, had lost so much. They felt for her. There was a kind of transfer taking place within them. They loved Jack so much and now that they understood how much he loved Veronica, they suddenly cared a great deal about her. They looked at the baby with adoration. Very little was said. Any talk at that moment would have been superfluous. Everything that needed saying was said by the eyes of the people involved. Veronica looked radiant. Her long dark hair silky, her eyes, in glancing from the Conroy's to her baby, said she loved Jack as much as he'd loved her. Here was the proof of that love, this gift of a child, which was their gift to share. She handed the baby to Catherine again.

Catherine held the baby and adored him. She glanced at Alexander. She turned toward Veronica and Veronica's mother. Then she gazed for a long, silent moment, into the baby's eyes, just barely open. She cradled the baby; let his head rest on the top of her left elbow.

"When I look into his eyes, I see Jack," Catherine said.

# 35

Almost four months had passed since they bought MILLFENN GRACE. In that time, the estate had taken on a different look.

First, the cleanup crew had finished their work. Gone was the sprawling addition to the main house that had taken up so much of the yard. In its place, the gardens were extended. So that now, two sides of the house adjoined wide tracks of garden, making the house look, from a distance, like it had flower beds for arms. The cleanup crew had also scraped off a green film of moss from the poured concrete blocks of the old house, removing what began to look like a shroud. With the moss gone, the old house looked new, clean and bright. All the eaves had been replaced, too, and were also clean, white and new. And the red tiled roof, washed and repaired, shone like fresh-dried pottery—a smooth terra-cotta blanket draping the house.

With the help of The Women of Claremont Hills, who came back and continued working until it was finished restoration of the gardens recovered their ancient beauty. Patterns discerned became visible and then visibly improved by revived beds of flowers. The gardens now grew marvelously all around the house in rows of color and light, sun-dappled, green and full.

Closest to the house a Mountain Laurel alley sat, two stands of Mountain Laurel arching toward each other over a shady lane between them. Below the Mountain Laurel, beds of yellow roses were added in a design taken from a page out of one of Jack's college notebooks. Also added, was a track of evenly spaced Firethorn bushes, burning orange. Together with the yellow roses, the Firethorn filled the space between the Mountain Laurel alley and a long narrow channel of luxuriant grass located above the interior gardens.

Elephant-ear hosta and rhododendron framed the outer wall of the interior garden. Inside the wall at the top of the interior garden the wisteria covered pergola, now pruned and neat, resembled a three dimensional cross of wood, stone and vines. The vines had been cut back and their ample green leaves neatly covered the wooden rafters and beams of the pergola.

Benches positioned underneath the wisteria, along the cinder path, provided places to rest and take in the full measure of the interior garden.

Laid out in a pattern taken from one of Jack's notebooks, the interior garden formed a giant square enclosed on all sides by a four-foot high red brick wall. Two brick walkways formed a cross at the center of the garden. A stand of lilacs grew just beyond the south wall of the interior garden. Over the north wall stood the dense woods of The Revolutionary Preserve. Those woods ran north to east and were interrupted beyond the east wall of the garden by a passage way between them. A center section of brick wall on the east had been removed and fitted with an iron gate. That gate sat in line with the center of the interior garden. Standing above the garden under the pergola, one could look straight across into this passage way and far beyond it for a great unimpeded distance.

Standing there together this morning Alexander and Catherine felt that the garden had its own spirit. Beyond the garden, too, the spirit of history beckoned. With the back gate opened, it was as if the spirit of the past from the historical preserve joined that of the present in the garden making it all one.

They knew history was with them today. For it was the day of the memorial. The memorial had been planned after their visit to Veronica's. They initially were going to make it small but then decided to open it up to honor all of the people in the community who had lost their lives on September 11th. They set the date for the memorial as September 11th, 2002. Eventually, more than one community joined in and the event became something of a regional commemoration.

To begin with, it was a procession of color. First, a line of police cars came up the drive, their lights swirling. Behind them, the line continued, extending down the driveway a quarter mile onto Jockey Hollow road and then down that road another half mile. Fire trucks stood out behind the police cars. One of these had mounted to its grill a red, white, and blue light in the shape of a star. And as it came into view, the star spun around, so that red, white, and blue loomed from the face of the truck. Behind the trucks, firefighters and police officers marched in parade dress, looking like soldiers.

Striding in perfect step after the firefighters, a pipe and drum corps marched. Their shirts white and kilts green, and from their bagpipes Amazing Grace filled the solemn air. Then came a group dressed like Minutemen, in Revolutionary War garb. These men looked uniformly young and Alexander recalled some of the faces of the young police men and women from New York City who he'd read had perished on September 11th. The connection resonated and Alexander could not help feeling upset.

All through the crowd and along the procession, Old Glory blazed and blazed and blazed. And the faces of the people marching, and those who stood to watch, as well as Old Glory, shone. But more than Alexander had, Catherine suddenly felt bombarded by association. All the youth of the parade echoed her son. Gradually, she started putting this huge puzzle of pride and honor the celebration meant together with the woven pattern of immense sorrow it signified. Catherine fought herself to try and understand the full scope of the event taking place around her—not just a small town's tribute, not just the tribute of several towns gathered together, but the collective outpouring that follows large scale tragedy coupled in this instance with the kind of patriotism normally associated with a country at war. The country in all of its cities and hamlets, towns and villages, needed to purge itself of sorrow at the same time it let go its rage against the anathema of terror. This event was the Claremont Hills piece of the funeral shared by the nation and the Country's need to honor freedom. It was bigger than the loss of any one person, greater in scope than the suffering of a single family but Catherine could not fathom that, could only condense the meaning of all of that went on around her into the absolute confirmation of the death of her son. She stood hurt and bereft, near the point of breaking down again. Of course Alexander knew and he skirted the intensity of his own sorrow by looking after his fragile wife.

The procession continued. A great gathering streamed in, a parade of regular citizens marching slowly up the drive toward the house. The honor guard of firefighters and police officers were first to the house. After them came the local monsignor and the district Congressman. The Women of Claremont Hills came next. Mrs. Donogan followed closely behind with a double column of school children, some twenty-one uniformed children from St. Theresa's School. Most everyone held small American flags. Many carried flowers. All were quiet. All looked both proud and sad. It seemed a holy communion of people.

Where the driveway crossed into their yard, Alexander and Catherine stood to meet the line of citizens. This was not easy and didn't last. Catherine, after not very long, moved away. Alexander followed. They went into the interior garden where a podium had been placed at the center of the crossed walkways. There, they waited. The monsignor led in the people.

There were so many people that the garden overflowed with them and they spread out onto the terrace and into the yard behind the house. Everyone in the garden and in the yard, on the terrace, and along the stone wall bordering the yard, now looked toward the center of the garden to the podium.

Next to the podium on the ground, a salmon-colored marble stone, four-feet high and three-feet wide, had been erected. On the face of the stone, half way down, a mounted bronze placard listed the names of the 21 people from the community lost in the Towers. Above the placard, on a small golden shelf affixed to the face of the stone and covered by thick, transparent, glass was Jack's ring and cross bound together as found. They were illuminated by a small spotlight. The Congressman moved next to the monument, gazed out to the ready throng and began the ceremonies:

"History takes it all in, just the way it did out there beyond the wall for those who fought in the Revolution. History made there, in those woods and fields beyond the walls of this garden, two hundred years ago comes back to us today. That fight for freedom gave us our America. And what happened last year recalls what the fight was for: our Liberty.

"Ours is a country of free enterprise. We can choose where we work and what we do. That became possible when we became a nation. It is one of those inalienable rights we cherish and sometimes die for. Those who perished in the towers last year enacted that right and died for it. They were at their work as Americans. And the police officers and firefighters were too. I cannot praise them enough as sad as it is.

"I like to think that in their bravery and goodness the blessed angels of that day ascended all the way to the top. Up they went. . . up so high that they could not come down. And though the Towers fell, and they did too, their spirit rose-rose ever higher and soared above our land holding open the golden door. Now let us dedicate this memorial to them, once again to realize the price we pay for freedom. Never shall we forget, that those who died before her eyes. . . with Liberty reside."

After the congressman finished the local monsignor spoke. "Good morning, everyone, good morning on this glorious and solemn day. I ask your permission to attest to a miracle. Not too long ago a recovery at the site of Ground Zero took place that has had a great spiritual impact upon me. Today, when you look at this memorial stone, you will be blessed to see what I mean. At the site of all that devastation something that belonged to one of the young men lost, was found. Hidden under a steel beam, Jack

Conroy's college ring and gold cross necklace were found. They were found bound together.

"In speaking with his loved ones, I learned that Jack held both ring and cross dear. He wore them every day. Perhaps that is why, in the seconds before he died, he joined them. Perhaps what he meant to say is that these two things are me.

"They were discovered not just bound, however, but carefully bound, bound in such a way that the cross of the necklace fell over and perfectly covered the blue stone of the ring. Chance, perhaps, but I doubt it.

"In looking at them now, I see more than just two precious possessions of a beautiful young man. And I believe Jack did too. These two precious and precisely bound things of his serve; it seems to me, as symbols of his estate and our own. THE CROSS covers the world and is inextricably bound to it. It is a Cross estate, and our mutual inheritance. But it also confirms Jack's belief, I think, that ultimately, by way of the Cross, life prevails over death.

"Now, as we contemplate our own mortality in the face of the death of our brothers and sisters, let us also look to our inner light and be bound to our belief in the same way that, over there," the monsignor pointed to the memorial stone, "the cross is bound to the ring."

When the priest moved away, Alexander walked toward the podium. The plan was to have family members come up and say something about whomever they lost. Alexander started toward the podium but stopped when he noticed Catherine hesitate and then move away. In the momentary pause that followed an awkward silence filled the air. Then Catherine, not Alexander, meekly moved toward the microphone. Her hand trembled as she laid it upon the mike.

"I am trying to be unselfish about my son, trying at last and too late to let him go, not keep him only to myself. But it is hard. I listened to our Congressman and to the Monsignor. Both are good men, wise and holy. But in all honesty, they are too abstract for me. And as to God and Glory, I just don't know. But I do know this:

"There is a whole in my life like there is a whole in the skyline of New York. No place on earth could be as empty as my heart today. And yet it's full. It never occurred to me before, but this year eternity felt much too long. I can speak about my boy, Jack, only as a mother speaks of her son. The rest of it I can make nothing of.

"I miss him beyond an ability to tell you. And as I look at the world now, irrevocably different, all I can see is his absence before me. I miss his eyes, his ready smile, his sweetness, his form. . . and his golden hair. I miss him standing with me, sitting with me, laughing with me. I miss being with him and his father, all of us together. I cannot tell you how much I miss seeing him. I long in a way that only parents can understand to hear his voice-his happy and optimistic voice-my golden boy.

"His life seems to me like a dream now with the golden door shut. Wherever it is that goodness goes, there Jack has gone for good. And I feel him gone in the pit of my stomach and deep in my soul. And it is as if my heart is torn in strips and scattered in the wind across the universe in search of him. Even while I know that he is in my heart always. What can we do about that which cannot be replaced, but die trying?"

When Catherine came away Alexander followed her and, once away from the podium, Veronica joined them. Veronica had found it difficult all day to feel the spirit the occasion had sought to engender and that everybody else seemed to share. But seeing Coach Ross and Bob Evans and some other Duke swimmers and then, especially, seeing Mr. Bellini, had made her think of a world of lost possibility. That world was gone and, as with Catherine and Alexander, a big part of her had gone with it. They three went off alone for a moment. Even the beautiful flowers around them brought with their beauty a referential pain-funeral flowers is what they were to them. It was supposed to be in some grand way, an affirming experience, the festivities, yet for them; once again, it confirmed death and in that way only affirmed negation. They were at the point where they wanted death to die but it was too soon yet to accept the spirit of the thing.

Back at the ceremony a strong breeze blew and in the microphone you could hear the sound of the wind blowing by. Tossed were the heads of flowers, bent the still-green limbs of trees, and bowed the summer grasses-all with that speaking breeze and the singing birds sang silently.

At last a final song marked the end of the memorial: God Bless America. The St. Theresa's children sang the song. The loaded words of the song rang out over the crowd and carried far beyond the crowd to the woods in the distance which are part of the Revolutionary preserve. The woods of the preserve acted as a shell and brought the words of the song back in an echo, as if the woods were singing too. When the drums played and the children sang, more echoes came and it was as if in singing God Bless America, America sang.

Towards the end of the song each child from St. Theresa put a yellow rose next to the memorial stone, forming a large circle of roses around it.

The sun shone as the music rose in a crescendo before subsiding. And the garden brightened as the children finished their singing. Light touched the flowers of the garden and the faces of the children. And farther away, light shone against the trees of the preserve— over the wall. In the meadow behind the garden more light spread and the grass looked golden again.

Now as the music sank to silence the sun shone even more brightly and the roses glowed. Voices rose again, spirits soared . . . resonance of the perfect-pitched sun. In the great distance, a muffled roar of a canon sounded; shadows died, echoes lived. All over. . . Light!

# 36

Duke's fifth birthday brought the family together at Uncle Browne and Aunt Millicent's on Taylor Island. His actual birthday was in June but in trying to arrange the party Uncle Browne gave good reasons to make the celebration take place in July. July on the island is the best month he said. He also pointed out how he'd be done teaching and Veronica would be finished with her classes too. So they made it July.

Three cars were parked in Uncle Browne and Aunt Millicent's driveway when the party took place. Two were on the dirt driveway and one was pulled up at an angle off the driveway onto the grass. The Mercedes Coupe, its convertible top all the way down, was first in the driveway, closest to the house. Behind it was Jack's old Jeep which now belonged to Veronica. The Jeep had Massachusetts plates. In the back seat of the opened Jeep, a small swim bag sat. On the grass was the Conroy's old Ford. It had a new paint job. Uncle Browne and Duke had gone down to the cove swimming. Veronica and Catherine had been down watching them and were coming back up to the house.

"I wish you would let us help you more," Catherine said to Veronica.

"We don't need it. The victim's fund money is ample; thank you so much for that, Catherine," Veronica said, sounding grateful but clearly not wanting more.

"It's not enough, Veronica; Jack was just starting and the cost of your medical school and childcare? Won't you let us help more?"

"No, Catherine, Tufts has given me a grant. I'm fine, really." Veronica gazed at Catherine considerately as if she were afraid by refusing additional help she might be hurting her and didn't want to.

"It's hard to believe you're in your third year already," Aunt Millicent said, joining the conversation.

"It's a tremendous accomplishment," added Catherine.

"Thank you," Veronica said quietly. Then she turned and watched the Conroys's pug dog, Louis. Alexander had just finished walking him and let him off the lead. Louis started dancing in front of Alexander and then scampered to the middle of the lawn. He ran animatedly in a short line, back and forth, repeatedly, barking at nothing and pawing the air. The silly dog seemed obsessed with the wind and light as it moved in a stream across the yard. He squealed in frenzied play utterly engrossed in his invisible game, continually looking up at nothing and pawing the air.

"Louis is hysterical," Veronica said.

"He is, isn't he?" Catherine agreed. "He's always barking at nothing." As she said that Louis took off again and headed down toward the water below the crest of hill, out of view.

"Would anyone like more coffee or tea?" Aunt Millicent asked.

"I'm fine," Catherine said.

"Me too," said Veronica.

"Well, I'll drink alone then," Aunt Millicent said and walked toward the kitchen door.

"I think what you and Alexander are doing is wonderful. I mean donating your property," Veronica said to Catherine.

"We've thought about it a lot. It's what we really want. And we're ready to move. It will be nice living in Falmouth, too, so close to my brother and it will be nice to be closer to you and Duke."

"Will you continue with that charity you started, the Patriot fund?" Veronica asked.

"We will, that means a lot to us," Catherine answered.

"It's a great idea," Veronica said. "I wish I could help you with that more than I do."

"But you're doing so much, so well. Duke's a wonderful boy and I think becoming a pediatrician is terrific," Catherine said.

"Well, now that you're coming up here, you'll see more of Duke. He'll love that. He's really starting to understand that his daddy died. Having you two nearby will be great for him."

Catherine looked out toward the water as if studying it, took in the wide expanse of the sound, then turned to Veronica.

"How about you, Veronica, are there any men in your life?"

"No, I don't want that yet," Veronica said, her body giving a quick shiver of rejection.

"Are you lonely?" Catherine whispered.

"You know."

"It's not easy," Catherine said, "is it?"

"No, it's not," Veronica said, staring off at nothing, her voice somewhat laden.

"It's good you have your boy."

"He's a blessing."

"Yes."

After a momentary silence during which both Veronica and Catherine looked out at the water, as if the water held answers to questions not asked but thought, Veronica said, "We're coming down for the ceremony. It's going to be a big deal, I hear."

"Good. Yes, we're turning the property over at the ceremony," Catherine said.

"Will the whole estate go to the National Park Commission?" Veronica wondered.

"That's what Alexander worked out. They'll use the house for administrative offices and lectures and the garden will become part of the preserve. It's funny what they are starting to call it down there."

"A Cross Estate, is that right?"

"Yes."

"Is that because of what the monsignor said on the first anniversary?"

"That and what you still have," Catherine said.

"I keep them like that, too. I will, always," Veronica confirmed.

"Jack was lucky finding you," Catherine said to Veronica, meeting Veronica's eyes with her own affectionately.

While they talked, they didn't notice Uncle Browne pass. He had gone inside to change out of his wet suit. When he came back out and Duke wasn't with him, Veronica questioned him.

"Where's Duke?" she asked matter-of-factly.

"I left him inside when I went to my room to change. Didn't he come out yet?" Uncle Browne asked. Alexander had now joined Catherine and Veronica.

"Haven't seen him out here since you left to go swimming," Alexander said.

"He must be still inside, perhaps watching TV," Uncle Browne said. Aunt Millicent had just come out with a cup of tea and heard what her husband said.

"He's not inside, Browne. I just came from there, and the TV isn't on."

Veronica showed mild concern. She left the others and went into the house. When she came out seconds later she was less composed.

"Hasn't anyone seen him?" Her mood spread to the others and now everyone became serious. Catherine pulled on Alexander's shirt sleeve as if she were pulling on an alarm. Alexander took charge.

He pointed to the house looking at Uncle Browne. Uncle Browne went back inside the house, checking once more to be sure. Aunt Millicent in her purple sun dress flew over the back yard like a scared peacock squawking the boy's name, "Duke . . . ! Duke!" Then Catherine and Veronica joined in and the backyard rang with a chorus of Dukes. Presently, Louis barked and everyone remembered the dog was gone.

"Louis's down at the water," Alexander said. All of them hurried to the water.

The sand was white along the high part of the beach and brown where it was wet near the water. There were the large footprints of Uncle Browne and behind his the small ones of Duke still visible. But now the tide was starting to come in.

"Duke!" Veronica called loudly. Louis ran up to Alexander and Catherine. He jumped up at Alexander and then ran down to the edge of the water. In the cove, the current rolled strongly into shore. Louis ran in circles at one point on the shore. Veronica ran to where Louis was and saw Duke's yellow seahorse goggles lying wet in the sand. "Duke!" she screamed.

Uncle Browne and Alexander were now in the deepening water. Uncle Browne surfaced some forty feet down away in the middle of the cove. He saw Louis racing along the water's edge to a point where a tongue of red clay jutted out from the land like a natural barricade separating the beach of the cove into two sections. The tongue of red clay was some fifteen feet high and bulky and no one standing where the others did could see beyond it to the rest of the beach. From where he was Uncle Brown couldn't see past the red clay either but he was closer and thought he heard someone. He swam farther along the cove to where he could see past the red clay.

Before he saw him, he heard Duke. Duke was calling out, "Liberation, Liberation." Uncle Browne got out of the water and came up to Duke. Duke was alone except for Louis. Louis turned and scampered farther away up into the woods above the beach at that part of the cove where a catwalk sat. Duke looked at Uncle Browne and laughed.

"Your ears are funny," the little boy giggled.

Uncle Browne stared at him, marveled at him. "Did I tell you about that?" Uncle Browne asked the boy curiously. Then he called to the others. "He's here and okay."

Veronica arrived instantly. She grabbed her son and hugged him without saying anything. After a while she brought her head up. She held Duke and looked around. She had a strong feeling of Deja vu. She saw the grass just off the shore on that side of the red clay and how it was low in places and luxurious and soft and how a spot of land sunk above the shore after the woods. She knew the place and sobbed. Soon the others arrived and everyone gathered around mother and child.

"Oh my God, we're so happy to see you," Catherine said, stroking Duke's arm with a trembling hand.

"What on earth would we do without you, little fellow?" Aunt Millicent sang out. Alexander and Uncle Browne stood by as Veronica held Duke as if they were guards but enthralled by the boy. There was joy and relief in their eyes. Veronica gazed at the group, released a sigh and then gave Duke to Uncle Browne to hold. Uncle Browne, with Alexander joining in, lifted the boy up and raised him above the crowd like he was a victorious champion or a rescued prince. Then all of them marched down the line of the beach, Duke raised up high toward the sky so that in the sunlight he appeared to be glowing.

"You are our world," Uncle Browne said to Duke.

"Nothing must ever happen to you," Aunt Millicent added.

"Oh, God, we do love you so," Catherine added, tears welling up in her eyes.

"My son's son, our promise is to keep you safe," Alexander said.

Veronica reached up and brought Duke down again into her arms. Then she looked at him and with motherly counsel said, "You must never go off by yourself. Do you understand me? And never go to the water alone, okay?"

Duke studied his mother, sensing her anguish. Then softly, almost inaudibly he said, "Okay, Mommy, but I wasn't alone."

Duke looked at Uncle Browne and then squirmed to get out of his mother's arms when he saw Louis returning. Uncle Browne zoomed in on Duke. "I don't remember telling you," and he bent down and kissed Duke.

Later that evening at sunset everyone went back down to the water. The sun, bigger than the world, cast a golden stream over the placid waters of the cove. In the distant sky, low on the horizon, its vermilion cloak draped down, the declining sun dipped from their vision like a fallen rose. Its wake, vermillion light, shone on. Along the edge of the water, their faces reflected in its mirror-like calm; those whom he left behind asked each other questions that couldn't be answered as they still sought Jack somewhere in the clouds.

Then by the shoreline under the bright sun Duke raised his small hand to the sky. Veronica cried a little, wondering. Catherine too cried, knowing. Aunt Millicent then announced that she wanted a photo. She called the group together and set up her camera with a timer on a tripod, pressed a button after adjusting the shudder, and then moved into the group. Later, from the photo, she painted them. The painting was lovely, replete with affection, vibrant with rekindled possibility, but most remarkable for what it could not disclose and yet still revealed. There was a space large enough to hold a man between Veronica and Duke, a golden space suffused with light from the Sun. Aunt Millicent called the painting Liberation.